## THEY RODE TO THE SHOWDOWN
## IN TULSA

**Jim Land**—A hard-eyed lawman, he'd ridden a lonely trail, until he found himself torn between his love for a married woman and his hunt for a savage hardcase who had marked him for death.

**Beth Converse**—She had followed her husband to the wild Oklahoma territory, but she never knew how wild it could be until she met Jim Land.

**Bill Doolin**—He plundered the rich territory with his gun-tough gang, riding roughshod over the law—all for the sake of a woman he secretly loved.

**Turk Freese**—He killed men for the pleasure it gave him, and the greatest pleasure of all would be killing Deputy Marshal Jim Land.

**The Stagecoach Series**
Ask your bookseller for the books you have missed

# STAGECOACH STATION 26:

# TULSA

## Hank Mitchum

 Created by the producers of
Wagons West, White Indian,
and Saga of the Southwest.

*Chairman of the Board: Lyle Kenyon Engel*

BANTAM BOOKS
TORONTO • NEW YORK • LONDON • SYDNEY • AUCKLAND

STAGECOACH STATION 26: TULSA

*A Bantam Book / published by arrangement with
Book Creations, Inc.*

*Bantam edition / November 1986*

*Produced by Book Creations, Inc.
Chairman of the Board: Lyle Kenyon Engel*

ISBN 0-553-26229-7

*Published simultaneously in the United States and Canada*

PRINTED IN THE UNITED STATES OF AMERICA

KR    0 9 8 7 6 5 4 3 2 1

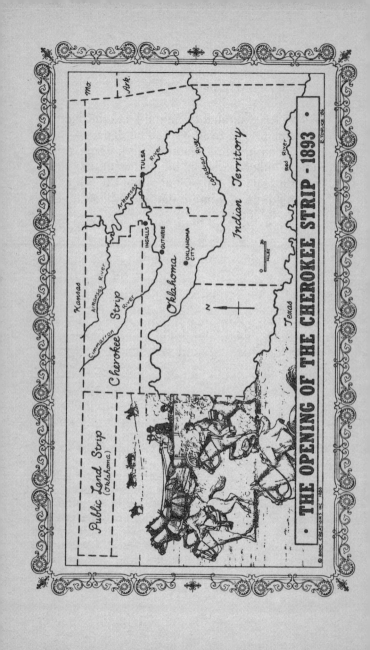

· THE OPENING OF THE CHEROKEE STRIP · 1893 ·

# Chapter One

Though it was not yet nine o'clock on this Friday morning—September 1, 1893, according to the calendar on the wall—the federal marshal's office was a busy place. One of the two women workers was occupied with a file cabinet while the other worked at her typewriter; a man with the look of an accountant had his books open in front of him. Despite the open windows, the heated air of summer moved sluggishly through the second floor of the Herriot Building in Guthrie, the capital city of Oklahoma Territory.

The clerk in charge wore the harried look of a man with urgent matters on his mind, but he spoke respectfully to the one who faced him across the counter dividing the office. "Just when did you get in, Mr. Land?"

"Last night, pretty late," Jim Land told him. "That's a long stage ride from Texas."

"I know the marshal's going to be sorry he couldn't be here to meet you," the clerk said. "These are hectic times, what with the Cherokee Strip being thrown open for settlement week after next. Marshal Nix is up there now, taking care of a million details. He left orders that if you showed up and decided to take the job he wrote you about, I was to see to getting you sworn in and give you this." And he laid a highly polished, five-pointed deputy U.S. marshal's badge on the counter. "Of course, I realize you've worn one of these before."

1

"On a couple of occasions," Jim Land said. "Down in Texas."

"Between jobs as a sheriff and with the Texas Rangers or the Pinkertons or on your own," the clerk said, and the other man nodded. "We're aware of your record, Mr. Land, and it's a good one. That's why Evett Nix sent for you." He eyed the taller man with clear admiration—the well-built frame, the gray eyes in a clean-shaven face that was sun darkened from a life spent mostly in the open. The hair that brushed the collar of Jim Land's coat was thick, a dark yellow in color, and a trifle long because he was some weeks overdue for a barber's chair.

The clerk continued in a serious tone: "Believe me, the marshal needs all the expert help right now that he can get. Today's the first of September; Ev Nix has now been in office for exactly two months—and already, you wouldn't believe the pressures that man is under! Naturally, the Cherokee Strip opening is bringing landrushers by the thousands pouring in, every one of them bent on grabbing off a chunk of the last free land in the territory. That spells trouble enough. But for the marshal's office, it's only the beginning!

"The next step will be statehood for Oklahoma—and the government in Washington is giving notice there's to be no more delay in getting rid of the outlaws who have always run things more or less to suit themselves. Once it was the Daltons—only, they obliged us by getting themselves wiped out last fall at Coffeyville, up in Kansas. But now we've got Bill Doolin! He's taken over what was left of the Dalton outfit, added some new ones, and put together a gang of his own. And he's turned out more dangerous and a bigger thorn in our side than the Daltons ever were!"

"That's what I've heard," Land said. "According to the letter from your boss, the Doolin gang is the chief reason I'm here."

The man nodded. "Too bad you couldn't have gotten here a day earlier!"

The clerk's statement made Jim Land ask, "What do you mean?" But just then a messenger hurried in with a handful of telegrams. The clerk excused himself as he quickly sorted through them. Seeing his frown, Land asked, "Bad news?"

The clerk tossed them aside, shaking his head. "No news at all—at least not the news we've been hoping for, since around midnight. As you might guess, it's Doolin again. We tried to set up a trap for him. If it worked, we should have had some word before now. This silence can only mean something's gone wrong."

"Any way I can help?"

"I don't see how." He mopped sweat from his forehead with a nervous hand. "There's a little burg called Ingalls about thirty-five miles northeast of here in Payne County, just below the Cherokee Strip. Lately it's been a favorite place for the Doolin gang to hang out. They've got friends there, and it's only a hop and a jump from their hideout somewhere near the Cimarron River, so I guess it's felt safe enough to them. But we've got a spy of our own who managed to tip us off yesterday that Doolin and his top men would be spending the night there so a local doctor could do some work on Doolin's leg—it got shot up in a train robbery a few weeks back.

"There wasn't much time to work in, and we couldn't get in touch with Marshal Nix to ask for orders. So it was decided to go ahead anyway and work up a little surprise for Bill Doolin. A couple of wagons were outfitted to pass for homesteaders' rigs headed for the Cherokee Strip. It was arranged by telegraph, with one wagon leaving from here and the other from Stillwater—that's the county seat of Payne County. They were to rendezvous at Ingalls sometime around midnight. And between them, hidden under the canvas, they carried the men and guns and ammunition to do the job."

"How many men?" Jim Land wanted to know.

"A dozen, altogether. It should have been enough." The clerk hesitated. "But the problem is, this is a new staff, and it's spread pretty thin. We just don't have that many trained and experienced men on hand. As it happens, Marshal Nix has been authorized to hire up to a thousand temporary deputies to help manage the swarm of landrushers expected into the Cherokee Strip, two weeks from tomorrow. Naturally, he's had to take whatever he could get; not many are what you would call qualified for this kind of work. And I'm afraid that most of the men that went in the wagons to Ingalls fit into that category."

"I see. . . ." Frowning, Jim Land thought he could indeed see the potential for disaster—a hasty and complicated plan that had to rely, in the end, on a green, untrained crew thrown up against dangerous and seasoned outlaws. Obviously, something *had* gone wrong, and in the face of that, Land's weariness after the long stage trip from Texas and a short night's sleep hardly mattered. Gruffly, he said, "Sounds like I'll have to start work a little sooner than I'd figured! How far did you say it was up there?"

The clerk stared at him. "Are you serious? It's thirty-five miles. You'd never make it in time to do any good."

"I might if I push it. I'll find a horse and be on my way."

"Well, I wish you luck! When you get there, look for deputies Speed and Hueston. They're the two staff men in charge of the expedition."

Land nodded. "All right." An impulse that was too strong to be ignored made him add, "By the way, I'm wondering if the name Freese would mean anything to you. Turk Freese . . ."

From the look he got, he could tell he had drawn a blank. The clerk shook his head. "I don't think so." He must have sensed Land's disappointment, for he added, "I'm sorry I can't help you. This man you're asking about—would he be an outlaw, by any chance?"

"By every chance," Land said grimly.

"It really doesn't mean much that I've never heard of him. Because if you're looking for an outlaw, you've probably come to the right place. Sooner or later, they all manage to gather in Oklahoma Territory!"

Land said, "That's what I was thinking."


For some time Jim Land had been listening for the sound of gunfire, but when he finally heard the first hint, carried on the scorching September wind, he almost thought he was mistaken. Flagging senses came quickly alert; he straightened in the saddle as he peered ahead through the haze.

Moments later, as the tired bay carried him on, he found

he was looking at a huddle of buildings across a quarter mile of rolling, sunbaked prairie. A shimmer of sunlight bounced off shingled roofs and clapboard sidings and reflected from the scattered windowpanes of the town that lay before him.

Even louder, now, the ground wind brought him the sporadic sound of rifles and handguns issuing from among that cluster of houses. *It sounds like a pitched battle!* Jim Land thought. He drew rein. The bay horse was the second mount he'd pushed almost to the limit to reach this place in the shortest time possible; now, while Land sat listening, the bay drooped its head, the breath from its nostrils pumping up swirls of roadbed dust.

Land couldn't make any pattern out of the shooting. For long moments it would cease; then some weapon would pick it up again, and others would join in, as though in answer. All it told him was that he must have found the town of Ingalls, Oklahoma Territory. And the surprise raid, planned for the previous midnight, was clearly a long way from being wrapped up.

He thumbed the hat back from his forehead while he debated his best move. He had come prepared for anything—a belt gun buckled at his waist, a rifle in the saddle holster under his knee. It was the new, nickeled badge pinned to his coat that worried him a little, and he fingered it thoughtfully. If he happened to run into Bill Doolin's men, the badge would be a handy target; on the other hand, if he took it off, he could wind up shot by the very people he wanted to help.

He shrugged and left the badge where it was; he would take his chances. He set the hat more firmly on his head and loosened his belt gun in its holster. A kick started the tired horse moving forward again.

Ingalls could hardly be more than a year old—probably one of many such hamlets, plotted and ambitiously laid out by someone with hopes of seeing it become an urban center in the newly settled territory. Those hopes didn't seem likely to be fulfilled anytime soon. Warily approaching, Jim Land rode in past undeveloped streets and staked-out lots that boasted nothing but brush and weeds and a bit of straggling timber. The sporadic banging and echoing of gunshots became increasingly loud, until he found himself nearing what looked to be one of the few principal streets. Some of the rifle fire seemed to be concentrated just beyond the line of buildings to his right. Land decided this was as close as he wanted to get on horseback. He pulled in near a corner building that appeared to house a blacksmith shop and dismounted.

A buckboard with one wheel removed stood tilted at a crazy angle outside the shop. He tied the horse's reins to one of the grab irons, where the thirsty animal could reach the brackish water in a nearby trough. Sliding his rifle from its saddle holster, Land moved quickly forward to try and get some clear idea of what was going on.

Just now, for some reason, the shooting had fallen off again, and in the sudden stillness dry weeds crackled under his boots. He put a shoulder to the rough outer wall of the shop and inched up for a cautious look around its corner.

To his right stood Ash Street, named by a crudely lettered sign fastened to the outside wall of the shop. The street lay still and silent, with nothing moving under a scorching sun directly overhead. Easing around the corner, keeping the rifle ready, Land cast a glance through the wide front door of the blacksmith's shop—it, too, was empty, the forge cold and tools scattered about as though someone had dropped them and left in a hurry.

Another step, and suddenly he froze.

A body lay facedown out in the rutted dirt street. There was blood on the man's clothing and on the ground. His hat rested on its crown beside him, a rifle almost in reach of one limp, outflung hand.

Even as Jim Land regarded this scene with narrowed eyes, there came the sharp report of a rifle, and something slammed into the front of the shop, close above his head—too close! His reflexes took over and sent him to the nearest shelter— back to the open entrance of the blacksmith's shop, where he took cover behind the door timbers. Even as he did, another bullet came searching after him, striking the anvil and glancing off in a crazy ricochet.

Land swore and jacked a shell into the breech of his own weapon. Thanks to that second bullet, he now had the sniper spotted.

Where it rose behind the smaller houses directly across the

street, he could see what must be the only two-story building in town—the hotel, most likely. It stood broadside to him and a little to his right, giving him a view of the upper story, with its slanted roof, and a glimpse of a window under the gable in the rear end. He supposed there would also be a window or two in the front, which wasn't visible from this angle, but he could see no other openings at all along this blank side of the second story.

Except that it appeared someone had just created one!

It was a stabbing reflection of sunlight on metal that caught his eye, lifting his gaze to the jagged hole that had been punched out through the shingles of the roof. The barrel of a rifle jutted from it, pointing straight at the blacksmith shop; Land thought he could almost look right up its muzzle. He could see a film of powder smoke dissolving from those two quick shots at him, and he almost flinched, thoroughly expecting a third one.

But the sniper must have decided against it. Instead the rifle was withdrawn, and now Land caught a glimpse of an arm and shoulder as its owner began using the weapon's butt to enlarge his makeshift rifle port, knocking loose still more of the sun-warped shingles and sending them clattering down the steep pitch of the roof.

His face gone hard, Jim Land whipped his weapon to his shoulder, intending to give the man a taste of his own medicine. Before his finger could tighten on the trigger, there was the lashing report of a rifle somewhere farther along, on this same side of Ash Street. Yonder at the hotel, a shingle was knocked free and sent flying by the bullet; the sniper ducked instantly from sight. Land frowned as he lowered his unfired weapon.

It began to make sense: Some person or persons must be under siege up there on the top floor of the hotel, in what looked like an unfinished attic—at least it didn't have any ceiling, making it possible for the sniper to get at the roof and open holes to shoot from and compensate for the lack of windows up there. A day like this would make it hot as hell under that shingled roof! On the other hand, the hotel was the highest point in town, giving the sniper a commanding view over all the rest of the settlement. With the windows at front and rear and with improvised rifle ports knocked through on either side, a determined marksman might hold off a sizable number of enemies coming at him from any direction.

Jim Land decided that standing here was accomplishing nothing at all; he had to find someone to clue him in on the situation. But having been shot at once, he certainly wasn't taking another chance of joining that dead man out there in the middle of Ash Street. He looked around for a safer way out of the shop and discovered with some relief that the place had a back door. Quickly he crossed to it and pushed it open.

More trash and broken equipment discarded by the blacksmith lay out back. Land stepped outside. He could see nothing moving; he imagined he would have a better chance to find what he was looking for nearer the center of town. So carrying his rifle, he started across the back lots, paralleling Ash Street as he let its buildings screen him from sight of the sniper in the hotel.

A little past the blacksmith's was a barnlike structure with the smell and look of a livery stable. He glanced into its gloomy interior and saw the street entrance up front, framing a blast of midday sunlight. But as far as he could tell, there was no one inside. He continued past it and had taken only a few steps farther through the back lot when he heard a voice say sharply, "You! Hold it right where you are!"

Land froze. There was the scrape of a boot sole behind him. The voice spoke again, and this time he caught a note of tense excitement: "Mister, I got you covered. Get those hands in the air and turn around—careful!"

He didn't need the warning; the owner of the voice was too tightly strung for him to want to take any chances. Both hands at shoulder level, one of them hampered by the weight of the rifle, Land slowly turned.

The man standing in the rear doorway of the barn was of medium height, with a derby hat pushed back from a florid, sweating face. He was in shirt-sleeves, and his unbuttoned waistcoat sagged with the weight of a deputy marshal's badge. The hands that held a rifle pointed squarely at Jim Land showed the white-knuckled tightness of his grip, and his eyes held a hint of wildness.

Jim Land drew a shallow breath and then said, "Take it

easy, friend. If you'll be kind enough to point that thing in some other direction—"

He probably wasn't even heard. His captor was staring at the badge that was identical to his own. "I don't get this!" he blurted. "Are you one of *us*? I can't remember seein' you before." Turning his head, he shouted into the barn, "Hey, Walsh! Come out here, will you?"

While Land waited, uncomfortable under the menace of the nervous man's rifle, two other persons emerged from the rear door of the barn into the back lot. The one he judged to be Walsh had a rifle and also wore a badge; he was trailed by a smaller man, who had neither badge nor gun.

Land's captor demanded, "Walsh, do you know this fellow? Was he in the bunch you came with, in the wagon from Stillwater?"

The deputy named Walsh shook his head. He looked pale and agitated; there was a smear of burnt gunpowder across one gaunt cheek. He said hoarsely, "Never seen him before this minute."

"If you'll just give me a chance," Land told him, "I can explain. I only got here a few minutes ago. I arrived at Guthrie this morning. The clerk at the U.S. marshal's office told me what was going on here, and I grabbed a horse and made it as fast as I could. My name is Land. There's a letter in my pocket from Marshal Nix, if that will help."

The eyes in the florid face widened. "You're *Jim* Land? Hell—I couldn't have known that!" His captor turned to Walsh. "You must have heard about a special agent the marshal was bringing in from Texas."

Looking suitably impressed, Walsh stared at the stranger. As though suddenly remembering that he held the newcomer under his rifle, the red-faced deputy let it drop downward.

Land felt considerably more comfortable as the muzzle of the weapon in those nervous hands left him. He didn't really need to be told that these two, with their shiny deputy's badges, were some of the new men the clerk had told him about; he could recognize the look and manner of raw recruits from his army days.

His hunch was quickly confirmed: The one who had challenged him at gunpoint—his name was Bentley—said in a complaining tone, "Damned if I even know what I'm doing here! I only signed on 'cause they said they'd be needing some temporary help during the Cherokee Strip doings. Sounded like it might be good for some excitement—but nothing like this! Nobody said I'd be sent out to trade lead with the Doolin gang!"

Land saw Walsh nod in agreement. He thought both men looked in bad shape—cheeks unshaven, eyes hollowed by tension and anxiety following a sleepless night. Just then a fresh round of rifle fire crackled somewhere, and they both winced visibly.

With a nod of his head toward the sound, Land said, "I understood the plan was to take them by surprise, sometime around midnight. One of you want to tell me what went wrong?"

Everything that could have, apparently. They both started talking at once, and as the words tumbled out, Land pieced the story together.

A defective axle fitting had delayed the wagon from Guthrie so that, instead of arriving at midnight, it hadn't made the rendezvous until daybreak. At that time, the lawmen's informant brought word that the gang was up and had left their bunkroom in the attic of the O.K. Hotel. Doolin and the rest had eaten breakfast and gone over to Ransom's Saloon for some morning drinking and card playing. The chance of surprise being lost, the deputy marshals' only option had been to surround them there in the saloon and try to force a surrender. Instead, a gunfight broke out; and knowing they would need more help if it turned into a siege, the leaders had sent a rider off to the county seat at Stillwater, eight miles away, to try to get the sheriff to come with a posse.

"But there wasn't any siege," Bentley explained. "All at once, from out of nowhere, a rifle began picking us off—and damned if we could spot it! In a matter of minutes we'd lost three of our people, including both of the men in charge. Poor Deputy Speed is lying dead out in the middle of the street right now 'cause nobody can figure how to reach him and not get killed himself."

Jim Land interrupted, "Speed was one of the two men I

was told to contact once I got here. The other was called Hueston."

Bentley shook his head. "He was one of the others to take a bullet."

"With nobody left to give orders," Walsh added, "and a sniper working us over, I'm afraid most of us panicked. We were busy trying to keep our heads down, when the whole gang busted out of that saloon and grabbed their horses and headed south for the Cimarron. Hell, we *tried* to stop them— one or two of them might have got shot up some. But they were all soon out of sight."

Walsh went on to explain that the sheriff had later arrived from Stillwater with a posse and that they had promptly set out on the trail of the Doolin gang. A few of the now-leaderless recruits from the marshal's office had wanted to join the posse, but they were talked out of it by a man named Duff Penner, who said he had a better idea.

"Now wait a minute," Jim Land interrupted. "Who's Duff Penner?"

"He's just another rookie like the rest of us," Bentley answered. "Though I did hear him say he once spent six months on the police force up in Wichita. But he located the sniper. Turned out it was a member of Doolin's gang, a man called Arkansas Tom who'd been feeling under the weather this morning and gone back to bed in the hotel. I guess the shooting must've woke him up, and he saw what was happening and went to work on us. No wonder we couldn't tell at first where the bullets were coming from! But then Penner spotted the holes he'd punched in the roof to help him get at us."

Walsh added, "Duff Penner said we could still grab one of the Doolin gang and salvage something out of this operation. He had us put what he called a cordon around the hotel, and we've been trying to hold our own ever since. When the bastard runs out of ammunition, we're hoping to rush the place and take him."

Just then another burst of gunfire broke out upon the heated stillness. Bentley said roughly, "Maybe we ought to get back to work! Unless maybe you got a better suggestion for us?"

"Not offhand," Land said. "I'd like to talk to this Duff Penner. Where can I find him?"

"Probably down there somewhere." Bentley pointed in the direction Land had been headed at the moment he was stopped. "Wherever, he's bound to be at the center of things." With that, Bentley and Walsh turned and hurried back to their positions inside the barn at the street entrance.

Jim Land found himself alone with the civilian. This man, he had learned, was the one who had acted as the law's informant here at Ingalls.

Ed Smith was the owner of the barbershop. He was not particularly impressive to look at—a small man, hatless and coatless, the neckband of his candy-striped shirt buttoned but without a collar. Thinning strands of black hair were combed across his bony skull. He blinked nervously behind rimless glasses as he said, "Mister, I'm damn well relieved to see another sure-enough professional turn up! Will you be taking charge now?"

"If I have to. For an amateur, though, this fellow Penner seems to be using his head." He changed the subject. "How are the townspeople holding up, with a gunfight going on in their midst? So far you're the only one I've seen."

The smaller man shrugged. "They're lying low," he said. "Staying inside their houses—or their storm cellars, those who've got them. You know, it really ain't fair to blame the town," he went on with a touch of defiance. "A little place like this, there ain't a lot of loose cash in anybody's pockets. If the Doolin gang comes riding in and throws their money around, it's only natural some of the businessmen will be happy to oblige them. As for the rest . . . well, we ain't heroes. And we have to live here. We learn to play it safe and keep our mouths shut!"

Jim Land looked at him with interest. Ed Smith might not look impressive, but there was a surprising amount of spirit behind the blinking eyes and timid manner. "You didn't play it safe," he pointed out. "I'd say you took quite a risk, going to the law."

"*Somebody* had to have pride enough to do something and try to take our town back! Actually," Ed Smith went on, "Bill

Doolin don't seem all that bad, himself. But some of his crew are downright vicious!"

Land's eyes narrowed as another thought struck him. "Would I be right to suppose you know all the members of the gang—personally, or by sight?"

The barber gave him a sour look. "I ain't bragging about it, but—yeah, I know most of the leaders, anyhow. Newcomb, Little Bill Raidler, Tulsa Jack—they've all sat in my shop at one time or another, holding their guns in their laps while I tried to keep my dumb hand from shaking and the razor steady! Can't say I know every last one that may have rode with Bill Doolin. The territory's full of outlaws that would hanker to work with him, and he can take his pick.

"Doolin's tough," Smith went on, "and he's smart. Most any job he plans pays off for the men that follow him. Of course, even Bill Doolin ain't a hundred percent perfect. During his last train robbery, up in Kansas a couple weeks ago, he took a bullet in the leg, and he's pretty badly laid up with it. But a thing like that could happen to anybody, I guess."

Land said, "Would you know if he has a man with him who might be described as swarthy, heavyset, with a scarred face? One eye—the left one—is damaged and gone milky."

That got him a quick stare. "No question about that—that's got to be one of the newer men. He was in the saloon this morning, took off with the rest. He strikes me as a killer, and mean as a skunk. I don't mind saying I'm scared as hell of him!"

Jim Land felt his pulse quickening. "Does he have a name?"

"I dunno as to a proper name. I guess on account of being dark complected, I've heard the others call him Turk. Turk Freese," he added.

"That's the one." To himself Land added silently, *So he never even bothered to take another name when he left Texas!*

In almost ten years of dealing with outlaws, Jim Land had thought himself well acquainted with the worst of humanity. But he had never experienced anything like the sight that met him when he walked into the house of a small rancher in the western part of Texas, near Pecos, after Turk Freese had

had his brutal way trying to torture the old man and his wife into revealing the hiding place of a nonexistent cache of coins and greenbacks. The place had been ransacked, both the man and the woman left dead, their futile sufferings finally ended.

It had taken weeks of hard and relentless trailing to run their murderer down. Land almost would have felt justified in executing him out of hand. Instead he had made the extra effort of taking his man alive—and it had proven to be a mistake. Once turned over to local authorities, Freese had broken jail and made his escape, committing another murder in the process. Jim Land was left knowing that his own strict code was to blame for a hair-trigger killer still being loose somewhere, still laying a trail of violence and death.

Now, two years later, upon being offered this appointment by the new federal marshal for Oklahoma to help combat the spread of outlawry in Oklahoma Territory, something had told Land he should accept. It was little more than a hunch, but his hunches were generally good. Conditions in Oklahoma in this year of 1893, with Indian tribal lands being thrown open one by one to white settlement, were chaotic enough to seem made to order for a man like Turk Freese.

And his guess had been right! Ed Smith's news meant that fate was giving him another chance to close the unfinished chapter. This time, Jim Land was determined nothing would stop him.

# Chapter Two

There was an interruption as another man wearing a deputy's badge came hurrying across the back lots from the center of town. He gave a curious, probing look at Jim Land, but his mind was on other matters, and it was Ed Smith he had come looking for. Without preliminary he told the barber, "Penner sent me to find you. We think maybe we've got one of the gang!"

The barber stared. "What do you mean, you got one? Where?"

"Down at Ransom's Saloon—he was hiding behind the bar. The rest must've left him behind when they cleared out."

"I don't believe it. There were six of them in the saloon, and they all got away together. I counted!"

"Just the same, Duff Penner asked if you'd come have a look, see if you can identify him."

"Oh, all right," Smith said impatiently. "Take me to him. But there's some mistake!"

Still grumbling, Smith allowed himself to be led away, the messenger retracing his steps. Curious about this development, Jim Land went with them.

As they emerged from the back lots, the hotel came into view. Penner's messenger hesitated a moment before going farther; he glanced uneasily toward the two-storied hotel building. From here they could see the front of it. Just as

Land had guessed, it had two windows in the gable above the doorway. A jutting signboard named it the O.K. HOTEL.

Nervously, the messenger said, "I got a feeling that bastard up there is just waiting for me to show myself. I made it past him a minute ago, coming the other way, but I got a feeling he's gonna nail me going back!"

"Maybe not," Land said. "The two of you go ahead. Just don't bunch up—and keep moving. I'll follow. If he starts anything, I'll try to discourage him."

The others looked at the rifle held ready in the Texan's grasp. Ed Smith said, "Let's go, then," and started across the dusty expanse at a trot. The messenger drew a deep breath and went after him.

For his part, Jim Land took his deliberate time—not letting himself be hurried, with rifle poised, and his head turned so he could keep a careful watch on those front windows and the gaping hole in the roof. At first there was no sign of the sniper, but then, suddenly, Land saw a flicker of movement behind one of the windows. He instantly halted, spinning about and whipping the rifle to his shoulder.

The two shots sounded together. A bullet struck the ground only inches from Land's boot, gouging up a spurt of dust. He knew his own bullet had gone wide, merely striking the window frame; but it drove Arkansas Tom back from the opening long enough for Land to cover the remaining distance and join the pair waiting for him behind the corner of Ransom's Saloon.

They stared at him, wide-eyed, but all he said was, "At least we know our friend hasn't gone to sleep up there!"

Ransom's Saloon turned out to be a tiny frame building, located on a corner lot and identified by its sign and by a Pabst beer shield nailed to the wall. A saddled horse lay dead at a hitching rack in front of it—limbs stiffening, reins still anchored to the crossbar. It gave mute testimony to the gunfight that had raged between the deputy marshals and the Doolin gang, holed up inside, a short time earlier. Land thought the horse might have taken a stray bullet or been deliberately shot to get it out of the way.

The saloon had a side entrance, and they circled behind and entered that way, beyond reach of the sniper at the hotel. The inside of Ransom's Saloon didn't amount to much. It was poorly lit and woefully cramped, barely large enough for a cheap counter and back bar, plus a few card tables and chairs that had been overturned and scattered. Signs of the fighting that had taken place while the members of the Doolin gang were pinned down here were everywhere. The stench of gun smoke and spilled whiskey was strong, and the floor was littered with broken glass and empty cartridge cases.

Two more of the deputy marshals were here with the prisoner, who sat slumped on a chair with hanging head. He was unshaven and dressed in filthy clothing. Catching the smell of booze from the man, Jim Land thought, *He looks less like an outlaw than the town drunk!*

But the deputy who stood over the prisoner, with arms akimbo and a stern look on his face, didn't seem willing to accept that. He was telling the prisoner in a threatening tone, "We're not going to fool with you! Look at me and answer me straight. I want to know, once and for all, who you are and what you got to do with the Doolin gang."

The derelict lifted his head; his whiskered cheeks were sunken, and his mouth trembled with fear. "Why, nothin' at all, mister!" he protested. "I ain't nobody. I was just havin' a few drinks and watchin' a poker game. All at once the shootin' broke out, and I started huntin' a place to hide. That's all I know about it—honest!"

"You expect me to believe that?"

Ed Smith broke in then. "You've made a mistake, Penner," he told the deputy. "This here is Jack Boggs. He's no outlaw; he spends his time in bars, mostly. I've heard that when one town gets tired of him and kicks him out, he just goes on to find another. He's harmless."

Deputy Duff Penner was obviously unconvinced. Penner, about thirty, was a man with blunt features and a stubborn jaw. Something of the six months he had spent with the Wichita, Kansas, police force appeared to have rubbed off on him. He seemed intense and determined as he said, "If this man's no outlaw, what was he doing with the Doolin bunch?"

The barber shrugged. "He usually tried to hang around when they showed. They were generous with their drinks, and they didn't seem to mind him."

"And *you* seem to take a lot for granted! How can you be sure he wasn't a spy, keeping tabs on the town for them?" Penner laid a keen glance on the prisoner as he added pointedly, "Maybe a little time in a cell would help us get what we want out of him."

Jack Boggs had been peering about, blinking fearfully at the guns and badges surrounding him. Now his head swung back, and his whole body jerked convulsively. "No!" he cried in sudden terror. "You can't do that! I'd go crazy, locked up!" Tears began to stream down his whiskered face. "Please! You don't want me. I ain't nobody!"

That was when Jim Land decided it was time to step in. Duff Penner was well intentioned, if overzealous in this instance. Land spoke mildly but in a way to show he meant business. "I think you're wasting time on him, Penner. It's obvious there's nothing here. Let him go."

The deputy stiffened, and he turned. "So who are *you*?"

But when the newcomer introduced himself, Duff Penner's attitude changed. His belligerence faded and his tone held respect as he said, nodding, "I've heard about you, Land, and I heard you were coming. Only wish you could have made it sooner!" He added, indicating the prisoner, "You're right about him, I guess. But I figured it wouldn't hurt to lean on him a little before we let him go."

Land glanced at Jack Boggs and gave him a dismissing jerk of the head. It was all the derelict needed. He was off his chair at once and heading in shambling haste for the side door and freedom.

While the other men looked on, Jim Land and Duff Penner faced each other in the littered wreckage of the barroom. Penner appeared bitterly frustrated. He mopped a hand across his sweating face and said, "With a little luck, I think we might have brought this thing off today—finished the Doolin gang in a single stroke and taken all the heat off the U.S. marshal's office. If we could even bring in *one* of them, it would help—especially the one that shot down three good men, without giving them any chance at all. . . ."

For someone who had only been sworn in a few days ago, Penner seemed to have taken the duties of a federal officer deeply to heart. Land was impressed, and he said so. "From

what I've seen, you're to be commended for keeping the rest
of these people together. I understand none of them have
had any kind of training or been under fire before today."

Penner passed off the compliment. "We haven't been getting anywhere," he insisted. "If that bastard in the hotel lasts
it out until dark, he can still slip out of our hands entirely.
Damn it, something's got to be done!"

Still reluctant to exercise his authority by taking matters
completely out of Duff Penner's hands, Land asked, "Do you
have any ideas?"

"Maybe." Broken glass crunched underfoot as the deputy
turned to stare moodily through a bullet-smashed window
into the street. "I been looking at that hardware store across
the way," he said suddenly. "Thought maybe I'd go on over
there—assuming I don't get picked off on the way."

"Go right ahead," Land encouraged him. "I can watch
those windows for you." Penner nodded. With no further
hesitation he wrenched open the door and started across to
the store. No sniper's bullet met him; the front windows of
the O.K. Hotel remained empty.

When Jim Land saw that the deputy had entered the store
safely, he lowered his rifle. He told Ed Smith and the two
other deputies, "You'd better stay here." Curious to see what
Duff Penner had in mind, he started after him across the
sun-drenched street. He also made it safely.

The hardware store, like the saloon, was a false-fronted
crackerbox of a building. The main room held a counter,
shelves cluttered with merchandise, and crates and boxes
that took up much of the floor space. Entering, Land noticed
two women seated on a bench against the wall, silently watching Deputy Penner and the storekeeper. A stoop-shouldered
man with thinning hair, the storekeeper was staring at the
deputy and stammering his answer to a question Penner had
just asked him: "Dynamite? Hell, I ain't got any dynamite.
What call would I have to stock that stuff?"

"All right." Penner made an impatient gesture. "Kerosene,
then? You're bound to have that on hand."

"Naturally. People have to keep their lamps filled. There's
a couple of unopened tins in the back room."

"Get 'em." Not waiting to see if his order was obeyed,

Penner turned and saw Jim Land standing by the street door. He explained, "I figure there's one sure way we can bring that killer out. Unless, of course, he'd rather fry up there in the attic!"

The words were barely out of his mouth when one of the women let out a shriek and sprang up from the bench, starting forward as she cried, "No! You can't burn down my hotel!" She was not young, her graying hair pulled back and tied up in a knot. Her face had gone chalk white, and her hands trembled as she lifted them and pressed them to her cheeks.

Duff Penner turned to her. "Lady, I don't like doing it. But," he pointed out bluntly, "you've opened your doors to men you knew were wanted criminals—and I don't doubt you were well paid for it. Do you think you deserve any special treatment now?"

She seemed unable to answer that.

Duff Penner gave a sharp look at the storekeeper, who hadn't moved from where he stood, openmouthed, watching this drama take shape. "What are you waiting for?" Penner snapped. Then turning again to Land, he stated, "Dry as this summer's been, it shouldn't take much to get a blaze started. If the rest of the boys will help keep the guy occupied, I'll try sneaking up on his blind side and set it off."

"No!" The second woman was on her feet now. She was taller and much younger than her companion, Jim Land saw—barely twenty perhaps, with black hair, a trim figure, and attractive features. Her chest lifted, and her cheeks flamed with anger. She confronted the officers, dark eyes flashing scorn at all of them.

"Every stick and thread Mary Pierce owns is in that building! When you ordered us out, you didn't give us time to bring anything with us. And now you intend to put a torch to it! Is it nothing at all to you, if she's left destitute?"

The older woman shook her head in despair. "Don't argue with him, Edie," she warned miserably. "You'll only make trouble for yourself!"

Jim Land knew the time had come to end this. He didn't like to reprimand someone who was only trying to solve a hard problem, and he spoke quietly. "Penner . . ." When the deputy looked at him, he continued, in the same tone: "You may very well be right, but I'd rather hold off if we can and only use the kerosene as a last resort. Every building I've seen here looks ready to go up like tinder—all it would need is a spark. I'd rather try something else."

Penner didn't seem to feel any resentment. "That's up to you, Mr. Land. Whatever you say."

"Fine. Tell the others to be ready in about five minutes to back my play. I'm going over and see if I can't take that fellow out of there."

The other man stared. "Not *alone*. . . . Hell, let me go with you!"

"No. This is a one-man job—he'll be taken by surprise or not at all. I want everyone else primed to draw his attention. Above all, he has to be kept away from those windows while I move in on him."

Duff Penner looked dubious and concerned, but he gave no further argument. "It'll be done," he promised.

Mrs. Pierce seemed too dazed by events to realize her place of business had been given a reprieve. If the young woman named Edie understood what Jim Land had done, she showed no sign of gratitude. Her angry eyes, briefly meeting his as he turned to leave, seemed as hostile as ever.

A minute or two later, as he waited in the shadow of a building across from the hotel for the moment when he could go into action, Land wondered about that young woman. There was something about her and her apparent hostility toward lawmen that puzzled him; somehow he felt it was a question that would be worth trying to answer—but at some other time, not now!

He had put aside his rifle, and now he drew his belt gun, which would be of more use at close range. And as he did so, the stillness suddenly exploded in a burst of gunfire concentrated on the hotel's opposite side.

The moment he saw an answering spurt of smoke rising above the roof, Jim Land broke from cover and headed at an angle across the sun-filled street toward the entrance of the hotel.

There was no porch, merely a broad wooden step and double doors standing open toward the dark interior. The

screen door squealed when he started to pull it open;
he froze, wondering whether that sound had carried. Then he
quickly drew it wide enough to slip through and stepped
inside. He let the screen close against his heel as he stood
alertly listening.

After the blast of daylight, the hotel lobby was dim and
shadowed. The stink of burnt gunpowder hung heavy in the
air. Directly ahead a flight of steps rose to the second floor.
He started up them, one hand on the banister and the other
holding his six-shooter ready.

The sound of a rifle being worked in a deliberate, steady
rhythm grew louder as he mounted. A step squealed under
his boot, and at once the rifle fell silent. Land halted, waiting. When the firing resumed, he took two more cautious
steps, which brought his head above the level of the opening
in the floor above.

Here the trapped heat was stifling, the air blue with stinging smoke. This upper story had never been finished off or
partitioned into rooms. It was a single large space that held a
table or two and a scatter of chairs; a half dozen unmade beds
and several untidy piles of clothing indicated that a number
of men had been sleeping here. As Land had guessed, there
was no ceiling at all, only the roof, explaining how the lone
rifleman had been able to punch holes directly into the roof
shingles. From these holes, bars of sunlight streaked down
through layers of smoke and dust and heated gloom.

Land could see Arkansas Tom crouched on a table beneath
one of those gaping holes; he rose up to throw a shot at his
enemies and then ducked back again while their weapons
answered him. Bullets rattled and thudded into the wall and
the dry shingles over his head.

A box of ammunition lay on the table within easy reach
while the besieged rifleman worked lever and trigger with
steady precision. Considering all the lead that had been fired
at this man since the battle began, it was amazing that some
of it hadn't found him.

Jim Land stayed where he was, silently watching. The
moment he was waiting for finally came—a last spent shell
flew from the rifle's chamber, and the man dropped to his
knees, groping for the box for fresh loads. And in the sudden

stillness, Land pulled back the hammer of his six-gun, the sound of its action startlingly loud.

He said, "Sorry, Tom. I'm afraid it's over. . . ."

The man called Arkansas Tom froze in that awkward position, only his head turning. All he could see of Land was his head and broad shoulders rising out of the stairwell, and the gleam of the revolver steady in his hand.

Land continued to speak in his calm but firmly weighted voice. "Be careful, Tom. Forget about the shells. That's an empty gun you've got, remember—no use to you at all. Just lay it aside and come down from there."

The outlaw must have weighed his chances and decided they were all against him. He did as he was told, the flimsy table creaking under him as he braced a palm against its top and jumped down to face Land empty-handed, poised, and wary. He was a well-built man, with a narrow head, a flowing mustache, and deep-set eyes crowding a long nose. Apparently, when the shooting began that morning, he had grabbed up the rifle but left a revolver and holster belt dangling at the head of his bed.

Land saw him shoot a swift look in that direction, and he warned sharply, "Don't even think about it! Stand easy, right where you are."

Land came up out of the stairwell then and approached his prisoner cautiously. Arkansas Tom watched him come. His piercing stare took in the deputy U.S. marshal's badge. Suddenly he demanded, "How many did I manage to get out there?"

"Three of them, that I heard of."

The other man shrugged. "I thought maybe more. Well, anyway, I kept them busy for a spell—long enough for the rest of the boys to bust out of that saloon and—" He broke off, his head lifting and turning.

"Listening for something?" Land asked. "If you're waiting for your friends to come back and get you out of this, then I'm afraid you've got a long wait! I don't doubt they appreciate you covering their getaway, but they're gone now. You've been left on your own."

He hardly expected the reaction he got with that. Arkansas

Tom stiffened, his sweating face reddened with anger. "That's a lie! They wouldn't run out on me!"

"Oh, come on—use your head! What choice did they have? From what I've heard, a couple of them got shot up before they broke clear. There's no way they could help you now, even if they wanted to!" His voice hardened. "Turn around," he ordered.

Scowling, Arkansas Tom obeyed.

Land was already drawing a pair of handcuffs from his coat pocket. He holstered his gun long enough to snap the irons in place; he felt the prisoner go tense as the steel touched his wrists. But Jim Land worked quickly and had both of the man's hands captured and secured behind his back before he could offer any real resistance. Satisfied, Land again drew his revolver. "Let's go," he said.

Arkansas Tom swung around, and for the first time he revealed some sign of fear. He exclaimed, "You know if you take me down there, I won't have a chance. I nailed too many of them. Those bastards will be waiting to shoot me on sight!"

"No, they won't." Land took his prisoner by an elbow and shoved him relentlessly toward the stairs.

The lobby felt degrees cooler after the attic's trapped and sweltering heat. At the street door, Jim Land motioned for the prisoner to stay back. The continuing racket of rifle fire had eased, and it was into a comparative lull that he sent his shout through the doorway: "Penner? Tell everybody to hold off. The fight's over—I've got our man, and I'm bringing him out."

Gradually the last of the guns fell silent. When Land was sure the shooting was over, he cautiously shoved the screen wide and held it for his prisoner. As the two of them eased out onto the slab of wood before the door, Arkansas Tom turned his head in quick jerks, showing high tension.

The other deputies began to appear then—out of doorways, from behind buildings, and in a dead hush except for the shuffling of boots in the thick street dust. Land counted nine, all with their weapons at the ready and the hot sun picking out their badges. They halted, centering on the pair in front of the hotel, and the very silence was heavy.

Then Deputy Penner stepped forward, his honest face

showing relief and ungrudging respect. "You did it!" he exclaimed. "I've got to admit, I didn't give too much for your chances!"

"Well, it's over. You can all put your guns away—he won't be giving any more trouble, with those handcuffs on him." Land slid his own six-shooter back into the holster and saw the relief pass through this harried group as their long ordeal finally came to an end.

He told Penner, "You're in charge. I want you to put this man and the ones he shot into the wagons and take them to Stillwater. From there, you can wire the marshal's office at Guthrie for further orders. This is one prisoner they're going to want taken real good care of! Here—you'll need the key to his irons," he added, taking it from his pocket and passing it over.

Accepting the key, Duff Penner asked, "You're not coming with us?"

"I figure to get on the trail of that sheriff's posse and see what luck they've had, if any. One last thing," he added, looking the other man in the eye. "I like the way you performed today. Everyone here did all that could have been asked of him, but you did something more. You kept your head, and you held a bad situation together. I think you may have the makings of a lawman, if that's what you want to be."

A compliment, when it was deserved, needed to be given. Land saw how the other man flushed with pleasure, and he smiled. Duff Penner nodded his thanks, and Jim Land turned away.

By now more townspeople were starting to appear, venturing out of hiding as they realized the siege of fighting that had held their town in its grip was over at last. As Land set out to retrieve his horse from the place where he had left it, he almost collided with the gray-haired woman and the younger one called Edie. They were hurrying to the hotel, no doubt to see how much damage it had suffered. He quickly stepped aside, touching his hat brim.

Mrs. Pierce gave him a glance and a timid smile, which he took to be in gratitude for saving her place of business from the torch. There was nothing of the sort from the younger woman, however; her eyes met his in a look of defiance and

unbending dislike. He was left staring, puzzled by such behavior. But when the hotel's screen door slammed behind
them, he dismissed the matter, impatient to be on the trail.

The bay seemed rested and in good enough shape for more
travel. Not knowing how long he might expect to be in the
saddle, Land stopped at the grocery for emergency supplies,
which he bought from a man who seemed resentful of him
and eager to see him gone. Afterward, heading out of town,
he passed the saloon again and saw Jack Boggs leaning his
shoulders against its clapboards; the derelict watched him go
by with no expression on his whiskered face. Across the
street and a little farther along, Ed Smith stood before his
shop, ornamented by a white-and-red striped barber's pole.
An impulse sent Jim Land over there.

The other man spoke first. "Well!" he said with a shrewd
look. "Going after Turk Freese? You know, you can't hope to
catch up with him."

"Worth a try," Land said. But the barber shook his head
emphatically.

Land was forced to admit he was probably right. He picked
up the reins to ride on, but then he paused. "By the way,
that girl at the hotel—Mrs. Pierce called her Edie. Something in the way she acts, I can't help being curious. What
can you tell me about her?"

He wasn't prepared for the reaction he got. The smaller
man stiffened; the expression froze on his face. "Mister," he
said crisply, "don't ask me any more questions, okay? I've
said too much already! Remember, I have to *live* in this
town—and after my part in this business today, I'm going to
be in trouble enough as it is!" And with no more than that, he
wheeled about, strode into his shop, and slammed the door.
Jim Land was left staring after him.

A half mile south of Ingalls, Land met the Stillwater sheriff
and his posse returning, empty-handed, from their pursuit of
the Doolin gang. To a man they sounded weary and disgrun-
tled after their hurried summons and futile chase—but most
of them, he suspected, were more than a little relieved at not
actually overtaking their quarry.

"They didn't even bother trying to cover their trail," the
grizzled sheriff said in answer to Land's questions. "They had

a couple of wounded with them, but even so all they wanted
was to make time. Once they had to stop and do some repair
work—we found a bloody shirt they threw away. But we
never got in sight of anybody.

"We followed them to the Cimarron and upstream for a
couple of miles. Then the trail crossed the river, and we had
to turn back. That's the Sac and Fox reservation down there;
we got no authority to go outside the county."

Jim Land wondered if that wasn't really an excuse for not
riding into unfamiliar country, with the constant risk of running into a rearguard action or an ambush. It would be a real
feather in the cap of any county sheriff's posse to succeed
where federal officers had failed by capturing Bill Doolin, but
it was a privilege these men all seemed willing to forgo.

Land watched them ride off through the heat haze. After
that he picked up the reins and, with a nudge of his heel,
sent the bay forward again along the trail that the sheriff's
posse had made clear for him. Man and horse had recovered
well enough from the hard ride they had made in reaching
Ingalls that morning. In any event, nothing could have kept
Jim Land from the trail he followed now.

Pummeled by searing wind and careful not to push the bay
too hard, he came after an hour's ride to the Cimarron River.
It was shrunken by the long summer's drought. When he
found where the posse had turned back, he paused to let the
animal drink; after that he took the same crossing that the
Doolin gang had used earlier, past the unmarked boundary of
the reservation.

South of the river, the men he followed appeared to be
setting an easier pace—he didn't know at first if it was out of
consideration for the wounded or because they now felt in
less danger of pursuit. But then he suddenly pulled rein and
frowned. One of the horsemen had peeled off to the left and
another to the right, pulling away from the group. Peering
about him, he thought for an uneasy moment a rear guard
might have been sent out to set up an ambush, but the
ground here appeared too open to make that feasible. So it
seemed he was faced with three separate trails. He had no
choice but to keep after the main body.

This was empty country, and the fugitives were deliberately choosing terrain that grew steadily rougher and wilder, broken with stony outcroppings, making the trail more difficult to follow. But soon he came upon a stretch of softer ground, where the tracks were easier to see. He was following no more than two of the original half dozen riders now.

His jaw set as he recognized what was happening. Somewhere up ahead, the remaining two riders would probably split up, leaving him with only one of the half dozen men to follow. Meanwhile a glance at the sun showed him it was already too late, with dusk approaching, for him to turn back and try to pick up one of the other trails he had passed up. By morning, of course, they might be obscured.

So he had seen proof of what the barber meant when he called Doolin a smart leader and a dangerous man. But there would be other days, Jim Land promised himself grimly. He had taken a job and a challenge; before he was through, he intended to come face to face with Bill Doolin. And when he did, he was determined to bring Turk Freese, along with Doolin, to justice.

# Chapter Three

The train from Kansas City had hit another poorly ballasted stretch of road and was making slow time over it. The crowded day coach creaked and groaned; heated air swirled through open windows, carrying the smells of coal smoke and steam and cinders. Beth Converse endured the discomfort while she listened to the voices around her, hearing mostly talk of but one subject—the long-awaited opening of the Cherokee Strip for settlement, now only a couple of days away.

When the train conductor came bustling through, sweating in his heavy blue uniform, he was greeted by complaining voices, all wanting to know the same thing: "Any idea what time we'll get into Tulsa?"

He repeated the same answer: "We *should* be there in thirteen more minutes."

Beth turned to her husband, sitting between her and the window. "Did you hear? It can't be very long now." His face was turned from her; he made no answer. Thinking he might have dozed off, she placed a hand on his arm. "Charlie?"

Charlie Converse jerked his head irritably. "Yes, yes—I heard," he muttered. "That should make us only an hour and a half late—just because they refuse to get any speed out of this hayburner!"

She studied his profile against the blaze of sunbaked prairie sliding past, in hot daylight, beyond the window. When he had one of his petulant streaks, she found it increasingly hard to say anything to him; yet she knew if she didn't at least make the attempt, he was apt to settle deep into a mood that was even harder to deal with. She tried now to answer with a soothing confidence.

"I know how you feel. We've come an awfully long way, and the trip hasn't turned out any easier than we thought it would. But just wait—once we're off these cars, with our feet on solid ground again, everything will look different."

He turned to give her a sudden sharp stare. "Different? What do you mean by that?"

"Why, nothing." Beth almost stammered, dismayed to learn that she had apparently said the wrong thing. "Except that when anyone's as tired as we are just now, it's easy to be fretful or discouraged."

"So now it comes out." Charlie Converse's mouth tightened at the corners. "Already you're discouraged. You think what we're doing is a mistake! Why don't you just admit you were against it from the start?"

"That isn't so!" she protested. "You know I've supported you every way I could!"

"Oh, you've gone through the motions, but you weren't honest about it. The truth is, you don't have faith any longer in anything I undertake!"

He whipped the words at her with such anger that, taken aback, she couldn't stop the tears that misted her vision. "You aren't being fair!"

For a moment the words hung between them, both oblivious to the hubbub of voices around them. Then just as unpredictably, Charlie's manner changed. "I'm sorry," he said, suddenly contrite. All at once he was smiling, and his face had become that of the darkly handsome young man who had swept her off her feet three years ago. "You're right, of course. I think I'm too close to exhaustion to know what I'm saying. But you'll see," he added, and squeezed her hand. "Everything's going to work out. This time, I *know* it! It's got to!"

He turned again to the window, but Beth continued to look at him, disturbed by this scene between them.

In their years of marriage she had become thoroughly

familiar with his behavior—these wild swings between enthusiasm and despair, as his feelings changed toward the various
schemes he concocted for lifting himself from the curse of
poverty.

Today she couldn't say for sure when her initial confidence
in the success of his dreams had finally been eroded away by
failure. There had been too many disappointments—too many
promising jobs lost or impatiently thrown over, businesses
begun on borrowed capital only to fail, until there was no
more money in all of St. Louis available for Charles Converse
to borrow.

To be completely honest, she had to ask herself if the loss
of faith might have begun with a wife's hurt pride and disillu-
sionment, the first time it was forced home that he had been
less than faithful to her—and that time had been only the
first! For all her determination not to let the knowledge
destroy her marriage, something had been lost then that
could never quite be recovered; she was no longer able to
look at him in quite the same trusting way she had before.
Even now the thought of it was too painful, and she shied
away, not wanting it to color her judgment or make her
unhappier than she was.

As she looked now at this man she had once admired and
loved, holding back nothing as a romantic young woman was
prone to do, she knew that she would need all her wisdom
and courage in the days ahead. A long wail of the train's
whistle reminded her that they were nearing their destina-
tion. She was farther than she had ever been from home,
committed to the realization of Charlie's latest dream and, if
it was still possible, to the saving of what was left of her
marriage.

The train stood at the station, panting gusts of steam, coal
smoke, and heat while the day cars disgorged their boisterous
passengers. The Converses held back, at last stepping down
onto the cinders, where they stood with the suitcases holding
their limited possessions while they got their bearings.

Beth had heard somewhere that this place on the north
bank of the Arkansas River had originally been a tribal center
of the Creek Indians, but if that was so she saw little to
suggest it. This resembled any photograph she'd ever seen of

a typical Western cattle town—rutted dirt streets and false-fronted wooden buildings, hitching rails and saddled horses. To complete the picture, a racket of lowing cattle, squealing horses, and shouting men rode the dust cloud that lifted above nearby shipping pens, where cowpunchers were shoving reluctant beef cattle up a ramp and into a boxcar destined for distant markets.

A stagecoach, in to meet the railroad, rolled past behind its four-horse hitch. Charlie swore, and Beth ducked her head as its dust whipped over them both, briefly blinding and engulfing them. As she rubbed the back of a hand across her stinging eyes, Beth found herself thinking that she had just witnessed another symbol of a passing era—the railroads spelling doom for the old Concord coaches of which she'd heard so many romantic stories. Just as surely, opening the Indian lands to settlement, in this year of 1893, constituted a final chapter in a long history of the white man's encroachment on another race and its ancient way of life.

Her husband's words broke in on these sobering thoughts. "Main Street seems to be down that way." It ran perpendicular to the railway line, a little to the right of where they stood. "Let's give it a look," he suggested, and they started walking in that direction, weighed down by their luggage.

It was good to stretch muscles that had been stiffened by hours of sitting in one position. Solid ground had a strange feel though, after the constant sway of the cars, and for a moment Beth was uncertain of her footing. The sweltering heat was enough to make one gasp; she was glad when they stepped up onto sidewalk planking and into the shade of an occasional wooden awning.

Traffic here was nothing compared to the streets of St. Louis, yet she still found herself confused by the bustle of the place, by her exhaustion, and by uncertainty as to where they were heading. Charlie appeared to know what he wanted, however. She asked him, "Just what is it you're looking for?"

"This," he said, as they halted before the wide doors of a verandaed building. Beth saw the word HOTEL stenciled on the glass.

She held back, frowning. "You want to stop *here*? It looks as though it would be expensive!"

"We haven't slept in a bed or had a decent meal since we left. This could provide us with both."

*And a bath!* she thought. It was almost like a prayer. "But can we afford it?" she protested. "We don't have an awful lot of money. We're going to need every penny before we're through."

"You want to spend the night in a hayloft?" he snapped. "We deserve better than that! Let me worry about the money." And he mounted the steps, plainly expecting her to follow.

Knowing it would be useless to argue, Beth could only let herself be led across the veranda and into a lobby that looked considerably more ornate than might have appeared from the hotel's exterior. Wide doorways led into a parlor and a dining room; from the latter came sounds of tables being cleared and someone using a broom on the carpet.

As he signed the register, Charlie asked, "Are they still serving?"

"I'm afraid you've missed the noon meal," the clerk said. "Supper will be at six."

"I suppose we'll wait then."

An aged bellboy collected their luggage and preceded husband and wife up the stairs to a room at the front on the second floor. Charlie Converse tipped him generously; Beth noticed, but determinedly made no comment.

She made a quick assessment of the room's furnishings and afterward stepped to the window, where she could look across the veranda roof to the buildings on the opposite side of the street. She noticed a bank, a lawyer's office, and other business establishments. Farther on, south and west of Tulsa, the flat and looping course of the Arkansas River shone like beaten metal under the high sun.

Despite the open window, this room was musty and breathless. Turning away, Beth drew her pins, removed her hat, and laid it on the dresser with a sigh as she observed in the mirror the wrinkled state of her traveling dress. It seemed to her that her face looked deathly pale with heat and fatigue. She stood a moment pushing at her heavy crown of dark brown hair, trying to worry some order into it.

Beth thought again, longingly, of a bath. But other things were more important. She looked around for her husband, to discover him stretched out on the bed and looking wonderfully relaxed. His eyes were closed, the dark, curly hair fallen across his high forehead in a way that made him look as young as the day they first met. Just now he seemed content to stay where he was, indefinitely. The thought that he might actually have fallen off to sleep sent her over to the bed. She hesitated and then spoke his name.

She had to repeat it before he opened his eyes and frowned up at her, plainly annoyed. "Well?"

"Don't you think we should be getting busy?"

Charlie groaned. "Busy! Why? I'm just beginning to feel human again. And the big event is three days away."

"Not quite—today's half gone," she reminded him. "It seems to me we need to be thinking about supplies. And then there's transportation. This close to the deadline, such things may not be too easy to find. Everything available may have been snapped up already."

He considered that. Reluctantly he said, "Yes, you could be right." He groaned and levered his legs across the side of the bed, sat there a moment as though gathering his strength, and got to his feet. "I'll go have a look around. You stay here and try to get some rest."

"I want to come with you."

She was already reaching for her hat. She had thought he might object for some reason, but Charlie only shrugged. "Suit yourself." Yet she felt a sort of distance between them as they left their room and went down the stairs to the lobby, neither speaking.

Out on the busy street, Charlie scouted the signs on business houses they passed until he found an all-purpose establishment that advertised groceries, general merchandise, and ranch and farm supplies. They joined the stream of people through its propped-open doors, but as they made their way along the aisles, looking at the prices on the sacks and boxes and bins, Beth couldn't help a gasp of dismay; she saw her husband's face grow grim.

A man who had been watching them from behind a counter asked, "Something for you people?"

Charlie said, "Are you the proprietor?" And getting a nod

he demanded, "What sort of markup do you call this? It's robbery!"

"It's just good business," the man replied blandly. "You won't find any cheaper in Tulsa—or anywhere else hereabouts, right now. Not with the territory crawling with boomers that are stocking up for the opening on Saturday." He gave the pair a shrewd look. "Would you two happen to be amongst them?"

"That's hardly your affair," Charlie reminded him.

"Oh, sure. I just wondered, is all, how you're planning to make the run. I hope you've got yourselves a conveyance—if you ain't, you can save some money because you sure won't have any use for supplies!"

"I do happen to be in the market for some sort of wagon," Charlie Converse admitted shortly. "Can you sell me one?"

"Hell, I couldn't even sell you a wheelbarrow. Look—do you have any idea how many they expect to have on the starting line come Saturday noon? I've heard figures high as a quarter million! I made the other run, in eighty-nine. I'm just as glad to be sitting this one out!"

Beth asked him out of deepening concern, "Do you know any place where we might hope to find a wagon?"

He shrugged. "You can try the liveries around town or the public corrals. Sometimes one of them will pick up a rig from someone and have it for sale. But I wouldn't be too hopeful, this late in the day."

Charlie said stiffly, "We have money. I'm sure we'll find what we're looking for."

"Well, it's nice to be sure!" the man commented dryly.

He gave them directions, and they set out. Beth was apprehensive after what they had just heard; her husband sounded confident, but she suspected he was bluffing. Now, as they made the rounds and the places left to visit grew fewer, and they met nothing but curt denials, her discouragement grew. It seemed the final irony—to have come so far and spent so much in money and energy and hope, only to find themselves thwarted.

Her spirits sank; she wondered if Charlie was beginning to suspect he faced one more in a string of failures and defeats. They found themselves near the railroad tracks, confronting the last place on their list. A barn that had HALSELL'S LIVERY AND PUBLIC CORRAL painted on its false front rose before them. And here, just within the entrance, they saw exactly what they had been looking for—a light but sturdy-looking spring wagon, almost new. But the attendant shook his head at Charlie's question, telling him curtly, "Sorry, but this rig's already spoken for. I understand the buyer will be in to pay and pick it up before the day's out."

Charlie caught him by an arm. "But supposing he doesn't? Look! I'll raise him; I'll pay double!" He dug the wallet from his coat pocket and thrust it under the man's nose. "I have cash, and I'm desperate. Just name the price!"

The man backed away, indignantly. "Hell, mister! I couldn't do that—I only work here, and once a deal is set, Halsell would never go back on it for any amount of money. I've told you I'm sorry, and that's all I can do!"

He turned his back and headed for his cubbyhole office. Beth and Charlie looked at each other, unable to speak in this moment of complete dismay. Charlie was pale, and his cheek muscles bulged to the clenching of his jaw; she knew he felt terribly defeated and was as completely discouraged as herself. And knowing how much he had depended on the success of this latest venture, her heart went out to him. She managed a smile as she told him, "It's all right. I know we'll think of something." He only shrugged.

Neither had noticed a man who stood a little distance away, watching them. Now, as they turned to walk away, he spoke: "Hey!" He was an unprepossessing figure, tall, bony, and slope shouldered, his whiskered cheeks sunburnt and peeling under a battered hat. He said quickly, "If you folks are hunting for a rig, happens I got one—*and* a team. Hadn't been thinking about selling, but if somebody was to make the right offer, I might consider it."

"Oh?" Beth could sense her husband's quick surge of interest. "Just where is this rig of yours?"

"It's around in back. You want to look?"

"Sure—why not?" Charlie took his wife's arm as the man gestured for them to follow.

Beth realized now that there were two of them. A second man stood in the background, shorter than the other but dressed very much the same in boots, coat, and pants that looked as though they had seen better days. She didn't particularly like their looks, and she had reservations about anything they might have for sale. But she and Charlie could scarcely afford to pass up any proposition without investigating it.

Her suspicions appeared to be unfounded. Their guide led the way around the side of the barn to the wagonyard and public corral in back. Sure enough, there was the wagon, with a fair-looking span of horses harnessed to it. He himself gave one of the wheels a kick to demonstrate its soundness. "Go right ahead," he invited. "Look it over. Take your time. I guarantee you won't find a thing to fault it."

Beth thought that, like herself, Charlie was wondering what the catch might be. He walked around the vehicle, frowning critically. The skinny man continued, "To be frank with you, I got a bad case of the shorts just now, and so I'd be willing to hear an offer. But I won't let you steal it from me—and I can't wait all day."

Someone said, "Watch out! That rig don't belong to him."

Everyone turned. A man had just stepped out of the livery barn. He wasn't young; straggling gray hair and mustache contrasted with the sun-darkened flesh of his face and muscled arms, where the sleeves of his work shirt had been hacked way. He wore a stable hostler's overalls, and he had a pitchfork, which he leaned on as he stood bareheaded in the sun, faded eyes peering at the group around the wagon.

Charlie Converse exclaimed, "What are you saying?"

"I'm just sayin' I know the owner, and this ain't him. The man you're talkin' to is a saddle tramp name of Sid Yount; don't remember hearin' a name for the other one. It looks like Yount come near to takin' your money for something that warn't his to sell!"

A glance at the skinny man's thunderous look told Beth all she needed to know. She saw the color rising in her husband's face as Charlie hastened to deny his gullibility. "You're wrong!" he told the hostler. "I wasn't born yesterday! I was merely letting him give himself away. I suggest now you go and find a policeman—I'll keep him here until you do."

"The hell you will!" There was a convulsive movement

from Sid Yount, and his hand came into the open holding a six-shooter that had been hidden beneath the threadbare coat.

Beth was scarcely aware of the scream that tore from her throat as she saw the revolver turned upon her husband. Her hands flew to her cheeks; she stood helpless, thoroughly expecting to see Charlie go down, shot to death before her eyes.

She had reckoned without the old hostler. His only weapon was the pitchfork in his hand, but without hesitation he loosed an angry shout and came charging, its polished tines leveled at the skinny fellow's chest. Sid Yount jerked his head around and gaped at him, as though too startled to think of using the gun.

It was his smaller companion who found presence of mind to act. He also suddenly produced a gun and without hesitation threw a bullet at the hostler. The sharp report echoed off the barn's siding. Stopped in midstride, the old fellow's head jerked backward. He dropped his pitchfork, and then his legs seemed to tangle and he went down. As he fell, Beth saw with horror the blood that streaked his thinning hair.

Jim Land had noticed the woman as he rode up to the livery stable. He didn't know what it was about her that caught his attention—something in the way she stood, the way she held her head beneath its wealth of brown hair and the feathered hat she wore. She seemed somehow both proud and vulnerable, and he looked more closely and saw that she was beautiful and, at the same time, obviously troubled.

Now she and the man beside her—the woman's husband, he guessed—turned and started walking toward the corral at the rear of the lot, accompanied by two other characters so dubious in appearance he couldn't help but wonder what she could have to do with them. Land rode on to a hitching rack near the livery entrance and dismounted, thoughts of the woman strangely remaining with him even as he paused to lift one of his mount's rear hooves to check the seating of its iron shoe.

The horse was a good one—a sorrel—that he had bought

the second day after his arrival in this Oklahoma country; it
had carried him a lot of miles in the two weeks since then.
After the day when he lost the trail of the Doolin gang in that
country beyond the Cimarron, he had been following every
hint or rumor that might point him toward one or another of
Bill Doolin's many hideouts, but nothing ever came of it.
After the raid at Ingalls, he thought Doolin must be lying low
and nursing the crippling leg wound he was supposed to have
taken during the course of his last railroad holdup, on the
Santa Fe line in Kansas. If that was the case, there seemed
little anyone could do but wait for him to come out of hiding.

One final clue had brought Jim Land to Tulsa. He had little
confidence in it, but it was the one lead he still had, and a
livery seemed as likely a place as any for asking questions.
Satisfied with the shoe, he set his animal's hoof down and
ducked beneath the pole. As he did he heard a woman's
sharp scream near at hand and, immediately afterward, a
single gunshot.

Somehow he knew that the scream had come from the
woman he had seen so briefly a moment earlier. At once he
ran toward the sound alongside the raw boards of the livery,
with the depot and railroad tracks on his left. As he approached the rear corner of the big building, two horsemen
suddenly burst into view, spurring past him at a dead run
across the tracks. Seeing a glint of gunmetal in the hand of
one of the riders, Land came to a halt and whipped out the
six-shooter from his own holster. But before he could use it,
the horsemen swept from sight behind a boxcar sitting on a
siding, and then they were gone.

Land had to forget them for the moment. He had come out
upon the open space behind the livery, where people in town
from adjoining farms and ranches were free to park their
wagons and put their saddle horses in a public corral. At once
he saw the woman kneeling in the dirt, heedless of soiling
her dress as she anxiously tended the motionless figure of a
grizzled, sun-browned man in overalls. Jim Land slid his gun
back into its holster as he walked over and placed a hand on
the woman's shoulder. He demanded anxiously, "Are you all
right?"

She lifted her head and gave him a distracted nod. She

looked pale, but she seemed unhurt; her whole concern was for the limp and bleeding figure beside her. "I think he's dead!" she exclaimed. "A couple of men were trying to cheat my husband and me with a wagon that wasn't theirs to sell. *He* stopped them, and—and they shot him!"

Land dropped down beside her to give the hurt man a closer look. He examined the damage the bullet had done just above his ear, felt for a pulse, and found one. He said quickly, "This fellow's not dead. Either he was lucky, or he's got a hard skull! At any rate, I believe he's already starting to come around; the bullet must only have creased him."

Her brown eyes flooded with relief. "You really think so?"

"I really do." He added gently, nodding past her, "If that's your husband, yonder, maybe you'd better take a look at *him*. He seems to be in trouble."

Her head whipped around, and she gasped as she saw the man who lay sprawled in the dirt. "Oh!" she cried out, and at once leaped up and hurried to him.

At that moment the man with the head wound moaned and stirred. Land put a hand on his arm and said, "You take it easy, partner!"

Interestingly enough, either no townsmen had heard the scream and the shot or they hadn't bothered to investigate. The four of them were alone here. The woman had an arm around her husband's shoulders and helped support him as he tried now to push himself into a sitting position. "Charlie! What in the world happened?"

"I don't know," he said petulantly, then corrected himself. "Oh, yes I do! It was that fellow Yount. He used the barrel of his gun on me. Next thing I knew I was on the ground, with my head full of fireworks!" He felt the side of his face and winced. "It's a wonder my jaw isn't broken!"

"And I never saw a thing!" she cried.

Her husband looked around. "What happened to that pair of thieves, anyhow?"

Jim Land listened to her say that they were gone; she had heard Sid Yount tell the other one, "Jeeter—fetch the horses!" There'd been a couple of animals tied to the corral fence, and in less than a minute the two men were in the saddle and heading away from there, fast.

Land watched the man called Charlie take in her story, his eyes still glazed in pain. Suddenly he shoved a hand into a coat pocket, and his face contorted. He cried out, "My wallet! It's gone! That was it—he knocked me down and took it. Oh, my God! They got every cent we had!"

The young fellow was trying frantically to lunge to his feet; but still feeling the effects of the blow with the gun barrel, he fell back as she seized his arm. "Charlie!" she protested. "Please! You can't stop them now."

It was at this point that the old hostler spoke up, drawing all their attention. His voice was surprisingly clear, for someone who had narrowly missed taking a bullet in the skull. "Did you say they took them two Bar Cross horses that was tied to the fence?" When the woman nodded, he said gruffly, "That figures. I was wonderin' who it was left 'em there, instead of putting 'em inside the corral like they was supposed to. Looked like somebody was expectin' to have to make a quick getaway. Which wouldn't be surprising—anyone connected with that Bar Cross!"

"Bar Cross," Jim Land picked it up. "A local ranch?"

The man nodded and then winced as though he wished he hadn't. "It don't amount to much," he grunted. "Fellow that runs it—name of Nels Antrim—he's got a bad reputation for playin' easy with other men's livestock and takin' in unsavory characters."

"Including Yount and his friend?"

"Sounds like it, if they were riding a couple of his horses. Unless maybe they stole them from him; now *that* would be a switch!"

Anyone watching Land would hardly have guessed, from his expression, that he had ever heard the name Nels Antrim. He asked, almost casually, "Where would I find this spread, supposing I was to look for it?"

"Ain't too hard. Just take the north road till it branches, some ten miles out. Follow the one that leads east."

Land nodded. "They could be headed that way, all right. I saw them go." Abruptly he got to his feet and walked over to the woman and her husband. "I'm going to see if I can catch up with that pair. If I'm able, I'll try to bring back your money."

"Yeah?" The man's eyes filled with quick suspicion. "It's almost five hundred dollars—every cent we own. How do I know you won't be tempted to keep it for yourself? Thanks, but I think I'd better contact the sheriff."

In that moment, Jim Land decided he didn't like this man. He said coldly, "Suit yourself. But by the time you get around to doing that, it will probably be too late." He turned away, too angry to say anything more.

But the woman cried, "Wait!" She was on her feet facing him with an anxious look. "He shouldn't have said what he did," she told him in apology. "I know you made a sincere offer. Even so, we'd have no right asking a stranger to take risks on our account!"

With a half smile he answered, "I intend to be careful."

"And we haven't even told you our name. It's Converse. Charlie and Beth . . ." She held out her hand.

The hand felt strong when he took it briefly in his own. He gave his own name in response and afterward said, "Maybe these men should have a doctor look them both over, just to make sure no serious damage was done."

"I'll see to it," she promised. "Good luck, Jim Land!"

He took that with him, as he hurried to the hitchrack where he had left his sorrel.

# Chapter Four

The Bar Cross was a fairly poor excuse for a ranch. From the looks of it, Nels Antrim could have been here for some time, squatting illegally on land belonging to the Indians. A weather-beaten house and grain shed and a few smaller out-buildings were scattered near the thinly timbered bank of a creek, which was bone dry just now. The yard was a litter of broken equipment; a small mountain of rusted tin cans stood within throwing distance of the kitchen door. Only the corral seemed to be in decent repair. It held a half dozen horses, and a couple more stood outside it, under saddle, their reins knotted to one of the poles.

Those two horses were the same ones whose trail Jim Land had followed all the dozen miles from Tulsa—the ones he had seen being spurred away from the wagonyard where Beth and Charlie Converse had been robbed of their savings.

Land had approached cautiously, following the dry creek bed to a spot directly behind the buildings; here he dismounted, tied his reins to a sapling, and pulled his gun while he gave the place a careful surveyal. There was no movement in the yard, no sound from the house. But now, even as he listened, he heard an ax starting up a rhythmic racket in some scrub timber farther along the creek bank. Somebody was chopping up firewood; whoever it was might be busy with that for some little while.

He came out of the trees and approached the grain shed,

keeping it between himself and the house windows. The shed had to be checked out; he found a door and opened it cautiously on its leather hinges, slipped inside, and stood listening. Bars of light from holes in the disintegrating roof streaked through the gloom; it had the feel of emptiness. But there was a loft, and he climbed a ladder and poked his head up for a look at that before he was satisfied.

No one was holed up in this building—not Bill Doolin or anyone else. Whoever was here would have to be staying at the house.

Satisfied he would not be leaving his back unprotected, Jim Land put the shed behind him and moved directly across the yard. He skirted the pile of rusted tins and the badly depleted woodpile. He heard no outcry, no gunshot or other signal that he had been discovered. The rear door of the house stood open, with no screen to keep out the flies. He placed his back against the wall beside it and heard a murmur of voices within.

Land drew a breath, held it, and stepped into the doorway with his six-gun leveled in front of him.

The room he looked into appeared to be the main living area of Nels Antrim's ranch house, with a few pieces of rough furniture and an iron stove for heating and cooking. To his right was a closed door. Land wished he knew what lay beyond that, but in front of him, seated on benches at a crude deal table, were the two men he had followed here from town. A leather wallet lay on the table, and they were busy dividing its contents, too intent to be aware of a newcomer's shadow filling the doorway. No one else was in the room.

The man who had been doing the counting finished his work, and the two started to gather up their shares. That was when Jim Land said, in a pleasant voice, "Are you boys sure it's all there?"

They froze, their hands gone motionless. Two heads came around and stared at him in the doorway, his gun leveled at them. The smaller of the men looked at his companion and demanded hoarsely, "Sid, who the hell is he?" The rawboned figure thus identified as Sid Yount could only shake his head.

"As far as you two are concerned," Jim Land answered,

"I'm the gent who followed you from Tulsa to get back the money you stole from those people in the wagonyard." He added, his voice hardening, "I want you to leave everything where it is. Just move away from the table—and keep your hands in sight!"

For a moment he thought they weren't going to obey. The one called Jeeter swore at him, but Sid Yount met his look with a wolfish stare, as though taking his measure. Land stared back, and as though convinced, the gaunt man shifted position on his bench, swung a leg across it, and moved to hitch himself up to his feet.

Considering Yount the most dangerous of the two, Jim Land kept a careful eye on him. And that was a mistake, for it was the scruffy-looking Jeeter who suddenly gave a cry of rage and made a bold move toward his holster. Instantly, Land swung his weapon over, with a sharp warning: "Don't try it!" But Jeeter was already committed. The derelict's fist came up holding a revolver.

Land held off till the last moment; then, having no choice, he fired—an instant sooner than the other, aiming for the man's gun arm. But in that same instant, Jeeter flung himself to one side, and the bullet struck him in the chest, driving him backward. His own six-shooter went off, and the bullet drilled uselessly into the floor. The two shots mingled, ear-shattering within the confines of the room. Jeeter tangled with the bench he had been sitting on and went down, falling loosely, like a broken doll.

"Son of a bitch!" Sid Yount gritted his teeth. "You killed him!"

"Does look like it," Jim Land agreed coldly. "Your turn, now. Drop your gun on the floor—or use it!"

The bony face twisted, but Yount wasn't going to make Jeeter's mistake. He lifted his weapon from the holster and let it fall. Land picked up the gun and, keenly conscious of that other door so close beside him, took a couple of strides and gave it a kick that flung it open. A quick glance showed him a second, smaller room, with a half dozen crude wooden bunks lining the walls, most of them bare but a few holding straw ticks and blankets. There was no one in the bunk room.

As he turned back, satisfied with that, Land was suddenly

aware that the strokes of the ax that had been sounding
continuously up to now, out in the stillness of the afternoon,
had broken off. Quickly he stepped to the table and, one-
handed, gathered up Charlie Converse's wallet and money
and dropped them into a pocket of his coat. Then he turned
toward the front entrance as hurrying footsteps approached.

The man with the ax still carried it as he came bursting in.
The first thing he saw was the body of Jeeter, lying where
Land's bullet had dropped him. The newcomer gaped at the
dead man and then threw his stare at Yount, across the drift
of powder smoke. "What the hell?" he demanded. Not speaking, Sid Yount gave a sideways jerk of the head; the other
man followed his glance and for the first time saw the stranger
who stood with revolver in hand, covering him. He went
still.

That the man would feel he had to wear a shell belt and
holster while chopping up kindling on his own woodlot told
Jim Land something about him. He said, "You won't need
that gun or the ax. Get rid of them."

Nels Antrim glared at him for several moments before,
reluctantly, he turned and leaned the ax against the wall;
then he unbuckled his belt and let holster and gun thud to
the floor.

He was a stocky figure of a man, with a shapeless nose and
slightly walleyed. His hat was battered, stained, and sweated
through. He tried to sound threatening as he said loudly,
"You think you can just walk into a man's house and gun
down his friends?"

"Maybe they didn't tell you," Land said, "but these 'friends'
of yours robbed some people in town this afternoon. I came
for their money. Your friend on the floor wanted to argue
about it. D'you figure to give me some more argument?"

He could of course have shown them the badge he carried
in his pocket, but he preferred not to. Men like these would
be more impressed with cold audacity, he suspected, than
influenced by any respect they might have for the law. He
saw indecision now in Nels Antrim, whose jaw worked nervously, as though he were chewing at his lower lip. The
rancher finally gave way to bluster. "Whoever you are, you
better get the hell off this ranch! You hear me?"

"That's all right." Land touched the bulge made by Converse's wallet in his coat pocket. "I got what I came for, so there's no good reason to stay." But then an idea that had been stirring at the back of his mind firmed into decision. "Except for maybe one other thing. What do you say we step outside?" He gestured with his gun barrel. "The two of you walk ahead of me."

Puzzled, they let themselves be herded out of the house and across the barren yard to the corral where Yount and Jeeter had left the saddled horses tied to the fence. At a closer look, Land's impression that they were both good animals proved to be confirmed; in spite of Nels Antrim's Bar Cross brand, he hardly doubted they had been stolen somewhere.

Antrim didn't like the way this stranger was studying them. "What you looking at?" he demanded suspiciously. "Those broncs belong to me, in case you want to know."

"You don't seem too particular who you lend them to," Land remarked, with a pointed look at the glowering Sid Yount, "or for what purpose. So I've decided I might as well borrow them myself for a day or two. I may have use for a couple of good extra horses."

"By God, no!" The words exploded from Nels Antrim.

"Oh, don't worry. You can have them back, any time after Sunday. I'll leave them for you at the stable in town. Yount will know which one." Without further ado Land whipped the reins of one of the horses free and swung into the saddle. When Antrim surged forward, he was stopped by a revolver pointed at his head.

A sharp order made both men stand back. As they watched, helpless to interfere, Jim Land proceeded to drop the poles that closed the entrance to the corral.

He raised his gun and punched out a couple of shots into the afternoon stillness. A shout sent the animals in the corral streaming wildly through the opening, and they instantly scattered. Without hesitation Land holstered his gun, grabbed the reins of the second borrowed horse, and kicked his own mount into motion. Furious, frustrated yells rose behind him as he rode across the yard. Looking back he saw Nels Antrim whip off his battered hat and fling it into the dirt; after that both men started at a run toward the house—to get weapons.

That didn't greatly concern him. He could see little chance of their catching a horse in time to give pursuit. Land headed directly toward the place where he had left his own animal in the dry creek bed. As he neared it, there was the crack of a pistol behind him; he looked back and saw Nels Antrim at the rear door of his shack, smoking revolver in hand. But the bullet had missed widely, and in the next moment Land put the grain shed between them.

He jumped his borrowed horses down the bank of the dry creek bed, where the sorrel waited. He gave himself time to swing over onto the other saddle; then he was away at an easy lope, making distance with the borrowed animals following at their trailing reins.


The shingle above the door of the house a half block west of Main Street read JOHN ALLEN, M.D. The door stood open. When Jim Land stepped inside, he found the doctor bandaging up the hurt foot of a half-grown boy who appeared to have gotten into some broken glass. Land said, "They told me over at Halsell's stable that you're taking care of a man named Parsons. He got hurt there earlier today."

Allen was a spry and bright-eyed old man with a thick mop of white hair. He said, "You must be the fellow named Land that I heard about. Yes, Dake Parsons is here, and he's doing fine—the bullet he took barely grazed him, did no special damage that I can see. Still, I'm trying to keep him in bed until I'm sure." He added, pointing to a white-painted door, "That nice Mrs. Converse has been with him practically all afternoon—I guess she feels real concerned. She and her husband are in there now. Go right on in if you like; I got to finish this."

Land thanked him and left him to his work. He entered a room that apparently served the doctor as a small hospital. One of its two beds was vacant, but the other held the injured hostler. He lay propped against pillows, the bandage around his head contrasting sharply with his sun-darkened features. Beth Converse sat beside the bed, deep in conversation with Parsons; her husband stood looking out the window at the waning afternoon, his attitude suggesting impatience and boredom.

Dake Parsons greeted the newcomer. "Hey—you're back! Any luck?"

To answer, Land took out the wallet and handed it to Converse, who turned quickly from the window. "So far as I know, your money's all there," he said as the man opened the wallet to check its contents. "You can count it."

He thought Charles Converse wanted to do just that, but the man had the decency to say with a shrug, "That's all right. I guess I'm lucky to take what I can get."

Beth Converse had been studying Jim Land with an anxious expression, and now she asked, "But are *you* all right? Did you have trouble?"

"Not too much," he said evasively.

The man in the bed made an impatient gesture. "Well, ain't you going to fill in the details? Did you go clear to Antrim's? What happened, anyway?"

Land refused to elaborate. "You could say we reached a settlement." He had no intention of telling them about the death of the man called Jeeter. "I let it go at that. If I'd brought anyone in to turn over to the sheriff," he pointed out, addressing Converse, "you would have to prefer charges and give testimony. And if you're expecting to make the run day after tomorrow, I couldn't see how it would fit in with your plans."

"You thought right," the other man agreed, and slapped the wallet into the palm of a hand. "This is the only thing I was concerned about."

"How does that jaw feel?"

Converse touched it gingerly. "Couple of teeth feel as though they've been jarred loose. But no permanent damage done."

"To you either, I guess," Land told the hostler, "from what the doc says."

Dake Parsons said gruffly, "I'd be up and out of here right now, but the old fool won't let me!"

"You barely missed getting killed!" Beth Converse exclaimed. "And all on our account, too." She placed a hand on his arm.

Dake Parsons appealed to Land. "You see what I been putting up with?" It was obvious he enjoyed every bit of it. "In fifty years, I ain't ever had such a pretty woman make a fuss like this over me!"

Converse interrupted then, to say to his wife, "Haven't we spent enough time here? We haven't even had dinner yet."

She hesitated and then asked the hurt man, "Is there anything more we can do before we go? Anything at all?"

"Not a thing," he said promptly. He added, "But if you folks are here to make the Cherokee Strip run on Saturday, there just may be something I can do for *you.*"

Charlie Converse said, "I doubt it. Not unless you can supply us with a wagon!"

"I'm afraid that's beyond me. But what I *can* do is point you to one of the nicest little pieces of land in the whole Cherokee Strip."

"Oh?" Beth's husband suddenly looked interested.

"It's a fact! I know that country about as well as anybody," the old fellow explained. "Over the years, I've punched cattle for one or another of the outfits that leased grazing land there from the Indians. And if I had it in mind to claim myself a homestead, I know one particular quarter section where I'd want to sink my stake. I'm telling you, it's got everything: good soil, some timber, and most important of all, a dandy sweetwater spring that I never knew to fail, even in the driest year. And it's yours for the askin'."

Beth said, "But why share this with strangers? I should think you'd want it for yourself."

Dake Parsons shook his head emphatically. "Needs a younger man. I ain't about to lay claim to homestead land at my age. Been working cattle too long. I'm doin' all right with the job Mr. Halsell give me at his livery stable—one of the businesses he's gone into, now that beef ranching is about finished here in Oklahoma Territory. Anybody got pencil and paper on him? Maybe I could draw a map for you of this place I been talkin' about."

Land found both in a pocket of his coat and handed them over. Dake Parsons hitched himself into a more comfortable position and gestured for Beth to hand him a book from the bedside table, to use as a writing surface. He started to unfold the paper Land had given him, but suddenly he halted, and his expression seemed to ice over as he saw what it was he had in his hands. He lifted his stare at Jim Land then, and his gray eyes held cold anger and something very much like contempt.

Land had not looked for such a reaction; at any rate it was too late now to take the paper back. He knew by heart the bold words it contained: "$5,000.00 REWARD for Capture Dead or Alive of BILL DOOLIN, Notorious Robber of Trains and Banks."

Land met Dake Parsons's look as the latter demanded heavily, "You carry things like this around for fun? Or maybe you're in the business?"

"I suppose you'd say I was," Land replied.

The older man shook his bandaged head. "Somehow I'd thought better of you!"

Beth Converse had been looking from one to the other in perplexity. She blurted out, "What is it? What's wrong?"

"I'll tell you what's wrong," Parsons answered her, tight-lipped. "In *my* book there's nothin' lower than a lousy bounty hunter! For your information, mister," he threw the angry words at the tall man standing beside the bed, "Bill Doolin happens to be a friend of mine! Ten years ago, we rode together for Oscar Halsell's Double H. I can't condone Bill turnin' outlaw, but whatever he's done, no one can claim he ever killed another man. Which don't even put him in the same class with the kind that would hunt him down and turn in his pelt, to collect blood money on it!"

Jim Land took firm hold of himself; far worse than the bite of the man's furious words was the change he could see in Beth's troubled face as she listened to Dake Parsons. He kept his own voice under control as he answered. "I can understand your thinking, old-timer, but you're wrong. I've had to do some things I wasn't exactly proud of, but I've never yet collected a bounty on a human being. Maybe it will help if I show you this." He took the badge from his pocket and dropped it onto the bed.

Parsons picked it up and looked at it for a long moment. "Guess I stand corrected," he told the Converses, finally. "It seems your friend was hidin' something from us. He's a deputy U.S. marshal."

"I just never got around to mentioning it," Land corrected him. "The point is, if we aren't to turn Oklahoma Territory over to outlaws, then someone has to do something—in particular about the Doolin gang. I've been assigned to that job. I'll do it if I can."

Dake Parsons heard him out, his sun-darkened face unreadable. He said dryly, "You'll need a lot of luck," and tossed the badge back to Land, who caught it from the air.

Beth Converse, with her husband looking over her shoulder, was studying the reward notice. It did not tell them much. There was no photograph of the wanted outlaw—the law had never managed to lay hands on one—and only the most general of descriptions: "About 6 foot 2 inches tall, light brown hair, dangerous, always heavily armed." Beth looked at Land and at Dake Parsons. "Even in St. Louis we heard of Bill Doolin. You really know him?"

"Sure do. Met him first some ten years ago," Dake Parsons said. "He was just a young fellow Oscar Halsell picked up in Kansas, took a liking to, and brought down here to build fences for him. Bill was handy with an ax and a hard worker. Couldn't even read or write; Halsell taught him how, and before long had the kid keepin' his accounts for him. But Bill wanted to be a cowboy, so I sort of took him under my wing—showed him ropin' and let him ride with me until he got the hang of ranch work. Didn't take long before he was the best all-round puncher on the Double H. And even then, he was someone other men would be apt to listen to when he had occasion to open his mouth. Someone you knew you had to reckon with!"

Though Parsons directed his remarks to the woman, Jim Land knew they were actually meant for his benefit; he listened intently, because he was learning things he had not known before, and from someone who seemingly knew the facts.

Parsons continued: "After he put in a few more years, Bill seemed to develop a streak of fiddlefoot he had to get rid of. For a while there I wasn't sure what had become of him— heard that he'd drifted out to Wyoming or some such. Then he was back, ridin' for an outfit on leased range over in the Osage nation. I ran into him once or twice, figured he'd changed.

"That was right after the opening for the settlers in 1889, and Bill was full of talk about how the land was fillin' up, and he was watching the Old West dying with no place left in it for fellers like us. Next thing I heard, he'd got mixed up with the Dalton boys, in a train holdup. It's true I ain't laid eyes on him recent, but in spite of all I've heard, there's nothing will make me believe a boy like that could go really bad. Like I said before, he's no killer!"

"He's got men riding for him who are," Jim Land reminded him, and the thought of Turk Freese put an edge to his words. "I can't see making excuses for him."

That stopped Dake Parsons for the moment. His gray eyes narrowed in anger, but he couldn't seem to find an easy answer, and finally he gave it up with a shrug. He said sourly, "I ain't gonna argue it with you. I was about to draw these people a map." He took the reward notice out of Beth's hand and turned its blank side up against the book he'd propped against his knee. He licked the point of the pencil Land had given him and set to work, with no further mention of the thorny problem of his friend Bill Doolin.

As he drew his map, Dake Parsons kept up a running description. "This here is the southern boundary of the Cherokee Strip. You should be crossing the line somewhere about here—it don't exactly matter. You'll be headed north-northwest. Watch the creeks; they'll mostly be dry, after the summer we had. Third one you hit, turn and follow it up. It'll curve west. When it swings due north, start keepin' an eye out for running water—that'll be the spring I told you about. Don't see how you can miss it." He handed the paper to Converse. "Think you can follow that?"

The younger man scowled at the crude pencil marks, in a way that told Jim Land he was completely baffled. He could only shake his head and admit, "Well, I just don't know. . . ."

"May I have a look?" Jim Land said. The stabbing glance he got was weighted with suspicion, but after a moment's hesitation Converse reluctantly handed over the map. To Land, an outdoorsman himself, what the old puncher had drawn seemed clear enough. He commented, "I rode over some of that country only last week. I'm pretty sure I could find the place."

Converse said sharply, "I didn't hear it being offered to you!"

At that, Jim Land almost lost his temper. "Here!" He shoved the map into the other man's hand. "Go find it on your own, then."

Beth's protest was torn from her. "Charlie! Can't you see he was only offering to *help*? As if he hadn't done enough for us already—and as if he didn't have a job he has to get back to!"

Her husband had the good grace to look embarrassed as the truth of what she said bore in on him. Land didn't expect an apology, nor did he want one. He said gruffly, "I'll be honest with you: As far as the job's concerned, I hardly seem able to do anything more just now. I'm up against a blank wall. It's been two weeks since anyone has seen or heard of Bill Doolin."

"Two weeks?" Dake Parsons cut in. "I think you're talking about the raid over at Ingalls. Hey! Were *you* in on that?"

"Yes, I was at Ingalls," Land admitted. "Ever since then, I've been tracking down any clue I could get, but without a sign of Doolin. I'm here in Tulsa now because someone suggested he might be holed up at Antrim's place. Today, using the stolen money as an excuse, I had my chance for a look at Antrim's without having to let on what I was really after. I saw enough to satisfy me that Doolin wasn't there."

"I could've told you that much," Parsons exclaimed. "Hell, Bill wouldn't waste the time of day on the likes of Nels Antrim!"

Land nodded. "I believe you. I'm convinced Bill Doolin has gone to earth, probably nursing the leg wound that's crippled him since his last train job. Until he decides it's time to come out in the open, there doesn't seem much I can do. Meanwhile, the run that's scheduled to happen on the Cherokee Strip at noon this Saturday is something I would surely hate to miss. Tell you the truth, I'd like to have a part in it. Nobody who does is ever likely to forget it!"

There was bitterness in Charlie Converse as he said, "We

came a long way, my wife and I, just for that purpose. But it looks like it was for nothing, since we haven't found a soul who's willing to sell us a wagon, at any price."

The moment had come, Jim Land decided, to present the idea he had been holding in reserve. He was still hesitant, not being able to guess how these people would take to it. But he said, "Tell me, Converse. Just how good are the two of you at staying in a saddle?"

Converse showed his puzzlement. "Why, we're both pretty good—quite good, I'd say, for townspeople. Why?"

"Happens I've got a couple of extra horses putting away a healthy feed of grain over at the livery. I brought them back from Antrim's; they're the same ones Sid Yount and his friend were riding when they made off with your money. They're a good, solid pair of animals. Naturally I only borrowed them—I'm not a horse thief—but I just had a hunch you folks might be needing them."

Beth Converse stared. "You mean you brought them for *us*? To use for the opening?"

"But how could we carry supplies?" her husband wanted to know.

"If you take my word for it, you'll do best to travel light and figure to rough it at first. Take blankets and enough grub to last until you find whether you turn out to be among the lucky ones that stake a claim. You should have a much better chance than you would encumbered by a loaded wagon."

As Converse pondered this, scowling, Dake Parsons spoke up. "The man makes a lot of sense. If I was you I'd listen hard—and take him up on his offer!"

Beth left it for her husband to make the decision, though from the look she gave Land he was sure she heartily favored his suggestion. Finally, Converse said gruffly, with a shrug, "We've got no other options. I guess we'd be fools to pass up this one."

At once, Jim Land went on to make final arrangements. Learning that they had a room at the hotel, he told the pair, "Get a good night's sleep if you can. I'll be by early with the horses. We've got a long ride tomorrow, if we expect to reach the starting line and be ready for the signal gun next day at noon."

And so matters were left, as Dr. Allen came in just then to say, "I have to go out on a call, and I'm going to ask you folks to leave—my patient has got to have some rest." Jim Land said good afternoon and walked out into the waning afternoon, hearing Dake Parsons sputtering and protesting over the doctor's orders.

The thing that bothered Jim Land was the thought of Beth Converse's warm smile and sincerely voiced thanks as she put her hand in his. He didn't like to admit the strong impression that had been made on him, in a matter of a few brief hours—by a woman he knew to be the wife of another man.

# Chapter Five

The Cherokee Strip . . . six million acres of virgin land, a huge block of it two hundred miles long and sixty miles wide, the largest single piece remaining of a great sea of land and grass that had stretched all the way from Texas to the Dakotas. The next day, at noon, this too would be swallowed up to feed the needs of a steadily growing nation.

During their day-long ride west from Tulsa, Jim Land and the Converses found themselves a part of a seething and restless tide of journeyers, riders in almost every conceivable type of vehicle, who clogged the roads as they made their way toward the starting line. Land explained to his companions that an equal number were piling up against the northern edge of the strip, along the Kansas border. When the signal gun went off, those two lines would go pouring, from both directions at once, onto the waiting land between.

Beth Converse asked, "But what happens when they meet in the middle?"

"Why, then," Land said with grim humor, "I guess that's when some hopefuls will be turning around and going back where they started from, empty-handed. Even six million acres aren't anything like enough to go around. There'll be a sizable number of disappointed folks, I'm afraid, by the time tomorrow is through."

It was a sobering thought, and nobody said anything for some time afterward. Land wondered if Charlie Converse, for one, was beginning to get some idea of the size of the thing he had optimistically taken on, with hardly any preparation.

By now, Land had observed how well his companions shaped up on horseback. Beth seemed to fare better than her husband; though she had no proper riding clothes, she gamely sat astride and spread her long skirts as well as she could and made no complaints. Toward late afternoon she showed weariness at last in the tense set of her features, under the brim of the man's hat that Land had suggested she buy to protect her from a scorching sun.

Charlie Converse, for his part, let everyone know of his discomfort. He grumbled about the heat and about the long hours of riding; he wanted to know why no one had told him that, after leaving the train at Tulsa, he would still have to travel west another day before reaching the jumping-off point into the Cherokee Strip. Jim Land felt like suggesting that he might have looked at a map, but he held his tongue.

Finally they pulled up in the scant shade of a pecan tree, to rest their horses and drink from the canteens Land had specified they should all carry on their saddles. He told Converse, "It's not too much farther now. Meanwhile, here's a chance to get out of that saddle and stretch your legs a bit. Yonder is the place where you register."

Converse looked to where he pointed, squinting against the glare of the low sun. He frowned as he saw the ramshackle wooden booth, the long queue of people snaking toward it; though they scarcely seemed to inch forward, a yellow ball of dust hung above them, kicked up by many shuffling boots. He demanded crossly, "Now what's *this* all about?"

"Unless you carry a registration slip tomorrow, even if you manage to stake a claim you won't be allowed to file it. It's someone's bright idea for dealing with what they call sooners—people who try to sneak onto the strip ahead of time. Sounds foolish to me," he added. "All an ambitious sooner would have to do is collect his slip first and *then* head over the line. He'd still have all the time he needs before tomorrow noon."

Converse rubbed a palm over his sweating, dirt-streaked face. "You sure there's no way around this?"

"Afraid not. Not if you want to make the run and do it legal."

The man swore wearily. With a shrug he climbed down from his borrowed horse and passed the reins to his wife. "All right," he said gruffly. "I'll go check it out. Don't go anywhere without me." They watched him stride away through the rank grass and weeds, dodging the constant stream of riders and vehicles that went by in a steady and unbroken current.

Watching him go, Beth wore a frown of anxious concern. Jim Land suggested, "We may be waiting here awhile. We might as well make ourselves comfortable." She nodded without speaking and let him help her down from the saddle. But when he had tied their animals to a tree limb, she suddenly revealed the thoughts that were bothering her.

"You have to understand that Charlie's under a lot of pressure. He's gambling so much on what happens tomorrow!"

Jim Land couldn't keep from saying, "And I suppose you're not?"

"He's my husband!" she replied. "He's had so much bad luck in these three years we've been married that of course I try to support him any way I can."

"Even so," he told her, "I can't help wondering if either of you realizes the job you're taking on if you do get your claim. When I was a youngster, I helped my folks settle a homestead, so I know something about it."

That made her turn and face him. "Mr. Land," she said, meeting his look directly, "it's true enough that Charlie and I are city people, but we're both young and we're willing to learn. And don't think I'm afraid of hard work! My mother was never very strong. From the time my father walked out, she had to run a boardinghouse to support us, and I grew up doing all the heaviest chores. Believe me, I can carry my share of the weight."

"I do believe you." He also believed he had just gained an insight into her problem. The child of a broken home, Beth Converse would be determined that her own marriage would not fail, no matter what the cost. But even courage and determination such as hers must have their limits, and he wondered just how much she could take before her spirit

broke and patience deserted her. He asked himself, too, how
Charles Converse could be so insensitive as not to be aware
of the suffering he caused.

And then, unexpectedly, Converse was back, in high spirits as he strode toward them. "Well," he said, "I'm all signed
up. Let's be going."

Beth stared at him and at the registration booth with its
queue of landseekers stretching away from it. "You mean
you're through already?" she exclaimed, and frowned in disbelief at the paper he showed her. "I just don't understand—
slow as that line is moving!"

Charlie shrugged as he pocketed the registration slip. "I
wasn't going to stand for hours in that sun! So I used my
head: I started at the front of the line and kept asking till I
found someone willing to sell me his place. Cost me fifty
dollars, but it was worth it." He rubbed his palms together,
highly pleased with himself. "So why are we waiting? What
do you say we hit the saddle!"

Glancing at Beth, Jim Land saw her expression of dismay.
Knowing the state of their finances, and how great a hole fifty
dollars—spent for nothing—would make in the contents of
that leather wallet, he could guess what she was thinking just
then. Still, the money was gone; there was no getting it back
nor any use in making an issue of it. But he thought he saw a
sag in the line of her shoulders as Beth Converse turned to
lift herself once more into the saddle.

The sun lay like a molten ball on the edge of the prairie,
still pouring its searing heat across the flat, red-soiled land,
when they found a place to make camp and stake their
horses. Jim Land took down the canvas bag he had carried
behind the saddle, along with his blanket roll. It contained
the minimum of supplies he had known they would be
needing—food, utensils, and even material for a fire. He had
suspected that any place this close to the starting point would
already have been picked clean of firewood, and he was right.

Beth Converse insisted on taking over and preparing a
meal for them. Land didn't argue; he felt that it was important to her, even weary as she was after her day of travel. He
got a small fire going, by which time dusk was settling,
leeching color out of earth and sky. Other fires were begin-

ning to spring up in the early night around them, their flickering glow illuminating the canvas of wagon tops and the figures of people moving about their camps; there was a medley of voices in the growing dark, a continuous sound of wheeled vehicles and ridden horses still straggling past. Presently, as Beth worked, the aroma of brewing coffee and frying meat began to cut through other smells of dust and horse dung.

Charlie Converse had wandered off somewhere, and for just a few moments Land experienced the pleasant intimacy of being alone with Beth, in the midst of all this bustle and activity that was shut out by the circle of their own fire. They talked little—there seemed nothing much to say—but he enjoyed the sight of the woman busy at her cooking; it reminded him of simple domestic pleasures, which were all too absent from Jim Land's lonely way of existence.

The mood was shattered as her husband returned. Converse reported that he had been to look at the starting line, which was being patrolled by the military to keep the boomers from crossing over until the noonday gun should turn them loose. Seated cross-legged with a plate of food in his lap, he added, "But damned if it doesn't appear the whole Cherokee Strip is burning! You can see the glow along the horizon. A man I talked to said he'd heard the army had set the fires on purpose. He didn't know if it was to get rid of the sooners or burn off the grass and make it easier to spot the survey markers."

"My guess," Jim Land said, "is that trying to beat the sooners is a hopeless job. There must be hundreds of them in there tonight, all set to grab off whatever choice claims they've picked out for themselves."

"They're the smart ones, at that. Just look at all these idiots!" Converse gestured with his fork, indicating the teeming camps that surrounded them. "How many of them have any idea of what they're getting into? Would you believe, I saw lines waiting to buy drinking water—at a dollar a cup! Makes you realize how smart we were to bring our own!"

And watching Converse tilt the canteen that he himself had supplied, Jim Land refrained from saying, *Sure does, doesn't it?* He suspected the sarcasm would have been lost on Charlie Converse.

Land spent that night rolled in his blankets, with his horse staked nearby and his six-shooter under his hand—someone in that crowd of land seekers might well be tempted by a likely piece of horseflesh. Waiting for sleep, he was acutely conscious of Beth Converse beyond the embers of their fire, a motionless shape in her own blankets. Nearby, her husband muttered and fretted, trying to make himself comfortable on the hard ground.

The camps of the boomers seemed to take forever to quiet down; late into the night there was a continuing hubbub of sound, of sudden drunken, angry shouting, of the come and go of late arrivals at the starting line. But in time even this gave way to silence, the low-hanging stars giving a dim light, and the night wind off the empty strip carrying the scent of scorched earth and the occasional yipping of a coyote.

Saturday, September 16, dawned like the opening of an oven door as the sun rose above the eastern skyline. The mass of people camped below the strip were already up and hurrying through final preparations; the ones who had come in canvas-topped prairie schooners would be sorting out the things they needed to take with them, since they would have to travel light, by horseback, leaving the ponderous and slow-moving wagons to be brought up after their claims were duly staked.

Now, as the hour of noon approached, a seething movement began toward the jump-off line. As though by an understanding, the crowd of land seekers sorted themselves out against the invisible barrier; saddle horses jockeyed for position, and behind them were ranked wheeled vehicles of every description, many of them stripped down to the running gear for greater speed. As the minutes dragged out, the sounds that rose from thousands of throats began to take on a note almost of hysteria.

From the place he had maneuvered for himself, very near the front rank of horsemen, Jim Land twisted in the saddle and sought out the Converses, farther back in the pack. He had made it very clear that morning what he expected of them: "This is going to be more than a horse race. The stakes

are high, and it will be every man for himself. Some people
are probably going to get hurt, or even worse—and I don't
want to worry about it happening to you! The sorrel is fast,
and he's surefooted. I don't know as much about the animals
you're riding, or what luck you would have staying on them
in a flat-out run over this kind of ground. I think you know
the route we'll be taking; just set a pace you can hold to and
don't run any more risks than you have to. All I'm asking of
you, Converse, is to look after your own safety—and Beth's."

He suspected that Charlie Converse was still suffering from
his previous long day in the saddle and was more than ready
to make things as easy for himself as possible. He said only,
"My wife is my responsibility. I'll worry about that."

Now Jim Land spotted the pair and lifted an arm in salute
as he saw Beth's smile and wave. He faced forward again,
collecting the reins. He was on edge, primed and ready. To
save weight he had divided his gear and belongings between
the Converses to bring with them; the only spare items he
carried were his six-shooter and a length of hickory, one end
whittled to a point and the other fastened with a white strip
of cloth; this was the all-important flag and stake to mark
ownership of the quarter section he intended claiming on
behalf of Beth and Charlie Converse.

A smell of scorched grass rode the hot wind that breathed
against him across the empty strip. But he saw no smoke
from the fires the army had set; if they were out by now, they
probably had done comparatively little damage.

The moment was almost upon them. The noise about him
began to ebb; a strange stillness settled on the waiting mob.
Out in front, facing them, stood a line of soldiers with their
rifles at port arms, ready to pass the signal. Jim Land wondered if they were speculating on how they would escape
when that mass of land hunters was set loose to come charging directly at them.

Then somewhere a rifle cracked. The signal passed on
along the blue-clad line, muzzles pouring white smoke and a
rattle of shots rising toward the hot sky. And with a sudden,
deafening roar from a host of straining throats, the tide rolled
forth into the emptiness of the Cherokee Strip.

In that instant, as the sorrel leaped forward under him, Jim

Land lost all thought of the Converses. He found himself nearly swept up in the frenzy around him. He kept his head, and when the sorrel, catching fire from all the other frantic horses, tried to plunge ahead and match their headlong pace, he deliberately held it back. He knew the extreme risk of sending a mount at a blind run across unfamiliar ground. Though the sorrel fought the restraining bit, Land kept a firm hand, letting other horsemen surge into the lead.

If others wanted to break their necks and cripple their mounts, that was up to them. He had a definite goal and was determined to run his own race.

Impatient to pass, a rider coming up from behind ran his horse into the sorrel with an impact that nearly upended them both. The sorrel staggered, and Land pulled its head up, helping it stay on its feet. The man shouted an obscenity at him as he pounded by, his own horse stumbling and barely managing to keep its stride. Stinging dust engulfed them both, and then the other rider was streaking away, leaving Jim Land in his wake.

Glancing over his shoulder, Land saw that matters were already shaking out, the compact mass of the rush breaking up as less well mounted riders began to fall back. A few of the lighter rigs were moving up now, the men who drove them whipping their teams with reckless abandon. Even as he looked, one of these, a two-wheeled racing sulky, appeared to hit a partly buried rock. The whole contraption bounced high into the air, flipping completely over as it came down; the driver was thrown from his seat, though he still kept the reins. In the next instant a heavier vehicle, unable to avoid a collision, plowed into the wreckage in a sickening pileup of animals, turning wheels, and enveloping dust.

Jim Land winced and looked away; trying to turn back and help in the face of that relentless tide would be worse than hopeless.

Suddenly he was into a stretch of prairie that had been recently burnt over. The ground still smoked, and ashes flung up by shod hooves filled the air in a stinging, stifling cloud.

The sorrel tossed its head in protest and tried to break stride. Land held it with a firm grip and peered ahead through slitted lids. A smoldering brand that settled on his skin was instantly blown away. Visibility and sunlight were blotted out by the cloud of ashes; he clamped down on his breathing to protect his lungs.

Then, just as quickly as they had come upon that stretch, man and horse were out of it again, and just ahead a tree-lined creek bed was littered with stones and trash. The near bank had been deeply gouged, and now he saw that loose soil still trickled onto the man and horse that had piled up at the foot of it, having taken the jump too recklessly. The animal was getting to its feet, but the rider crouched motionless on hands and knees, head hanging as though in shock. Land thought he recognized the same one who had been so determined to get past him, a few miles back. Not pausing, he eased the sorrel down the crumbling bank, crossed the dry bed in a few steps, and scrambled up the farther side, picking up speed again, leaving the other man behind.

Breaking into the open once more, he saw that the field was thinning somewhat as men here and there began to drop out and stake their claims. He rode straight on, not deviating from his course. Once the hot wind brought him an unmistakable spattering of gunshots, which ended almost before he registered it; grimly he judged that one dispute over a claim had just been settled by the most direct of means. It wouldn't be the last, before this momentous day was over.

A coyote scuttled through the deep grass, cut across his route, and vanished. The sorrel had been breathing hard but by now had gotten its second wind, falling into a steady gait that was comfortable for it and that ate up the distance in a flowing rhythm. Even so it was heavy work in this blistering weather; the sorrel's withers shone with sweat.

They crossed a dry creek and then another, but when they reached the third one Land brought his horse to a halt and let it blow for a moment within the thin shade of a few pecan trees that grew along its banks. A wild turkey flopped down from a roost in one of them and vanished into the underbrush. Otherwise there was no sound that could be heard here above the dry rattling of windswept branches. Somewhere, he had left the land rush behind.

This time Land put his animal directly up the bed of the watercourse, following the instructions memorized from Dake

Parsons's map. Moisture made the sand look black in places, but still he could see no evidence of the water he was looking for. He watched closely as he rode. As promised, the course of the creek bed took a gradual swing to the north.

Almost immediately afterward he caught a glint of living water. With a grunt of satisfaction he took the right-hand bank and climbed out upon a nearly level sweep of broken prairie grass, with a line of timber across the head of it—almost like a windbreak, planted against the onslaught of harsh northerly winds. As he rode up toward them, he kept seeing the glint of water struck by sunlight. Suddenly, there was the spring itself, gushing out into a small natural basin, which someone at some time—Dake Parsons himself, perhaps—had dug out and improved and lined with stones.

The sight of it made Jim Land thirstier than he thought he had ever been in all his life.

Quickly he stepped down from the saddle, knelt, and scooped up the water in one palm. It was wonderfully cool, with a faint metallic taste that was far from unpleasant. He drank briefly, and then the sorrel was beside him, anxious to reach the water. Rising, he slapped the animal's sweat-darkened shoulder. "Help yourself," he said, as the sorrel sank its muzzle into the spring. "But don't overdo it!"

While it drank, Land took down the flagged stake of hickory wood that he had lashed to the saddle strings. Satisfied that the sorrel had been allowed all it needed, he took the reins and led it over to a place where he had already spotted something he was looking for—the concrete corner marker showing range, township, and section, where the boundaries of four claims met. Dry grass and weeds rattled against his legs as he approached. Suddenly he halted, and now there was no sound except the shirr of insects and the rustle of the trees behind him. For a long moment Jim Land could do no more than stare at the stake, crudely flagged with white cloth, that had already been driven deep into the parched sod at his feet.

Then a sound caused his head to turn, and he saw the man who stood motionless at the edge of the trees a half dozen yards away, with a leveled six-shooter pointed straight at him.

# Chapter Six

The brim of a low-pulled hat hid the man's face. The horse that stood tied to a nearby tree limb showed no sign of having been ridden hard. Jim Land turned slowly, making no hasty moves and keeping his hand away from the gun in his own holster.

Across the stillness, the other man spoke: "This claim is taken. Looks like you're a little too late."

"Does it?" Land shook his head. "I'd say you were a little too soon! Just how long have you been camped here? It's clear enough that horse of yours hasn't traveled any today."

"What of it? I'm here—and my stake says this ground belongs to me. Don't give me any trouble!"

Land studied the gun pointed at him and the face, half visible below the hat brim, of the one who held it. There was a shade too much belligerence in the voice, coupled with a hint of uncertainty. Trailing the reins of his own animal, he started forward over the dry grass, careful to move without haste—aware of the danger in crowding a nervous man with a gun in his fist.

As he paced he said quietly, "Maybe I don't cotton to being run off by a sooner. Do you have any idea of the risk of what you're doing? It's not only breaking a federal law, but the fellow who gets caught at it will likely find that people aren't going to wait for a judge to settle matters. Haven't you heard what they like to do with sooners here in Oklahoma Territory?"

"Sure, I've heard," the fellow answered. "They hang 'em."

"To the nearest tree! I saw one already today, back a piece." It was a lie, but he thought it had an effect; the fellow's mouth tightened, and Jim Land pressed his point home. "Would you want to end like that?"

"And who's gonna do it to me?" the man with the gun demanded harshly. "You, maybe? Not with a bullet in you, you ain't!" They stood face to face, each with his saddled horse beside him. The scorching wind plucked at their clothing and moved the branches of the trees above them. Land felt a clotting in his chest as the other man's hand tightened on the handle of the gun. He took a shallow breath.

"Go ahead and shoot, then!" he said suddenly. "But there'll be witnesses. . . ."

A drum beat of arriving horses grew louder. The other man heard them in the same instant; his head jerked and lifted to peer behind Jim Land, down the gentle slope. Now full sunlight struck his face, and Land's guess was confirmed: It was a young face, pale from indoor living, and with only a beginning trace of sandy whiskers. He stared at the horsemen coming toward them, and in that moment his pale eyes were blank with indecision.

Under the cover of talk, Jim Land had managed to narrow the space between them. Now he was able to take a single step and, with his free hand, grab the other's gun wrist, giving it a twist and a sideward thrust. The gun went off in a flat crack of sound that was swallowed up in the immensity of the open prairie; jarred out of the man's fingers, it fell to the ground between them. Instantly, dropping the reins of his horse, Land brought out his own weapon, and at the sight of it the other man froze.

"Once you get the drop on a man," Jim Land reminded him gruffly, "it's just stupid to let him get close enough to take your gun away from you!"

His prisoner seemed to wilt at the sight of a revolver pointed at him; all his arrogance drained away. Jim Land turned then, to get a look at the horsemen whose timely arrival had likely saved his life. There were two of them; they had reined in their horses and were staring up the slope, as though unsure of their next move. They had probably heard the single gunshot and perhaps could see the weapon Land was holding. Now, as they debated, he took off his hat and circled it above his head—the frontier's warning to ride around. And though they might have been tempted otherwise, they apparently decided to heed the signal. They pulled wide of the two men at the spring and rode on out of sight.

The man Land had disarmed stood waiting, dispirited, with all the fight taken out of him. He was as young as Land had thought at a distance—a town kid by the look of him, no older than nineteen or twenty. He tried to sound belligerent as he said, "You going to hang me now or later?"

Jim Land gave him a look. "You're in luck," he said coldly. "As I said, what you did is a federal offense—and I happen to be a federal officer." And he let him see the badge from his pocket. "I'm just going to put you under wraps for the time being. Stick out your wrist!"

Hesitantly the other obeyed, and a manacle was unceremoniously snapped into place. Taking his arm, Land marched him over to the nearest tree, forced him to sit, and shackled his arms around its trunk, behind him. With his gun back in its holster, Jim Land said sternly, "Now, what's your name?"

"Vern Morley."

"How old are you—about twenty?"

"About."

"Maybe you'll tell me what you thought you were up to, trying a thing like this?" Morley's chin was sunk dejectedly on his chest. He muttered something inaudible; Land told him sharply, "Speak up!"

He repeated it louder. "I said, I took a dare." He raised his head and met the marshal's look defiantly. "I work in the drugstore, down at Stillwater. Me and some other fellers were having a few drinks. One thing led to another. Somebody said I didn't have the nerve to sneak past the army and find a claim and stake it. I said I did."

"And just what did you think you'd do with a claim once you staked it? You're underage."

Vern Morley's shirt scraped tree bark as he shrugged. "I dunno. I never thought that far."

"Well, suppose you sit there and think what's going to happen to you now. It should do you good. . . ."

Land left him with that and set about things that needed attention. He pulled up Morley's stake—telling the unhappy youngster, "The court will be needing this for evidence"—and replaced it with the one he himself had brought. He led his own horse over and tied it near Vern Morley's animal and afterward went to get the prisoner's gun, which still lay in the grass. As he straightened with the weapon in his hand, the full tide of the land rush struck this section of the strip.

He stood and watched, ready to meet a challenge. Riders thundered past, throwing up a reddish film of dust through which moving shapes were faintly seen. The dust and confusion seemed to go on endlessly, and yet in a matter of minutes the bulk of the stampede had passed on and vanished.

But now, as the dust screen thinned and lifted, he could see the ones who had dropped out of the pack and were scurrying about to find the corner markers, or simply pounding in their stakes wherever it struck their fancy. On a section to the east of him, two men tried to claim the same parcel of land, and he saw them go after it, swinging fists and tearing into each other with what looked like savage ferocity. In another direction, but out of his range of sight, there was a sudden spatter of pistol fire—several shots in a ragged pattern that ended abruptly as ownership of another disputed claim was settled in violence.

Jim Land, observing this mayhem, thought that even if they had tried, those in charge of disposing of the Indian lands couldn't have come up with a more ludicrous and wasteful method. Having seen the results of the 1889 opening of the central portion of the territory, he thought it was incredible that they should have gone ahead and repeated their error today in the strip. How many people would have to lose their lives before it dawned on the authorities that this was the worst possible way to do the job?

But for the moment, no one seemed to want to challenge him for the piece of land where he was standing. He realized that he had been holding Vern Morley's gun cocked and ready to use. He forced the tension out of him, lowered the hammer, and put the weapon behind his belt.

Almost as he did this, he saw a pair of riders emerge from the timber along the dry creek bed below the claim and pull up their horses as they looked about, as though unsure of themselves. They were the Converses. He waved, but they failed to notice him, so he turned quickly to get his horse and ride down to meet them. Beth saw him coming and eagerly answered his wave.

Though not caught up in the worst of the rush, they both showed signs of what they had been through. Their faces and clothing were streaked with soot and dirt, and the hot wind had loosened some of Beth's dark hair from its coils; she was trying to do something with it, pushing it up beneath the brim of her hat. Even so, she looked fine to Jim Land. He said, "Are you both all right?"

Charlie Converse merely nodded, but Beth was breathless—and appalled. "I never saw anything like it!" she exclaimed, almost like one in a state of shock. "I certainly never want to again! I didn't think it could be like this: wrecked wagons, injured people and animals! One man, I'm positive, was lying dead, but there was no way in all that madness that anyone could stop or try to help! Haven't they some better way they could go about distributing free land?"

"They don't seem to think so." Jim Land was struck by the way she voiced the very things he had been thinking. He added, "But come along and have a look at your claim. I think you'll find it's exactly as your friend Dake Parsons described it."

Since they both were townspeople, he soon found himself patiently explaining the virtues of the quarter section. Charlie Converse showed no particular interest in what he heard; what did rather astonish Land were the questions that Beth came up with and the understanding she showed when he answered in detail. She noticed the lush growth that lined the runoff from the spring—one of the few touches of green in this sun-baked landscape—and began to talk about the possibility of ditching in order to irrigate their claim.

When she saw the spring itself, she gave a cry of delight and at once slipped from her saddle and ran to kneel and sink both wrists into the water, bringing it up in her cupped hands. "It's delicious!" she declared, after tasting it. "And I can hardly wait to get a bath and wash my hair!"

"What in the world is *this*?"

Charlie Converse had suddenly discovered the prisoner, seated handcuffed to a tree with head hanging. Jim Land made a point of replying loudly enough for the pale young man to hear: "The fellow says his name is Morley. You've been hearing about sooners? Well, now you're looking at one! I'll say for him that at least he knew a good place when he saw it. I got here and found he had this one all staked out for himself."

They all studied the prisoner, who seemed ashamed to meet their eyes. Beth sounded troubled as she observed, "But he looks so young to be in such a fix! What will happen to him?"

"That's for a judge to say," Jim Land told her briefly and refused to discuss the matter further.

The thunder and tumult had died, leaving an odd quiet over this stretch of prairie land. The run—at least, the first stage of it—was ended; now many of those who had managed to stake out claims seemed to be seized by inertia, as though their exertions had left them stunned and sapped of energy. They seemed unable to do much more than squat beside their markers, with a gun and perhaps a jug of whiskey handy, as though waiting for someone to tell them what happened next.

Others, more industrious, stirred themselves to begin turning their quarter section of raw prairie into a semblance of home. A family in a wagon had moved onto the quarter section just west of the Converses, and Jim Land saw that they had taken down the overjets—the wagon box extensions to which the hickory bows were fastened—and had set the dirt-streaked canvas on the ground as a kind of temporary shelter. Now the man had harnessed one of his team horses to a grasshopper plow, which he carried lashed to the side of the wagon, and was running a furrow around his quarter section—perhaps to mark it off as his own, perhaps to serve as a firebreak in case the tang of fire-scorched grass, carried on the wind, should prove a threat.

With no tool except a hand ax, Land was able to do little

else than use it knocking up kindling from some of the down timber on the claim. And now, as the afternoon dragged on, there was a new tide of movement across the land as the losers in the race for claims began to come drifting back.

They had very much the look of a defeated army, beaten men and exhausted animals straggling away from a battle in which they had given everything, only to find it not enough. Most seemed glumly dispirited, but a few cast sour and envious looks, in passing, on their luckier rivals. Jim Land, at least, read a warning in this; he kept his gun handy. As a long sunset flared orange and gold, colored by the smoke that still hung acridly over the sweep of prairie, he wondered what the coming of darkness might yet bring before this momentous day could be considered over.

He built a fire at which Beth cooked a meal from their supply of food. A pleasant aroma of frying meat and boiling coffee spread through the early dark, and across the night other spots of brightness greeted theirs—there would be a campfire tonight on every quarter section of what, at sunrise, had been miles of completely empty land. When the food was ready, Jim Land released his prisoner and shackled his hands in front of him so that Vern Morley could feed himself. The four of them sat around their fire and ate in silence, while sparks streamed toward the mesh of stars and a few late fireflies wove intermittent patterns among the dark trees.

Looking at Beth Converse in the dancing light, Jim Land was painfully aware of time speeding toward the moment when he must leave, in all likelihood never to see her again. There were a dozen things he would like to say or to ask her, but he held his tongue. After all, she was another man's wife, and he had no business taking too much of an interest or feeling responsibility for her.

It was Beth who said, after a silence broken only by the snap of burning brands and the rustling of the trees behind them, "Now that we're here and settled, what happens next?"

"That's what I was about to ask," her husband said.

Land told them. "Officially, the next order of business is to register this claim. You'll do it at one of the new townsites that were settled today—I judge the nearest to be some six or eight miles due west of you. But that will have to wait until they've got their land office opened and functioning. Just now, the important thing is that you've only got a limited amount of supplies with you, to say nothing of the equipment you'll need. Tomorrow, when I head back to Tulsa, I'll see what I can arrange to have sent out."

"You're leaving us tomorrow?" Beth asked, and Land wondered if he heard a note of regret in her voice.

"After all, I do have my job," he reminded her. "And a prisoner to get rid of. Besides, there's a couple of horses to be returned to the man I got them from."

Charlie Converse's head jerked up. "You're not taking our horses?"

"They were only borrowed—at the point of a gun. I *am* a lawman, not a horse thief. I promised I'd return them, and I have no choice."

"But—my God! You can't just leave us stranded here, afoot!" the other man began, in protest. "Not in the middle of this wilderness—"

He broke off as Land raised a cautioning hand to silence him.

They all heard it then—a swelling sound of travel, as horses swept toward them in the night. There were a number of riders, coming in with a purposeful rush. At once Land was up and offering Beth Converse a hand. "Quick!" he told her.

"Who are they?" she stammered as she scrambled to her feet.

"Sounds to me like claim jumpers! I've been expecting them. I imagine they're out in force tonight, all through the strip!"

Charlie Converse swore in alarm as the hoofbeats grew steadily nearer. He cried, "Let's get this fire put out!"

Land vetoed that. "No! The more we're able to see, the better!" He had been using his saddle as a backrest, his rifle leaning against it. He asked, as he picked it up, "Can you use one of these?"

"I guess so."

Land levered in a shell and tossed the weapon over to him, saying, "Be careful where you point it, and don't fire unless I tell you. Now—everyone back into the trees." He indicated

Vern Morley. "Take him with you. And see that he keeps his mouth shut!"

Converse dragged the prisoner, hampered by the hand-cuffs, to his feet. Beth was already heading for the deeper shadows under the trees. Land stayed long enough to throw more wood onto the fire, setting up a greater crackling and a rush of sparks skyward. Then he grabbed up his saddle and lugged it with him as he hurried to join the rest.

Moments later the riders pulled up, somewhere out beyond the fire. Neither group could see the other, but the blowing of the horses and the jingle of a bit chain could be heard above the crackling fire. A voice bellowed, "We're giving notice: Get off or we'll clear you off!"

Land told his companions, "Don't answer. Let them stew!"

He heard Charlie warn the prisoner, harshly, "Keep quiet, unless you want the butt of this rifle used on you!" There was no sound from Morley.

The night seemed to hold its breath.

Jim Land could guess at the puzzlement of those night riders, finding a blazing fire with no one in attendance. They apparently decided to investigate. There was a stir of hooves moving through dry grass and approaching at a careful walk. Four horsemen shaped up out of the darker night, at first dimly visible and then more clearly, until they drew up just beyond the fire. Its glow faintly lined their faces and glinted off bridle chains and the eyeballs of their mounts and the metal of the guns in their hands.

Hearing no reply to their challenge, a couple of the riders moved as though to dismount. But at this Land called out, "You'd better stay in those saddles if you don't want to get shot out of them!"

He caused a stir. A horse started moving around as a nervous hand jerked at the reins. Then the one who had spoken before—Land picked him out, a big fellow whose face was all but hidden behind a thicket of dark whiskers—said loudly, "Don't try any tricks with us. Whoever is there, you better show yourselves!"

Land threw the challenge back at him. "*You've* already gone and made that mistake. We can see you, and we've got the lot of you covered. This is a federal officer talking," he added. "I imagine you know the penalty for claim jumping. I'm giving you just five seconds to get rid of those guns."

His answer was a curse; with it, the bearded leader threw a shot from his handgun into the shadows, aiming at the speaker's voice.

But Land had already moved aside, and at once he sent an answering bullet that plucked the hat from the man's head. With that the scene broke apart in yells and the squeals of horses and the guns on both sides of the fire. He could only hope that Beth had heeded his strict warning to take cover.

The claim jumpers had no more than the flashes of the opposing guns to use as targets, while they themselves were wide open, fully exposed in the fire's glow. Land had his own revolver as well as the one taken from Vern Morley, and he kept them both working as he moved about, never firing from the same position twice. Now, to the left, Charlie Converse opened up with the rifle; whether he was any kind of marksman or not, it would help create the illusion that the men in those saddles faced a considerable number of enemies.

One of the frightened horses wheeled in a circle directly through the fire, its hooves throwing up burning brands. All this confusion added to the claim jumpers' difficulties in trying to find targets in the shadows of the timber. Even so, a bullet clipped past Jim Land and thudded into the trunk of a tree close behind him. His answering shot took the horseman squarely. The man gave a cry of agony as he convulsively clutched the reins; the animal under him reared, squealing, and would have collided with another if the rider of that horse hadn't managed to catch the bridle and somehow pull it down, with the hurt man slumped helpless on its back.

Suddenly everything stopped. The claim jumpers lost their nerve, the gunfire petered out, and into the final echoes Jim Land said harshly, "This is your last chance. I want to see all those guns on the ground. Now!" And as the terrified horses settled, their riders tossed their revolvers into the dirt.

Into a tense silence, Land stepped forward. He had shoved Vern Morley's emptied weapon behind his belt, but his own was ready, and to his left Charlie Converse moved in step with him, the rifle held awkwardly in both hands; in the fire's glow he looked pale and a little wild-eyed, but determined.

The three who remained erect in their saddles eyed their captors sullenly. Even the bearded leader had nothing to say.

Then, before Land could speak, there came a shout of alarm from back in the dark of the timber. It was young Morley who cried, "Marshal! Look out for the knife! Behind you—he's going to throw it!"

Jim Land barely had time to remind Converse to watch the others as he twisted about to see what was going on. He heard a confused sound of scuffling at the edge of the trees. There was a curse, a muffled cry of pain. Even as he started toward it the scuffle abruptly ended, and the bulky figure of a man rose above the motionless shape at his feet.

An arm lifted. Remembering the shouted warning, Jim Land managed to swerve aside just in time and saw an errant gleaming of firelight flash along the blade as the knife flew toward him. It missed; he fired at the knife thrower, but all he saw in the muzzle flash was the briefest glimpse of the man turning away, to be lost from view amid the trees.

At that moment a disturbance broke out at the fire, behind him. Suddenly all the claim jumpers he had left in Charlie Converse's charge seemed to be in motion. He heard Converse swearing, and a flurry of shouting and hoof sounds that quickly receded—and only then, belatedly, Charlie's rifle streaked muzzle flame, twice, and fell silent again. By that time the drum of pounding hooves was already fading across the sounding board of the dark prairie. All Land knew, as silence descended, was that Charlie Converse had failed him; the claim jumpers had somehow managed to break and make their getaway.

It hardly seemed important, just then. As he hurried toward that motionless shape, lying in the fringe of the trees, all he was capable of thinking was contained in a single unvoiced, anguished cry: *Beth!* But as he reached the figure it stirred and gave a low moan, and he knew instead it was the young fellow, Vern Morley.

Next moment, Beth Converse was there beside him, and he demanded sharply, "You're not hurt?"

"No, no. But what about him?" She dropped to her knees. "I saw what he did. After warning you about the knife, he threw himself at the man to try to stop him—even hand-cuffed, the way he was. It will be a wonder if he's still alive!"

Morley mumbled a denial. "I'm okay. Jaw feels like he really gave me a good one. Must have knocked me out for a minute."

"He did more than that." Land had been making a hurried examination. "You're bleeding somewhere."

"My arm . . ."

Charlie Converse came up, still carrying the rifle. He spoke in bitter self-condemnation. "Dammit, they got away! I guess I don't know as much about firearms as I thought. Because somehow I let the thing jam on me—and while I was fighting to clear it, they saw their chance and rode off. Land, I'm really sorry."

He was so clearly apologetic that for once Jim Land felt sympathy for the man and didn't say any of the things he might have. Instead he passed the mistake off. "It doesn't matter too much. They had to leave their guns behind, so it doesn't look as though they'll be bothering anyone else to-night. Let them go." He added, "Give me a hand here—let's get this fellow where I can see better what I'm doing. He's taken a knife cut in his arm."

As Charlie Converse moved quickly to help, Jim Land told Beth, "Maybe you could fetch me some water. And see what you can find for bandages." She hurried to do this, while he and Converse carried the hurt man over to the fire and let him down in the glow of it. Morley's left shirt sleeve was drenched with blood. Land ripped it to the shoulder, telling Converse, "While I'm doing this, it might be a good idea to gather up the guns those people left behind and stow them somewhere, just in case."

"Right!" Converse agreed. He was all cooperation now and a good deal more civil of tongue than Land had yet seen him. The recent encounter, and his own poor part in it, seemed to have had its effect.

Using the water and clean cloth that Beth supplied, Jim Land worked over the wounded arm. "Only a shallow cut," he said. "It's already stopped bleeding."

"I said it wasn't anything," the prisoner repeated, but his voice held pain.

Tying off the bandage, Land told him, "It's going to be sore for a while, but try hard not to let it stiffen up on you. And now—hold out your wrists." And producing the key, he unfastened the handcuffs and slipped them off. "That should be more comfortable," he said and added, "After tonight, I think you deserve a break. I'm going to give you one."

In the firelight, the young fellow stared. "What do you mean?"

"You're free to go," the lawman answered gruffly. "You can leave right now if you want to. Or you're welcome to stick around till morning. It's a long ride back to Stillwater."

Vern Morley rubbed his wrists, stammering his gratitude. "Thanks, Marshal! I *would* like to stay till daylight, if nobody has objections. And I'll tell you one thing: That's the last time I play the fool. It's a promise!"

"I'll hold you to it," Jim Land said sternly. But as he rose and turned away, he found himself facing Beth Converse. There was a warm glow in her eyes. She said quietly, for his ears alone, "Jim Land, I don't think you ever really intended to turn him in! And I'm glad."

He shrugged. "The fellow was only acting on a dare when he rode onto the strip. I thought if I put a scare into him, it might teach him a lesson. It never occurred to me he'd try to be a hero, maybe get himself killed. I'm beginning to think I may have some things to learn about people, myself!"

"I know *I've* learned something," she said quietly, her eyes steady on his. "I've learned that they can give a man a badge to wear, but it doesn't necessarily have to turn him into a heartless machine. I thank you for teaching me that, Jim Land!"

# Chapter Seven

After the weeks of excitement building up to the opening of the Cherokee Strip, Tulsa appeared to have slid back into a stage of lethargy on the day after the run. The contrast was extreme. Riding in in the early afternoon, trailing the two saddled horses that bore Nels Antrim's Bar Cross brand, Jim Land found the village drowsing and its dusty streets nearly deserted. The only break in the Sunday quiet was the noise of bawling cattle and shouting men from the pens beside the railroad, where a saffron cloud of dust showed that the loading of beef onto the cars continued without a break.

Riding from the blast of sunlight into the dimness of Halsell's Livery, Land called out as he dismounted but raised no answer. In a couple of stalls horses stomped and rustled their feed in their mangers, but no one came from the office cubicle. So he found three empty stalls and put his animals into them, fetching generous scoops of oats from the bin.

On top of their exertions of yesterday, the horses had now covered the thirty-five-mile crossing of the big Osage reservation that separated Tulsa from the strip; all three horses needed a feeding of grain, especially the Bar Cross animals, which didn't look as though they often got one. He slipped the bits but left the saddles on for the moment.

He slid past the flank of a busily chomping animal and into the straw-littered central aisle of the barn, where he was starting to brush trail dust from his clothing when, out of the corner of an eye, he caught a dark shape silhouetted against the wide doorway. He went still as Nels Antrim warned harshly, "Don't make any sudden moves. You're covered!"

A second voice added, "From two directions!"

That brought his head around to discover the bony, slope-shouldered figure of Sid Yount leaning in the barn's smaller rear entrance. Like Antrim, Yount held a revolver trained squarely on him. Land drew a cautious breath as he saw how they had him bracketed. He blamed himself; his mind had been elsewhere.

"It looks as though you've been waiting for me," he said.

"Too damn long," Nels Antrim told him. "Sid and me had a little bet going as to whether you'd actually show up today the way you said. Personally, I'd about given you up."

"When I say something I generally do it," Land said coldly. "Anyway I brought your horses—assuming they *are* yours, which I doubt. I'm giving them a good bait of grain, at my expense. I figure they earned it."

Antrim's voice was heavy with sarcasm. "Well, now, ain't you just too damned generous!"

"The hell with the horses!" Sid Yount's words rang harshly through the stillness. "What about my partner that you murdered? And where's that money you took off me?"

"Where would you think?" Land retorted flatly. "The money went back to the people it belonged to. As for your friend, the one you called Jeeter—you know as well as me I didn't murder him. He insisted on what he got!" And then he went tense as Sid Yount started to lift the gun from his holster.

Suddenly Yount froze, and even in the dimness of the barn Jim Land saw the way the expression of the man's face grew slack. Next moment, as though propelled from behind, he took a stumbling step forward—and now Land caught sight of Dake Parsons behind him in the doorway, a shotgun in his hands prodding Yount between the shoulder blades.

"You can put that pistol away!" the hostler said, and when Yount failed to move fast enough, he added, "I think you heard me! I have enough trouble as it is, keeping this place clean. Nobody's gonna go spilling blood all over it—unless maybe I decide to do the spilling!"

At that the resistance went out of Sid Yount. His shoulders

sagged. He let his gun drop back into his leather holster—
whereupon Parsons murmured, "On second thought—so you
won't make any mistakes . . ." And reaching, he took the
weapon himself, disarming Yount.

In the same moment, as though by prearrangement, another man had appeared in the wide street entrance, armed
like Parsons with an ugly-looking, double-snouted shotgun.
Before Nels Antrim was aware of it, the weapon had him
covered, and its owner said sharply, "He means you, too."

Antrim looked at him, then at the shotgun, and then at Sid
Yount being herded forward through the barn with the hostler at his back. Grimacing furiously, the horse rancher con-
ceded defeat. When his revolver was back in its holster, the
newcomer with the shotgun nodded in approval and said,
"Dake Parsons told me the pair of you were hanging around
my stable, acting like you was up to some mischief. It appears
we checked you out just in time."

"We ain't done nothing to you, Halsell!"

"You better be thankful for that!"

Jim Land, with the threat against him unexpectedly ended,
looked with interest at this Oscar Halsell. A man of middle
years, he was dressed in the town clothing of a businessman,
but his movements and his appearance were those of someone who might be more at home in a saddle. He grounded
the shotgun now, but he looked as dangerous as when he had
held the other at bay.

He said crisply, "I've had my eye on you a long time,
Antrim. I've got a pretty good idea of the sort of things that
go on out at that place you call a horse ranch. If you'd once
given me reason to think you were after anything belonging
to me, I'd have taken care of you before now."

"Yeah?" Meeting his stare, Antrim tried a sneer of bra-
vado. "Talk comes cheap!"

"But not the beef and horseflesh with my brand on them! If
you know what's good for you, you'll go right on leaving the
Double H alone."

Angry color flooded into Antrim's battered face. His voice
was tight with emotion as he cried, "You can afford to talk
like that because you run a big operation, and I never been

anything but small fry. But one of these days you just might find yourself whittled down to size!"

Oscar Halsell heard him out in cold contempt. "Coming from you," he replied, "that doesn't even count as a threat. Right now you'll oblige me by getting out of my sight!"

"And your friend with you!" Dake Parsons added. He had been emptying the shells from Sid Yount's captured six-gun. Now he dropped it into the gangling fellow's holster and gave him a shove forward. He told Antrim, "You can take your horses, too, but we'll let you wait till they've finished the bait of grain Mr. Land was kind enough to put out for them."

"The hell with that!" Nels Antrim retorted harshly. "We'll take 'em now." He gestured to his companion. The others watched in stern disapproval as the two of them moved into the stalls, got the bridles, and dragged the horses away from their unfinished meal, swearing at the animals when they tried to hang back and tossed their heads in protest. They stomped out of the barn and were gone, leading the horses Jim Land had borrowed, and Oscar Halsell followed them outside.

Dake Parsons observed sourly, "That's one fine pair! The less I see of them the better! Didn't make me feel bad at all, just now, to hear about you doing in that other one—the one that parted my hair for me with a bullet. How come you never mentioned that you'd gone and killed that fellow Jeeter?"

Jim Land shrugged. "Didn't feel too much like talking about it that day in front of the Converses."

"I guess I can understand that. They might not have known how to take it."

Halsell came back then to report that Antrim and Yount had ridden out of town. "Looked like they were headed for Antrim's place," he said. "I'd say we can forget them."

"Maybe," Dake Parsons grunted darkly.

The rancher proceeded to introduce himself to Land, and as they shook hands the latter told him, "I have to thank you both. I should never have let those two catch me off guard the way they did."

Giving him an appraising regard, Halsell said briefly, "I don't doubt you could have handled them." He added, changing the subject, "I understand you're the man my friend Ev

Nix brought in to get after the Doolin gang. I got to wish you luck. Maybe you've heard that I'm the one brought Bill Doolin to Oklahoma in the first place—ten years or so ago. I saw a lot of promise in Bill. Helped him at the start, every way I could."

"That's what Dake has been telling me."

Halsell frowned and shook his head. "Always liked Bill—purely hated to see him go bad the way he did. But my feelings can't change the fact that something has got to be done about him. This just ain't the Old West anymore. We can't tolerate all this bank and train robbing—not if we have hopes to see Oklahoma grow up and take its place among the rest of the states. Too long this territory has had a name as a hotbed of outlawry. That's got to be changed, no matter what it costs or who it hurts. And much as I hate to say it, that has to include Bill Doolin!"

No one had an answer for that, and Oscar Halsell brusquely changed the subject. "Right now I better get back to the shipping pens. I got the boys putting beef onto the cars—the government ordered our stuff moved off the strip, to make way for yesterday's opening, and this is nearly the last of mine. Actually, these days I'm in the process of moving clear out of the cattle business. There's not going to be too much room left around here for stock grazing anymore, so I'm moving into other businesses of one kind and another. Do you two realize, we're only a few years away from heading into a brand new century? A man has to move with the times!" Halsell turned and headed for the railroad tracks, to the busy siding whence the restless sounds of men and cattle emanated.

"He's pretty badly upset over Bill Doolin," Parsons commented. "Purely hates to give up on him."

"Your boss strikes me as a good man," Land said. "And a fair-minded one."

"He's that, sure enough. All the years I've worked for him, he never gave me cause to doubt it. So it makes it kind of hard, to be quitting him now."

Jim Land gave the older man a look. "You're quitting?"

He nodded. "Told him this morning. I just don't think I can stand it around here any longer. Ain't the job I mind—it's just that I don't feel comfortable living in a town, knowing that all this country around me was open range that'll soon be gone for good. Like the man says, a fellow's gotta move with the times.

"You know," he went on, as though the thought had just struck him, "I reckon I feel a lot the same about it as Bill Doolin, only I couldn't have gone the way he has. Hell, I never was no rebel—it's just that I got a hankering to get off by myself, someplace where a man can still find room to swing his hat. Arizona maybe. Or Nevada—I ain't too particular. But I got to go!"

"Then there's no reason why you shouldn't," Jim Land agreed. "A man like you or me, with nothing to hold him down—no family, nobody dependent on him—I always believed he should feel free to do about as he pleases." He added, with a humorless smile, "Besides, being free helps make up some for the loneliness."

He drew a sharp look from the older man. Dake Parsons wagged his head. "So we both know about *that* side of it, too." He hesitated before he added. "Maybe you've wondered why I bothered tipping off those people—Converse and his wife—about that piece of land in the strip."

"A little," the other admitted.

"It was all because of the girl. Pretty little thing—and so damned concerned about me when she knew I was hurt. You saw how she acted, that day at the doctor's place—couldn't seem to do enough to help. A man needs some of that from a female, at least once in his life. But me, with no wife, no womenfolks of any kind—to tell you the truth, she was sort of like the daughter I never had and never will.

"But that husband of hers!" Parsons made a face. "*He's* sure no bargain! More I listened to him talk, the more I could see that, tied to somebody like that, she was in bad need of help, her own self. All *I* knew how to do was tell her about that piece of land. . . . But you ain't said—did they get it staked?"

Land assured him that both Converses had been delighted with their claim. The older man listened with deep interest as he was given a brief accounting of the run. When it was over, he scowled at his boots, shook his head, and muttered darkly, "I can't help thinking, with winter only a matter of weeks in the offing, this is a damned funny time of year for the government to tell a man, 'Here's a chunk of land. Take it and live on it—but be sure you got a house built and ten acres under cultivation by March, or by God we'll take it back!' What do you think, Jim?" he demanded earnestly. "Do they really have a chance to make a go of it?"

"I just don't know. If not, it won't be her fault. But I'm afraid I share some of your doubts about him."

"They're city people. They don't either of 'em know beans about the job they've tackled—but I got an idea she at least can learn." On a sudden impulse the older man added, referring to the pair of shotguns he was holding, "If you got a minute, lemme get rid of these things, and then there's something out back I want to show you. . . ."

Land waited while he deposited the weapons in the cubby-hole office, and they walked out to the corral. An ancient farm wagon stood there under a tarpaulin. As he untied the lashings, Parsons explained, "A feller showed up with this, earlier today. Just look at all this stuff!" He flung back the tarpaulin to reveal the things tumbled into the wagon bed. Land saw bags and barrels of food and other supplies. There was even a surplus army tent, a grasshopper plow, and other tools.

"A couple horses goes with the rig," the hostler said. "Not in the best of shape, but I been shoveling feed into them, and I dare say they'll fill out in time."

"Where's the owner?"

"You're lookin' at him!" Parsons punched a thumb at his own chest. "Feller I'm telling you about was planning to make the run, and he got together everything he thought he might be needing—I must say he sure didn't leave out much. But yesterday, before he even got to the starting line, he seen the mob he was up against and he plumb lost his nerve. Reckoned the odds were too long."

Which may have been good sense, Jim Land thought, observing the condition of the wagon. Try to take that vehicle into a desperate rush across uneven ground, jostled by other desperately driven rigs and reckless horsemen, and the chances would have been all too good of a smashup and possibly a broken neck.

"At any rate," Dake Parsons continued, "he didn't even wait to hear the signal shots or watch the run take off. He just turned around and left. Came tooling his outfit into town this morning, lookin' to sell the whole shebang and be rid of it—said all he wanted was enough for a stage ticket back to his wife's folks in Nashville.

"Looked to me like a real bargain. I had me a little money put by, so I took him up on the deal. Truth is, it was in the back of my mind that Beth Converse and her husband might be able to use these things."

"No question about it," Land quickly agreed. "They've got almost nothing out there—not even a way to get around. I've been worrying about what could be done for them. I'd say this could solve a lot of problems."

"I was hoping so. It's partly why I decided to quit my job today—while I was on my way west, I could drop it off for them. There's one thing gives me some trouble, though."

"What's that?"

"Money! I'm afraid I don't have so awful much laid by," the old hostler explained in an apologetic tone. "Not on my wages! And even though I got a bargain, paying for all this kind of left me strapped. So I was wondering, do you suppose there's a chance that feller Converse might be willing to reimburse me, at least partly?"

Remembering the fifty dollars that Charlie Converse had handed over to someone, just for a place at the head of the registration line, Jim Land said bluntly, "He damn well better! He's got no right to expect charity, on top of what you've already done for him."

The other man shook his head. "I just don't know about Converse. Trouble is, even if he don't pay, I suppose I'll have to end up leaving the stuff anyhow—for his wife's sake, not his. On account of her, I don't see how I could refuse."

Land suddenly found he had reached a decision. He wanted to know, "How soon could you leave? This afternoon, by any chance?"

"Why, I guess so." Parsons looked puzzled by the question. "Can't see nothin' to hold me, now that Halsell has been told I've quit."

"In that case, I'll ride along with you. It'll be a slow trip with a wagon," Land explained, "and I have to make as good time as possible. But I think if I'm there I can see you get some kind of payment out of Charlie Converse, whether he likes it or not. Knowing they have this stuff, I won't worry quite so much about leaving those people on their own—which I have to do. It's time I was getting to my own job—the one I'm being paid for."

"Bringing in my old friend Bill Doolin," Dake Parsons interpreted. He spoke without rancor; apparently he held no grudge against the marshal for a task that had been assigned him. "All right," he said. "Gimme an hour, and I should be ready to pull out. . . ."

It was still morning of the next day when they brought the Converse claim in sight—Jim Land riding beside the creaking wagon, Dake Parsons on the jolting seat and managing the team, and Parsons' saddlehorse, a rawboned dun, anchored to the wagon's tailgate.

Jim Land was surprised to notice the feeling of relief it gave him when he found everything in order, no apparent disasters having befallen these people in his absence. It gave him pleasure, too, to notice that Beth Converse appeared to be an efficient housekeeper, even camping in the open. The bedrolls were made up and neatly stowed, the few possessions in careful order. Since yesterday a good supply of firewood had been gathered, chopped into kindling, and stacked. A line of blue smoke rose leisurely above the cookfire. Land caught sight of the Converses themselves, gathered at the fire with two other persons who were strangers to him, all of them with coffee cups in their hands.

Coffee was forgotten as they turned to stare at the approaching wagon. When Dake Parsons halted his team and Land stepped down from the saddle, they were greeted with excited questions. The strangers proved to be neighbors from the adjoining homestead claim—a rawboned farmer named Vic Tuttle, who spoke with a decided New England accent,

and a half-grown youngster he called Bud, who was a gangling replica of himself. Land shook hands with them and left
it for Parsons to explain about the wagon and its contents.
For his part, he was satisfied to fill his eyes with Beth's
smiling face and enjoy her ecstatic expressions of gratitude
and disbelief.

Her husband's behavior was different. He listened skepti-
cally until he heard the price Dake Parsons was asking for the
wagon and its contents—an amount Land was sure must be
considerably less than what he had actually put out for it.
That was when Charlie Converse exploded. "Land, did you
let this old man suppose I would give him any such amount?
Perhaps you want to see me completely broke!"

Land had been prepared for some such reaction and was all
set to mount an argument. He never had to make it, for Beth
Converse spoke first.

"Why, of course we'll pay!" She turned indignantly to her
husband. "I should think you'd be ashamed! He's practically
giving us these things—things that can spell the difference in
whether we can get by or not!"

Charlie Converse's face turned red, either in anger or
embarrassment because of the truth in what his wife had said.
In the end he didn't argue, but shrugged instead as he
produced his leather wallet and started counting out the
money without any further comment. Looking at Beth, Land
wanted to say in approval, *Good girl!*

Having made her point, she quickly let the matter drop.
She walked around to the end of the wagon for a better look
at its contents, and after a moment Jim Land followed her.

He took off his hat and, holding it, tried to keep his
manner casual as he said, "I suppose this will be good-bye.
Not too likely I'll see you or your husband again, but I'll be
wishing you the very best of luck."

She turned to him, saying earnestly, "You know, of course,
we can never repay you for all you've done. We couldn't
begin to try!"

Jim Land passed that over. Indicating the Tuttles, father
and son, he commented, "I'm glad you've already met your
neighbors. It's good to have someone close you can call on."

"Yes, it is. Although," she added with a troubled frown,

"so far Mrs. Tuttle hasn't seemed very friendly. I only hope I haven't done something to offend her."

"She'll come around." He didn't want to say so, but he thought he could make a good guess as to what the problem was: He had been noticing Vic Tuttle's behavior. No matter what else was going on, the man's stare never seemed to stray far from Beth Converse. He seemed fascinated by her—something Jim Land could very easily understand. And if Tuttle happened to be married to a jealous woman, it wouldn't have taken her long to be aware of this and resent it. But all Land said was, "In this kind of situation, people get over bad feelings quick enough when they realize how much they have to depend on one another. . . . Well, then," he added, and put out his hand.

She took it and held it as she said, "So you're off again, hunting outlaws?"

"That's my job. Though it doesn't make me a bounty hunter," he added quickly, remembering when Dake Parsons had called him that. "It's just work that someone needs to do. Only, in this case there happens to be a little more to it than that."

She was studying his face, trying to read his meaning. "Are you telling me it's a personal matter, between you and this man Doolin?"

"Not at all, since I've never met him. From what I've heard, there could even be things about him I'd like. He's no killer, for one; and it speaks well for him that in spite of everything, an honest fellow like Parsons can still think of him as a friend. No, the trouble is in the men Doolin has riding with him—taking his orders, profiting by his brains and his leadership.

"There's one man in particular," and he heard his own voice go harsh with emotion, "a man named Freese. He's more than a murderer and the main reason I'm here—I followed him up from Texas. I won't shock you with the details of what happened down there; nevertheless I've made a promise to myself that, if I never do anything else as a lawman, one way or another I mean to see to it Turk Freese is put where he has no chance to do such things again!"

He still had her hand in his, and when she glanced down

he realized his grip must have tightened painfully and unintentionally. He quickly freed her, but she was still concerned with what she had been hearing. She said, "And this man Freese is now one of the Doolin gang? You're pretty sure of that?"

"I know it for a fact." He added, "The gang hasn't pulled a job since the railroad holdup in June, when Doolin was hurt. I'm convinced he can't afford to keep them holed up much longer, without coming out in the open and doing something to put money in their pockets; otherwise he'll lose control. It's got to be soon—my problem is that there's no telling just when or where it will happen."

"Or where you can expect your showdown with the one you call Turk Freese?" Beth finished. She added soberly, "However it works out, please promise me you'll try to be careful."

He ended their talk with a reassuring smile. "That's easy to promise. I'm always careful!"

They rejoined the others then, so Land could say his farewells. To his surprise Dake Parsons had an announcement. "Jim, I've done changed my mind. Reckon maybe I'll be stayin' on here awhile." At Land's puzzled expression, he explained: "It occurs to me, these people are gonna need something a lot more substantial than the army tent in that wagon if they hope to get through a winter on the strip. So happens that when I was a youngster, up in Nebrasky, I had some experience with sod houses. The things ain't much pretty, but if they're built right they make damn good shelter when the blue northers come whooping down from Kansas way.

"It ain't too hard to put one up if you know how. So I've been telling Converse that I'd be willing to stick around long enough to give him pointers and help him get a start on building one before I take off for Nevada. I won't charge nothing, excepting my grub while I'm working. Anyway, Converse has took me up on it."

Beth's husband seemed really pleased with the arrangement, and Land thought he well might. Now Vic Tuttle spoke up with enthusiasm: "Me and the boy are hoping we can learn something, too."

"Why, I think this is just wonderful!" Beth exclaimed.

Jim Land could only add, "It's a more than generous offer."

Parsons showed embarrassment at their praise. He shrugged and said, "Oh, well—a body wants to help where he can." But Land was sure he understood his real motives.

Once again, Dake Parsons was concerned primarily for the young woman. The thought of Beth here on this prairie claim, without adequate shelter and with winter only a matter of weeks away, had again roused all his paternal feelings and determined him to do his part, by at least seeing to it she had a decent house to live in.

As Land made to mount his horse, Dake Parsons said, "And one other thing: I was thinking it's time both these gents were gettin' their claims on file. Could you show them where that's to be done? Tuttle says he'll take his wagon, so I was thinking me and Miz Converse could stay here and get all this stuff unloaded and put in some kind of order."

Land hesitated. "It's all right with me, I guess," he said. "Not too far out of my way—and actually, it could be interesting to see what a town looks like when it's only two days old. . . ."

And so it was settled. Leaving, Jim Land turned for a final look at the claim he had helped these people to win and hold. He took with him the image of brown-haired, brown-eyed Beth Converse—and the guilty knowledge that it would be the better for him, the sooner that image was allowed to fade. . . .

# Chapter Eight

Jim Land wasn't even sure if the town had been given a name, yet it was clearly a place destined for considerable importance. Before the run, it had been surveyed and plotted in advance, as the seat of government for one of the seven new counties to be carved out of what had been the Cherokee Strip. Now he was seeing the result.

The place swarmed! Any attempt to hold it to an orderly plan had obviously broken down. On a flat where there was scarcely a tree for a shield against heat and blinding sunlight, population enough for a small city was jammed into and around an area no larger than a few town blocks. Lot lines were ignored, streets reduced at best to patternless lanes through a mass of temporary structures—hastily constructed tents, for the most part—that clustered and crowded one another, each guarded over by someone ready to fight for what he claimed was his.

In the long run, Land supposed final disposition of all these cases would have to be made in some courtroom or other; it promised to be a lucrative field day for lawyers. Some were already on the ground. Their offices were stools and folding tables or packing cases set up in front of their tents, where they carried on their business cheek by jowl with three-card monte and poker dealers.

Other men drifted through the milling crowd with no apparent purpose, unless it was to pick up anything that might be lying loose or in someone's unguarded pocket. Everywhere a continuous racket of voices rose along with the heat waves that shimmered above this expanse of sunblasted dust and sprawling canvas.

Land picked a way through the confusion, followed by Converse and Tuttle in the latter's wagon, both of them appearing subdued by the things they saw about them. He found at last what he was looking for—the only wooden structure so far on the townsite, put up by the authorities in advance of the run. It was the land office for this section of the strip, identified as such by a wooden sign and by the line of men trailing away from its entrance who waited to register the claims they had staked. Here Jim Land reined in beside the wagon.

"This will have to be where I leave you," he said. "You've got the permits you were given when you signed up to make the run. Those and the location numbers from your claims should be all you need to put you in business."

Vic Tuttle eyed the queue of homesteaders with a grimace. "Another damn line!"

"While you're standing in it, I suggest you don't forget to keep an eye on your rig—unless you don't mind making it back on foot."

"Nobody touches this wagon!"

Charlie Converse asked, "Where will you be off to, Land?"

"Guthrie, eventually," he answered. "Marshal Nix is supposed to be back in his office by Wednesday morning. I want to check in with him and while I'm at it have a look at one of the Doolin gang who's cooling his heels in the federal jail there—find out if the man feels yet like doing any talking. After that I'll have to decide on my next move."

"Well . . ." It seemed to take an effort for Converse to hold out his hand. "For Beth and myself, I guess I have some things to thank you for."

Land had given up looking for any spontaneous sign of gratitude from this man, and though it pleased him, it took him by surprise. He said briefly, "It's all right. I was glad to help." Converse's smooth hand contrasted with the heavily callused palm that the farmer, Vic Tuttle, offered him. Land gave both men a half salute in farewell. As he reined away they were already looking around for a safe spot to park the wagon and team while they took their places in line.

Land wondered if Charlie Converse would be using any of the dwindling funds in that leather wallet to buy his way to the head of this line. . . .

Moments later, Jim Land forgot them both as he was forced to pull hastily aside to make way for a freight wagon, whose cursing, sweating driver was having all he could do to maneuver his outsize rig and teams through the streets. Since this town was not on a railroad, it suddenly occurred to Land that every scrap of supplies needed to keep it alive—as well as the claim holders on all the quarter sections that surrounded it—had to be painstakingly loaded at railhead and hauled in and unloaded again, from an endless stream of these big freight rigs. It gave a further insight into the size and logistical complexity of this whole operation.

When, amid all the hubbub and bustle of movement around him, he suddenly heard himself being hailed by name, Jim Land jerked around with a start. It took him a moment to spot the tent that had a crude sign with the word SALOON erected over its entrance. Before the opening, a wooden plank propped up by two barrels served as a bar. Impatient men were clustered there, waiting for the bartender to pour their drinks from a jug into tin cups, at a dollar a throw.

A man who had just straightened from rolling a new barrel out of the tent waved and called again and stepped forward to greet Jim Land as he picked his way through the tangle of traffic. He was a brawny-looking Irishman, with a handlebar mustache and a dented derby hat pushed toward the back of his head. He grinned as Land said, "What are you doing here, Flanagan? I thought you'd still be tending bar in Guthrie."

"Why settle for that when I got a chance to start my own establishment here? Ain't a living man wouldn't rather work for himself. How about a warm beer on the house?" he offered. "We're gonna have to wait awhile for ice. Not that it matters to these people." He indicated the thirsty men clustered at the bar. "They're dry enough they'll drink any damn thing!"

"Thanks just the same," Land said, smiling. "I think maybe I'll hold out for the ice."

He had met Barney Flanagan shortly after coming to Oklahoma and had found him an invaluable source of information—the man had tended bar in a Guthrie saloon where Bill Doolin and, later, other members of his gang had hung out before their growing notoriety made the town unsafe for them. Flanagan had been able to give descriptions and personal facts about individual members of the gang, insights that made them something more than names in legends or on reward posters. Now Flanagan had something to report, and he came to it without any more preliminaries. "You recall, once, asking me about someone I had to admit I'd never seen? Name of Freese, I think it was."

Land nodded. "What about him?

"He just might be here. I seen one this morning that sure met the description—got a pretty fair look at him as he rode past, and it tallied. Dark complected, scarred up some. Way his hat brim was pulled down, I couldn't tell whether he had a damaged eye or not."

"When would this have been?"

"Maybe an hour ago," Flanagan said. "Not much more than that. It could just as easily been someone else entirely, of course. I sure wasn't watching for him—but then, I didn't expect to see *you*, either! So you never know!"

Jim Land peered thoughtfully into the clutter of the crowded street. He nodded. "Thanks. I'll have a look around, see if I can spot him."

"From what I remember you saying," the Irishman commented, "I don't think you'd want to let him see you first!"

But even as he rode on, Land's first stir of excitement was already leaving him. Even if the one Flanagan had seen was actually Turk Freese—a big if—how was he going to pick out one man in all this confusion? And again, whoever it was Flanagan saw, after the lapse of an hour he could already be gone from this town. If not it would be very dangerous riding blindly like this, hunting for him.

Land had a hand on his holstered gun, and his searching glance moved across the faces that tended to blur into one another, as he looked for the one that had become almost an obsession. . . .

So full was his mind of Turk Freese, that when he did come upon danger he almost stumbled into it unawares. His first warning was an angry shout that narrowed his attention suddenly to a quartet of men who had moved out into the street ahead of him, as though meaning to block his way. Land recognized their leader by his bulky size and the black growth of whiskers; then he picked out other faces that he had seen across the campfire two nights ago when they rode in on the Converse claim.

The would-be claim jumpers had known him instantly as the one who had thwarted their purpose, wounded one and disarmed and routed the rest. They'd had plenty of time since then to find other weapons; also, no doubt, to nurse their resentment. Now the bearded leader let out a roar: "By God, it *is* him! Get the son of a bitch!" As with one movement, guns began to slide into the open.

Against such odds, a moment's hesitation would be fatal. Jim Land didn't wait. His own gun was in his hand as he kicked the sorrel and sent it leaping forward, straight at the leader. The horse's shoulder struck the bearded man, sending him spinning off his feet, and by then Land was in the midst of the others. One triggered a shot nearly in his face. The muzzle flash was blinding; he felt the heat of it, almost thought he heard the bullet sing past. His six-gun arced down, its barrel clipped the man on the side of the head and drove him to the ground.

There was an uproar now, as bystanders in the crowded street yelled and scrambled to get clear of this burst of violence. Somebody stumbled over a tent rope and brought the canvas billowing down on top of himself and the struggling group trapped inside. Without pause, Jim Land was hauling the sorrel around, rear hooves digging dirt as the animal spun adroitly. The bearded leader, sprawled on his face where the sorrel's charge had dumped him, was fighting to rise. Quickly Land came down from the saddle, dropped a knee onto the fellow's back, and drove his face into the dirt; he put the muzzle of his gun against the back of the claim jumper's head and at once felt the starch go out of him, as he took the warning.

From the corner of his eye Land caught a flash of brightness. His head jerked up, and he saw the knife blade rising in the hand of another of his attackers. He'd been looking for this. At once his gun covered the man and he invited harshly, "Go ahead and throw it! You're a dead man if you do. You won't walk away like you did the other night!"

The man with the knife froze, staring into the gun muzzle. Slowly his fingers opened, and the wicked-looking blade fell into the dirt. Land swung the revolver toward the last of the four. Seeing himself suddenly alone, that one dropped his unfired gun without being ordered to and, face gone white, raised both hands above his head.

It was over as quickly as that.

Ignoring the excitement around him, Jim Land rose and nudged the bearded leader with his gun muzzle, saying roughly, "Get up from there. You're not hurt." The one he had clubbed off his feet was stirring a little and moaning faintly; the remaining pair stood motionless and seemingly bewildered as they watched their chief being prodded to his feet.

A couple of newcomers came bustling onto the scene, shoving through the crowd and bearing down on Jim Land. He saw their guns and the badges they both were prominently displaying. Not recognizing either one, he judged they must belong to the special corps of a thousand temporary deputies Marshal Nix had been allowed to recruit for policing the opening of the strip. They closed in on Land, and one of them warned him loudly, "All right, you! Throw down that gun, or—"

He broke off as he saw the badge Land took from his pocket; both were taken aback, but obviously relieved to find he was a fellow officer. To a stammered question Jim Land answered briefly, "I had trouble with these men earlier. They're claim jumpers—tried to run some people off the place they'd staked, but got run off themselves. Just now they were trying to get even."

With so many guns covering them, the prisoners looked

sullen and beaten. The deputy who had challenged Land said gruffly, "They don't look like much."

"They aren't—not with their fangs pulled. I'll turn them over to you, if you don't mind," he went on. "At the land office you'll find a man named Converse, probably still waiting in line to file his claim. He's the one they tried to jump that night. It's up to him to say whether he wants you to hold them so he can prefer charges."

"*Hold* them? Where we going to do that? You see any jail around here?" His gesture indicated the crazy conglomeration of tents that made up this place. "Hell, the two of us have got our hands full just trying to keep things from flying apart!"

Land shrugged. "Suit yourselves. You can turn them loose, for all I care—but you might hang onto their guns until I've had a chance to get gone. I've got more important things to do than waste time on them."

Nor could he waste it in continuing a futile hunt for the man Barney Flanagan had seen, he was thinking as he turned to mount his saddle. The odds of it being Turk Freese were poor enough; to find him in all this was obviously close to impossible.

Reluctant, but yielding to the pressures on him, he gave up the only lead he had yet received in his search for Turk Freese and set his sights for Guthrie.


From the shelter of a tent corner, Turk Freese had watched the brief battle in the street, held frozen in disbelief at what he saw. It was sheerest chance that put him there. For a half hour he had lingered near the rolled-up canvas siding, his saddled horse waiting nearby while he intently watched the gambling games going on inside. Fingering his holstered gun, he had eyed bills and coins scattered over crude gaming tables.

He was pulled in two directions. One was the temptation all that money offered to step inside, aim a gun at one of those tables, and scoop up the cash. He could fling a few bullets around to cover his retreat and be in the saddle and away from there before anyone recovered from shock. It was the kind of daring stunt that appealed to Turk Freese.

But even as he waited, there was also the awareness of time passing and of the long ride that lay ahead of him. Bill Doolin had made his plans carefully; he would have little patience with any member of the gang who spoiled them by arriving late for the rendezvous at the place called Woodward, over west on the Santa Fe railroad. Even as it was, Freese would probably have to burn up a couple of broncs in order to make it by tomorrow evening. And certainly, the job Doolin had in mind should pay him a hell of a lot better than the few odd bills lying there on the table, tempting him.

Nevertheless he stood where he was, torn by greed, unable to make up his mind—and that was when the uproar started in the street and pulled him over for a look, to find out what was going on.

All he saw at first was one man menaced by four others—a man who, without warning, suddenly took the fight directly to his enemies. In a blur of action nearly impossible to follow, he somehow bested them, downing a couple and forcing the others to throw up their hands.

And then he turned his head, and Turk Freese went numb in disbelief as he looked into the face of his nemesis, the man who had driven him ignominiously out of Texas two years before.

What quirk of fate could have placed that man here, not ten yards from where he stood? Could it be that through uncanny instinct and unswerving, bulldog purpose, the bastard had actually been able to track him down? As always in moments of agonized questioning, Turk Freese put up his hand to finger the scar above his damaged left eye.

Though he heard the angry voices out there in the street, he couldn't make out what was being said. Suddenly his mouth hardened, and he dropped his hand to his holster and brought up his Colt .45. He leveled the sights against Jim Land's broad back, but then, for just a moment, something he didn't understand—something very much like superstitious fear—kept his finger from tightening on the trigger.

It was a moment too long. Two men burst through the crowd, and he saw the badges pinned to their shirtfronts. He cursed, but it was too late; the chance was over. All at once he felt the sweat on his face and the shaking of the hand that stabbed the six-gun uselessly into the holster.

Suddenly the only thing he wanted was to get away from that place.

He turned and hurried back to where he had left his big roan horse. Trained as a cow pony, it stood anchored on trailing reins; Freese scooped them up as he hoisted his bulk into the saddle, the animal already turning under him. Had he glanced again into the tent he might have seen that the cardplayers had left the game he had been so avidly watching, to join the crowd in the street entrance. The money still lay, forgotten and scattered, over the tabletop.

But Turk Freese wasn't interested in that money now. He wanted nothing just then except to put distance between himself and the man he both feared and hated. He kicked the roan and settled into a ground-eating gait, across the rolling red earth of what used to be known as the Cherokee Strip.

When Jim Land walked into the marshal's office on Wednesday morning, Evett Nix greeted him with enthusiasm. "Land! Come in—come in. You're just the man I was wishing I could talk to. Let's go in my office."

Land followed him in, took a chair beside the flat-topped desk, and dropped his dusty hat to the floor. Through an open window came the busy sounds of traffic on Harrison Avenue, below them.

It was the first time he had been able to sit down with the marshal for Oklahoma Territory, here at his headquarters; their only previous meetings had been short ones in the field, during the frenetic preparations for the opening of the Cherokee Strip. A pleasant-looking man, with a luxuriant mustache and a level, intelligent eye, Evett Nix was clearly perturbed just now. He seated himself behind the desk and ran a palm across his scalp in a harassed way as he said, "Well, you called it dead right! You told us Bill Doolin was overdue to pull another big job—and that when he did, there would be no predicting where or when it was going to happen."

Jim Land said, "So give me the bad news."

"It's all in these telegrams." Nix shoved a fistful of them across the desk. "They've been coming in all morning, from up at Woodward—that's one of the new towns, over toward the western end of the strip."

Land nodded, having made himself familiar with the map of Oklahoma Territory and with the location of a good many places on it that he hadn't yet actually seen.

The marshal went on. "Even before the run, Woodward was a division point for the Santa Fe railroad, with a round-house and repair shop. And fortunately, we have a telegraph connection. So we know that a little past midnight this morning two men got the station agent out of bed and took him to the depot. He didn't know either of them by sight, but he's positive one was Doolin. The other . . ." Nix cocked an eyebrow. "This will interest you. The agent says he was dark and had a milky-looking left eye."

Land had straightened in his chair. "Turk Freese," he said grimly. "Then the other was Doolin, all right." He found himself making swift computations. If Freese was the man Barney Flanagan saw, by pushing hard he would still have been able to reach Woodward in time. But of course it didn't matter now whether Flanagan was right or not. That had only been supposition; *this* was positive!

Evett Nix continued. "The agent was forced to open the safe for them. And here's the funny part: Doolin claimed to *know* there would be ten thousand dollars in it—a payroll for the troops at Fort Supply, being shipped over the railroad line by Wells Fargo. What's more, he said he read about it in the newspaper! And d'you know, we've managed to dig up a copy, and by God he was right!" The marshal passed over a recent issue of the Kansas City *Times*, with the passage circled in pencil. It was no more than a paragraph, but the facts of the projected money shipment were there, in black and white.

"I don't know where a *Times* reporter could have got his information," Nix said in disgust, "or why in the world the paper would have printed it—they know things like this are supposed to be secret. But they gave Doolin all he needed to work out the logistics and know just when he could expect to find the money lying in the station agent's safe at Woodward.

It would take a smart man to figure it—but then we've always known that Bill Doolin is no dummy.

"Once they had the money, I guess the agent thought his time was up for certain. Your man Freese wanted to kill him right there and shut his mouth, but Doolin vetoed that. Instead they made the fellow go a distance with them out of town and turned him loose. When they rode off, he hurried back and spread the alarm."

"At least now the waiting is over," Jim Land said. He picked his hat off the floor, preparing to rise. "I'll get a fresh bronc and be on my way."

"I'm not sure there's any point in that," Nix told him. "One of my best field deputies, Jack Love, happened to be on the ground; this latest wire just came from him. He says that not far west of town he found where Doolin and Freese joined up with a half dozen others who had been waiting for them. The whole bunch took off for the Texas line, but they soon started to split up. Jack returned to put a posse together and send me word of what was happening.

"Looks like the same old story: Unless that posse has better luck than all the others, the sign will unravel on them and lose itself in those Panhandle breaks—and they'll be reporting back empty-handed. In any case, it's almost certain to be over before anyone from this office could get up there to lend a hand."

Land had to agree. Restlessness pulled him to his feet and to the window, to stare unseeingly out at the blank sky arching over this town of Guthrie—thinking of the manhunt even now in progress and the irony that placed him here, unable to take any part in it. There was no professional jealousy in this; he wished Jack Love every possible success. But knowing from experience the elusive nature of Doolin and his followers, he had grave doubts.

He turned from the window as, behind him, Marshal Nix said in a tone of some bitterness, "If Doolin does get away with this, all the papers will be demanding to know just what the marshal's office is going to do about it. The telegrams from Washington will be landing on my desk, hot enough to scorch the varnish. Yet those skinflints aren't going to let me keep any of the extra staff I hired for the Cherokee Strip opening, even though, with the turmoil still going on up there, I'm having to call in all my field deputies and send them in to try to get some kind of order. Meanwhile the rest of the territory can go to hell!" He shook his head. "All I know is, I'd never run a business the way the government tries to run this office!"

Land knew that Evett Nix was no professional law officer. His had been a political appointment—a businessman who had been given the job because of his management skills. But he had proved a good choice. He had assembled a staff of able field deputies, men of the caliber of Chris Madsen, Heck Thomas, and Bill Tilghman, and then backed them to the hilt. It was a question whether the territory knew just how good a man their marshal was.

Now he told Jim Land, "*Your* assignment remains unchanged. The Doolin gang is our biggest single problem, and you've been calling the turn correctly every time so far. The job last night was the big one you predicted that Doolin would have to try, if he wanted to keep the gang together. Well, if the loot was anything as big as the paper indicated, they've now got a nice piece of change to divide amongst them!"

"They won't take long going through it," Land predicted. "That kind never does. More likely it will only whet their appetites: A few nights in one of these Panhandle cow towns—a few hands of cutthroat poker—and they'll all be broke again and ready to head back to Oklahoma, looking for another score. And then the game starts all over."

The marshal nodded bleakly. "It starts all over. . . ."

From Nix's office Land went to the federal jail and had himself let into the cell where Arkansas Tom had been held, pending trial, ever since his capture during the raid at Ingalls. It was the first time Land had been to see him. He found the outlaw stretched out on his bunk shirtless in the breathless heat, eyes closed. At the clang of the slamming door, shutting Land in with him, he opened his eyes, but he didn't move; his narrow face showed no expression as he recognized the man who had disarmed and captured him single-handed.

"How are you, Tom?" Land asked.

The prisoner answered bluntly, "Bored."

"In that big a hurry for the hanging?"

"Nobody's going to be hanging me," Arkansas Tom said in the same truculent manner.

"Are you still counting on Bill Doolin to stop it?" Land asked him. "I remember he and the gang went off and left you stranded upstairs in that hotel. And now you've been sitting in jail for two weeks and still nothing's happened. The man's only human, Tom. He can't work miracles."

He waited for an answer, but the prisoner gave no reaction, merely continued to lie motionless and stare at the steel slats of the bunk just above him.

Jim Land gave a deliberate twist of the knife blade. "Of course, it could be Doolin doesn't think he needs you any longer. The gang pulled off a big job last night, up in the strip—had you heard? They're reported to have got themselves ten grand out of it—and it makes considerable difference, to men like that, when there's one less they have to divide with."

Now at last he got a response—a sudden hard, stabbing look, before the man's eyes returned to their blank stare overhead. "So just maybe you'd better start thinking about trying to cooperate with the marshal's office," Land finished. "You might do yourself some good."

"Oh?" Arkansas Tom turned his head fully toward the man in the doorway. He said with an edge of sarcasm, "How much good? Can you get me out of here?"

"After you murdered three deputies that day at Ingalls? I don't do miracles, either!"

"Then why should I tell you anything?" But now, suddenly, the man was roused enough to lever his legs over the edge of his bunk and sit up to face Jim Land. "Look!" he said. "I know what you want from me! You want to be waiting at the cave when the gang rides back in and pick them off one by one. Well, I'm not telling you anything—so forget it! And leave me alone."

Land considered him for a moment longer; it was clear he meant exactly what he said. Finally the lawman nodded. "All right," he said shortly and called for the jailer to let him out.

But as he left the jail, one word that the prisoner had spoken—probably without even realizing it had slipped out of him—continued to ring in the lawman's mind like the stroke of a bell: *Cave!* In romantic legend, every outlaw from Jesse James on down was supposed to have used natural caves for their hideouts; perhaps some few actually had. Jim Land had also heard such rumors about Bill Doolin, but had given them little thought.

Now, by an unconscious slip, Arkansas Tom had proved the rumor to be true. Moreover, Land had seen enough of this red earth and limestone country of Oklahoma Territory to fill in some details: A cave, hereabouts, would most likely be formed along the bank of a river or creek; for it to be large enough to serve as a hideout for a gang such as Doolin's, it would need to be a watercourse of some size.

So he knew now that somewhere in the tangled fastness of the Cimarron or one of its tributaries, in a region little known to white men, hollowed by nature into the side of a steep limestone bank, Bill Doolin's hideout was waiting to be discovered. All that remained for him to do was find it.

# Chapter Nine

Beth Converse sensed the coming of a change in the weather. This summer drought, which had dragged out for so long, was beginning to lose something of its grip on the land. Today she had awakened to find that a high thin scurf of cloud had slid across the blank sky, dulling the smashing force of the sun; a wind came with it that was different from the constant oven breath she had known during those first few days on the claim. This wind had the hint of teeth in it. It whipped the sun-dried grass and brought down streamers of dead leaves that had hung limp or rattled like paper on the tree branches.

It was a reminder that autumn was very near. And it made her realize, even more strongly, how fortunate she and Charlie were to have Dake Parsons on hand to help them.

The sod house was progressing, but it was a slow process. Parsons told her that in the old days in Nebraska, he had seen a family's neighbors get together in a communal effort and put up a house in a single day. It was a different matter when you did the whole job alone.

Dake Parsons took complete charge. He chose a location for the house and marked out its dimensions; he decided where the sod should be cut, in strips precisely a foot across. Beth pitched in with her share of the work with enthusiasm. She soon found she was able to guide the plow and draw an even furrow if someone else would keep the horse moving,

and afterward she helped cut the sod into eighteen-inch
lengths. That was the right width for the building's walls,
according to Parsons. Plastered with sand and clay and white-
washed, those walls would stand against any sort of weather,
hold warmth in winter and coolness in the worst of summer's
heat.

So the walls began to rise, one course upon another. Meanwhile, on the adjoining claim, another soddie was going up as
Vic Tuttle and his son put Dake Parsons' teaching to their
own use. But Charlie Converse, for one, found that handling
the heavy strips of sod was harder work than he'd expected.
After a half day at this sweaty labor, he protested, "Who
wants to live in a mud hut, anyway? We've got timber here.
A log house couldn't take this long to build."

"You ain't got trees enough for that," the old puncher
explained patiently. "You're going to want 'em left standing,
for shade and for a windbreak. As it is, you'll need to cut
some for roof poles and door and window framing, not to say
anything about furniture and firewood. But unless you figure
to spend the winter in that army tent, you only have one
good choice."

Beth tried not to let Charlie's grumbling upset her or spoil
her satisfaction in what they were accomplishing. It was
troubling enough to think about the months ahead, to tally
their limited supplies and try to judge how well they could be
made to last until spring, when she would be able to put in a
garden and begin to raise food for their table. But she tried
not to dwell on the future. They were committed; they had
done much with the aid of Dake Parsons—and of that quiet-
mannered and competent man Jim Land, about whom she
even now found herself thinking, wondering if their paths
would ever cross again.

Whatever lay ahead, she found the present strangely exhil-
arating. Certainly she had never expected to feel the thrill
she got just standing here on their own land, the wind
blowing her skirts against her while, shading her eyes with
her arm, she watched a skein of geese stitching a pattern
southward across the sky, their wild cries calling to her.

Charlie and Dake Parsons had raised the walls to the level
of the window frame Dake had nailed together, and now they

were setting the frame into place while Beth, at the campfire, looked to the iron pot of coffee she had been brewing for them all. As she settled it firmly into place amid the coals, she caught sight of a pair of riders approaching across the brown grass. She straightened, curious—they never had visitors here, except for their immediate neighbors.

These two came from the west; they had skirted the Tuttle claim, but now they veered and seemed headed directly for this one. When they reached the partially completed house, they drew rein for a moment, and then one came ahead while the other paused a little longer, watching the men at work there.

Beth stood and waited as the rider approached. He shaped up in the saddle as tall and slender of build, with a drooping mustache and—a feature that was apparently common to this country—a revolver at his hip, as well as a long gun in the saddle holster. He drew rein and with a respectful gesture removed his hat and held it on his lap; his hair was auburn, and the eyes that studied her were a pale blue. He said politely, "No intention of bothering you, ma'am. Our horses are in need of watering. All right if we use the spring yonder?"

Impressed by his manner, she could only say, "Why, of course. You're welcome to help yourselves."

"Thank you kindly."

Replacing his hat, he turned and signaled the other rider to come in. And suddenly the thought occurred to Beth that the latter could have remained briefly behind to serve as a rear guard!

By now Charlie and Dake Parsons had left their work and were walking toward the fire, their heads together as they discussed something about the job. Nearing, Dake Parsons raised his head, and the shielding hat brim revealed his face. Beth saw how he halted in his tracks as he and the stranger regarded each other in a silent stare.

The stranger spoke. "Dake! What are you doing out here?"

The old puncher's face was completely without expression. "I'm building a soddie. What are *you* doing?"

"Riding through. Thought we'd stop to take care of our horses. I remembered there was a spring here."

"I bet you did!" Parsons remarked cryptically.

The rider's gesture indicated the land that lay about them. "Good location for a homestead claim," he observed. "Yours?"

"Naw. I'm just lending these folks a hand, for a spell. They're friends of mine, the Converses. Beth and Charlie . . ." The rider acknowledged them with a nod and a touch at his hat brim to the woman. And then Dake Parsons finished his introductions, muttering shortly, "This here is Bill."

Even before he said it, pointedly not giving a second name, Beth had guessed the truth. The knowledge that this was the notorious outlaw Bill Doolin must have showed in her face, for she saw Parsons looking at her and caught a quick and warning shake of his head, meant to silence her. Her lips parted and then closed again, on a held breath. Her husband meanwhile stood looking on, giving no indication of knowing who their visitor really was.

And then the second horseman rode up to the fire. Beth's glance switched to him, and this time she could barely stifle a gasp as she saw the hideously scarred face, the milky, damaged eye. This could only be one man—Turk Freese!

Charlie Converse spoke with bland cordiality. "We've got coffee on the fire. You two take care of your horses and join us, why don't you?"

"Why, thanks," Bill Doolin agreed without hesitation. "It'll be a pleasure. . . ."

Trembling with apprehension as she got out tin cups for everyone, Beth kept an eye on the visitors. They rode over to the spring, Charlie accompanying them, and dismounted there to help themselves to some of the clear, cold water before letting their horses drink. On the ground they made contrasting figures, Bill Doolin being slender and about the same height as Jim Land, while Freese was stocky with heavy shoulders.

No one could possibly have mistaken Turk Freese, after once hearing a description of him, but Beth could understand why the law was having trouble pinpointing Bill Doolin: Without a photograph to go by, any description of the outlaw leader would sound like a hundred other men. The one thing she particularly noticed about him was the way he favored his left leg as he came leading his horse back from the spring. She remembered Jim Land telling about a train robbery early that summer in which Doolin had been wounded. The hurt leg was obviously bothering him still.

Passing out the cups and filling them from the smoke-blackened pot, she was acutely aware of Turk Freese watching her every move. She wondered how much of the feeling of evil she got from this man was an echo of the dark things Marshal Land had hinted at. *Worse than murder . . .* whatever he'd meant by that, she somehow knew Jim Land wouldn't have said anything that was less than the absolute truth.

They stood about the fire, drinking the hot brew while a rising wind whipped at the flames and sent sparks streaming. Flicking the last drops from his cup, Dake Parsons asked, too casually, "Just where are you boys headed?"

Bill Doolin's head lifted. "What was that?" He must have known he was being needled, and even if they had been friends once, it seemed to Beth a nervy thing to do. Parsons met the tall man's look squarely. "Don't I speak plain enough?" he retorted with the same hint of devilry. "I just asked where you're off to."

For a moment Bill Doolin's pale eyes rested on the older man's face. Then he said briefly, "Nowhere in particular. Yonderly." But it was plain he hadn't liked the question at all.

He turned then to Charlie Converse. "I told your wife," he said, "that you folks picked a good piece of land here—one of the best I know of in this part of the strip. You chose well."

"So everyone says," Charlie admitted. He had the honesty to add, "To tell you the truth, we more or less fell into it. Parsons told us about the place, to begin with. And then there was another man—"

"More coffee?" Beth broke in hurriedly, anxious to cut him off without appearing to. She was trembling so that she had trouble holding the big pot steady as she moved about the circle, refilling cups. When she came to Charlie, she tried to put an urgency into the warning look she gave him, but he only shook his head with no more than a glance and seemed oblivious to the message in her own. She sought desperately for a way to change the subject.

But Bill Doolin must have caught some overtone. He looked

at her searchingly and then turned again to her husband. "You were saying something about another man?"

"Yes, he helped us follow the directions Dake Parsons gave us. We might not have managed too well on our own. We were lucky, too, to have him around afterward when some claim jumpers tried to throw us off our place. It came in handy that this fellow, Jim Land, was a deputy federal marshal."

Beth groaned inwardly and shot an apprehensive look at Doolin and then at Turk Freese. It was what she saw in the latter's face that thoroughly alarmed her. The dark-skinned outlaw's undamaged eye had widened as he heard the name; then his whole face was contorted in sudden fury.

No one seemed to notice. Bill Doolin was looking at Charlie, his blue eyes frowning slightly. "Land," he repeated. "Seems I've heard of him. Texas, mostly. I had no idea he was a federal man or that he was working here in the territory."

"It's only been recently," Charlie explained while Beth stood by, helpless to prevent him. "He told us the marshal's office had brought him in to help deal with—" Suddenly the words stopped, almost as though a hand had been clapped over his mouth. His jaw dropped; he cast a glance at Beth and at Dake Parsons, and at what he read in their faces his own suddenly drained of color. "I—I think he said it was some special assignment," Charlie finished lamely, and after that there was not another word out of him.

Turk Freese, too, was silent, but the man's dark face showed that he was busy with savage thoughts. If Bill Doolin was aware, he gave no sign. He finished his coffee and handed the cup to Beth, thanking her. "Reckon we'll be getting on now," he said, and told his companion, "Fetch the broncs."

After a few more formalities and a last brief exchange with Dake Parsons, the visitors were mounted and riding off toward the dry creek bed below the claim. The three stood in silence and watched them go.

They were no sooner out of earshot than Charlie Converse turned on Dake Parsons, white with fury. "Couldn't you have given me some hint who I was talking to? That was Doolin, wasn't it? A wonder I didn't get myself into serious trouble before I finally caught on!"

The older man shrugged. "Not from Bill. He would have figured it a big joke! But you're right," he added. "I should have tipped you off. I seen that Beth knew, right away. Reckon I just figured you the same. I'm sorry."

Still shaken, Charlie said grudgingly, "Well, they're gone now. No harm done, I guess."

Beth could no longer hold herself in. "No harm!" she cried. "They didn't know about Jim Land before—and now they do! Did you see the look on that other man's face? I know about him! His name is Turk Freese, and he and Jim are deadly enemies. Now that he's been warned, he'll have the advantage—what's more, he'll be looking for a chance to use it. And we have no way at all to let Jim know the danger you've put him in!"

She wasn't prepared for the intent look her husband gave her or his tone as he said dryly, "So now it's Jim, is it? You seem very much concerned about a man you only knew for about two days—and will most probably never see again!"

That astounded her. "You mean, you're *not* concerned about someone we're indebted to, the way we are to Jim Land?"

"Oh, he's shown he can look after himself," Charlie replied coldly. "*I'm* beginning to wonder if I shouldn't be concerned that the two of you don't see each other again!"

At first she didn't understand him. Then she did; outraged by what he was suggesting, she gasped and felt a tide of warmth flood into her cheeks. Yet there was no way to answer without the risk of making matters even worse. Mouth gone tight, Beth turned from her husband and set about gathering the cups they all had been using and flinging them into the dish pan.

Dake Parsons stood by, a look of dismay on his sunbrowned face.


Bill Doolin pulled in and half turned his roan horse to face Turk Freese, who was also drawing to a halt. "All right," he said. "What about this Jim Land?"

The answer was cautious. "How do you mean?"

"I was just wondering. You both came up from Texas. And

I thought I saw a look on your face when that Converse fellow mentioned his name."

"You imagined it." Turk Freese generally considered it safer to tell a lie, on principle. "I've never had any dealings with the man. Heard of him, of course, same as you—nothin' more. If they've brought him up here and made a deputy marshal out of him, they'll be after bigger game than me. Hell, I ain't even known yet in Oklahoma."

The cold blue eyes continued to study him. "You figure *I'm* the one, then?"

"Most likely. But if it's so, from what I've heard you can't afford to fool around. Be smarter to kill him first chance you get and be rid of him."

"Like you wanted to do with that station agent over at Woodward, until I stopped you? I'm beginning to think you like the idea of killing a little too well. Seems to be your solution for every problem that comes up."

The other shrugged. "I dunno a better one. At least it tends to be permanent." He added in the same sullen tone, "If you want to fret about something, you might remember that the marshal has still got one of our boys in his jail. Long as the law hangs onto him, it's like they got a gun pointed at our heads!"

"You're suggesting Arkansas can be made to talk? Or that he might even cut a deal and sell us out?" Doolin shook his head emphatically. "No chance—they got the wrong man. Forget it."

"The boys don't want to forget it. They think we should be doing something about busting him out of that place—before the bulls really go to work to try and wear him down."

But Doolin again shook his head. "Have you *seen* that federal jail in Guthrie? Solid brick and stone; nobody's busting Arkansas out of there. And don't think for a minute I ain't laid awake nights, trying to figger a way to do it!"

They rode without talking after that.

Plainly, there was a feel of changing weather. The cloud ceiling had thickened until it lay over the prairie like the lid of a box. The riders settled their hats against the wind and pulled their coats closer and fastened them.

Presently, as they rested their horses for a moment, Doolin asked, "Which way you heading from here?"

Freese gave him a look of some surprise. "Why, I just assumed we'd be spending the night at Dunn's."

Bill Doolin had expected that answer. The Dunn family were ranchers, but they also had close connections with the gang and made its members welcome whenever they showed up. Doolin knew that Freese had a particular interest there—the four Dunn brothers had an attractive sister in her teens named Rosa, who had caught his one good eye. Doolin could have told him he had no chance with her at all, but he doubted Freese would listen. So he said now, "Suit yourself. I'm going on into town."

There was a note of alarm in the other's voice. "To Ingalls? Ain't that risky after what nearly happened last time? I don't figure we got many friends left there."

Doolin said bluntly, "There's somebody I have to see. Don't worry—I figure to walk easy."

"Should I look for you afterward, at Dunn's?"

The outlaw leader considered, deciding against it. "If I ain't showed by midmorning, don't wait for me—take off. I'll join the rest of you at the hideout by the next day at the latest."

"If you say so." On that dubious note they parted, Turk Freese swinging his horse southeastward toward the Dunn ranch; Doolin continued on alone.

When he had last seen Ingalls, it had been from the back of a speeding horse amid a rattle of gunfire, with bullets flying and the reek of powder smoke under a broiling sun. Tonight, by contrast, the town was a silent huddle of buildings with only scattered window lights to break the darkness and no sound at all except for the bluster of the chill night wind.

Bill Doolin rode into Pickering's grove, on the north edge of the settlement, and there dismounted and tied his horse to a low-lying tree branch. He loosened the cinch but left the saddle on, knowing the animal would be safe until he wanted it again. Then, limping on his painfully wounded left leg, which gave every sign of permanently crippling him, he made his way toward the blocky shape of the two-storied hotel.

It was bitterly ironic to be sneaking in like this. Over a period of many months the gang had virtually owned this town; the money they brought and spent here had bought them a welcome and comfortable haven, where they could relax their constant vigil against the law. But that would never be again. The raid had changed everything, so that now Bill Doolin found himself watching the shadows and never knowing which one might hold an enemy.

He picked his way carefully through trash and weeds and halted where he could study the rear of the hotel. Lamplight glowed behind the drawn shade of one of the windows flanking the closed back door. As he watched, he saw a shadow pass briefly across it; stooping, he found a pebble and lobbed it gently at the window, hearing the small sound as it bounced off the glass. The light was quickly snuffed out.

Doolin waited a moment and tossed another stone. Still nothing happened; then, with a slight noise, the hotel's rear door opened. A figure in white showed faintly there against darker shadows. At once he started forward. As he stepped onto the porch, the screen door was pushed wide; a warm hand clutched at him, and a voice spoke his name. He was led a half-dozen steps through a hallway to the darkened rear bedroom. Then that door closed behind him, and with a sob of greeting Bill Doolin's wife, Edie, threw herself into his arms.

Presently Edie exclaimed, "I've got to *see* you!" She broke away, found matches, and got the oil lamp on the table burning again. Its yellow light showed the bare walls and cheap furnishings of the tiny hotel room. As he stood looking down at his wife, a humorous quirk touched Doolin's mouth beneath its flowing mustache. "What's the matter? You want to make absolutely sure it wasn't somebody else?"

"Oh, you!" Edie cuffed his arm lightly with her fist, and then she laughed and came again into his embrace—this attractive twenty-year-old to whom he had been legally married, now, for over half a year.

No one else knew, not her parents or even hotel owner Mary Pierce, who was her closest friend. Edith Ellsworth's father, a part-time minister and notary public, had brought his family out from Iowa and become postmaster at Ingalls.

Doolin had met her while she was employed at McMurtry's drug store. Not long after they had been secretly married, her unsuspecting parents had moved to another town, but she had stayed on, ostensibly to keep her job with Mrs. Pierce in the hotel.

She had been upset at first when Doolin had told her where his money came from, but in time she had simply accepted him for what he was. She may have wept in private—he never knew. But if Edie lived with fears and uncertainties, it seemed to have no effect at all on her love for him.

Presently Edie leaned back in his arms to peer intently into his face, almost as though she were trying to memorize it. "Now what's wrong?" he wanted to know.

"I have to make a confession," she told him, quite seriously. "You're going to think I'm terrible, but when you've been gone awhile I find I'm not even sure what you look like! I try to remember every detail of your face, but all I get is a blur!"

"Guess that just proves you don't love me," he said, teasing, and kissed her when she indignantly protested. "Now I can see *you* anytime—clear as a picture."

"Wish I had *your* picture."

"Yeah—that's what the marshal wishes! But he don't, and I could pass him on Main Street in Tulsa, and he wouldn't know me from Adam. It's the advantage of being a plain, ordinary-looking sort of fellow."

"You're not! You're the handsomest man I know!"

She got another kiss for that, and then he limped over to the table and dropped his sweat-stained headgear on it. Edie frowned as she watched him favoring the injured leg. She asked anxiously, "Does it still hurt as much as ever?"

He looked down at it. "I doubt it'll ever be right again," he admitted gloomily. "I told you what the doc said—the Winchester slug that hit me in the foot smashed up too many bones; there's nothing anybody can do to fix it. Oh, well." He shrugged. "The luck of the draw. I'm learning to live with it."

Dropping the subject, he looked around him. The double bed, the table and chair and washstand and a curtained-off closet in one corner filled the little room. He said, "Don't suppose you'd have anything to eat?"

"There's no way to keep anything here," she told him. "But I can go across to the café and fetch you something."

"Not now—later, maybe. You and me have got too much to catch up on and not much time. I better be gone well before morning."

She agreed, unhappily. "You really shouldn't be here at all! You can't know how this town has changed since that awful raid three weeks ago. People who were your friends when you used to come here spending money now act afraid to admit it or let on they even knew you. They behave as though the law was watching every single move they make!"

"It don't surprise me. The kind of friends who can be bought with money are the first to turn around and start looking out for themselves. Next thing, they'll be studying how to turn me in for the reward. So the hell with them—let 'em go!"

She hesitated, and when she spoke again it was with a soberness that made her husband give her his complete attention. "Bill, there was one man in that raid I think you ought to be told about. It was him who came into the hotel alone and disarmed Arkansas and marched him out, when those others had given up and were talking about setting fire to the building. He looked like somebody worth taking seriously, and I heard it said that he was a special agent, brought in for the job of breaking up the gang."

Doolin asked, in an indifferent manner, "Did this fellow seem to have a name?"

She nodded. "The others called him Jim Land."

To hear that name, for the second time in one day, caused Bill Doolin's eyes to narrow dangerously. But all he said finally was, "I'll keep him in mind." And before she could press the subject further, he said, "Let's talk about something more important. I'm thinking about what you told me last time we was together. Do you still reckon it's so?" Her solemn nod answered him and made him demand anxiously, "How are you feeling?"

"Oh, I feel fine," she assured him.

"Have you been to the doc?"

"I can't do *that*! I can't even talk to Mary Pierce, since even she doesn't know about us yet."

Bill Doolin frowned as he considered that. He came to a quick decision. "Tell you what you do then. Have someone drive you up to Stillwater or some other place where you ain't familiar. Wear the wedding ring I gave you, and use a made-up name. We have got to know for sure, and whether there's anything special you're in need of. Don't worry about the cost," he added before she could protest. "That don't signify. Here . . ." From his pocket he brought out a thick wad of greenbacks held by a rubber band. He peeled off a few bills for himself, shoved the rest into his wife's hand, and gently closed her fingers over it. "This should be enough to take care of everything for now."

Edie eyed the money she was holding—she didn't know where it came from, but she could hardly fail to guess. Her expression troubled, she said in a hesitant and muffled voice, "Do you ever think it might be better if—? I mean, would you rather that I did—something else?"

"*No!*" Fiercely, he seized her by both shoulders and swung her about to face him. "Don't ever say that again! I want to have this kid, you hear?" He paused then, stricken by a sudden doubt. "Unless—you don't?"

"Of course I do!" she cried. "I guess I'm just scared. I'm trying to think about the future. You know, it ain't just going to be you and me, after this."

And as he looked down at her clutching the stolen money from the depot at Wentworth, Bill Doolin thought he understood. It was a new idea to him, and it sobered him as, frowning, he tried to think his way through it. He said slowly, "Maybe you're wondering what it's gonna be like some day, when it dawns on him who and what his pa must have been. . . . Don't fret about it now, honey. We got time. I promise I'll work something out—for all of us!"

Edie clung to him, burying her face against his chest as the chill autumn wind pummeled the window and shook it in its frame.

# Chapter Ten

It was definitely the changeover of the season—two days of clouds and chill wind and occasional rain, followed by a day when the skies cleared and the sun returned, bringing some late-summer heat. Now once again a chill mist lay over the banks of the Cimarron, clinging in the branches of leafless trees and turning them ghostly, while low scudding clouds obscured the upper stretches of the limestone bluff and seemed to muffle the creek that Jim Land followed, turning it almost to a silent sliding of colorless water.

Jim Land rode at a slow walk, every sense alert, his attention divided between the broken landscape around him and the rocky ground sliding past beneath his horse's hooves. This was a tangled piece of country, a remote area south of the Cimarron where no white man belonged. Yet there was sign of recent travel. As late as yesterday a shod horse had been ridden this way, and there were occasional older prints, half obliterated by the set he was now following. It marked this as a route frequently used, and it had to mean something.

An hour ago a drizzling rain had begun to fall, making him pause to break out the slicker that he carried behind his saddle. The clouds scuttling overhead seemed ready at any time to open up and turn this into a real downpour. If that happened, he knew it wouldn't take long to wash away completely every trace of the sign he was painfully following.

He was never sure if concern over losing the trail blunted

his caution or whether the slithering noise of the rain covered some sound that might have given him a warning if he'd heard it. The trouble, when it came, took him by surprise. One moment he seemed completely alone; the next, a rifle shot broke the stillness. The bullet whipped past him and slapped into a boulder face, and as echoes of the shot went bouncing away and were blotted up in the rain, a voice shouted, "Put your hands high! You've just had all the warning you're going to get!"

Already made nervous by the weather, his horse reacted to the shot, and Land had to curb it with the rein to settle it. He wasn't going to argue with an unseen rifle; he raised his arms, one hand holding the leathers. A new voice spoke, somewhere just behind him: "That's fine! Now you just stay that way. There's two of us—so don't think you ain't being covered every minute."

Jaw clenched with chagrin, he held himself motionless. There was a sound of someone approaching on foot. A figure that was shapeless in a glistening rubber poncho and rain-damp hat appeared beside him, holding a six-gun. A hand reached up and pawed at his slicker, jerked it open and got the revolver from Land's holster, and tossed it on the ground. Next the Winchester was snaked from the scabbard beneath his knee, and the one who had disarmed him stepped back. "All right—you can put 'em down," he was told. "But you best be damned careful." And as he lowered his hands his captor turned and called, "He's took care of, Annie. I got his fangs!"

Something about the voice made his head turn sharply for a closer look. Despite the big hat and bulky poncho, he had thought at first, unlikely as it seemed, that he must be in the hands of a young and undersized boy. The truth was even more startling. Though she wore boots and jeans, this was no boy, but a girl—perhaps fifteen or sixteen, so far as he could judge her age. She had a shell belt strapped around her waist underneath the poncho. Now she shoved the revolver she had been holding into a holster on her left hip, with its handle jutting forward, and covered the prisoner with Land's own rifle.

She was a pretty youngster by any standard, but the rifle

and the smoldering look in her level blue stare suggested nothing but danger.

And now a second girl came out of the brush into the open, leading two saddled horses and carrying a rifle, a finger through the trigger guard. She was about the same age as the other but a head taller, and instead of pants, this one—called Annie—wore a dress under her windbreaker, its long skirt rain soaked and bedraggled. She was well shaped and, if anything, even prettier than her friend; they both had an identical look of trying to impress the world with their rebellious toughness.

Jim Land thought, *It's true, then!* He had heard a story or two from the people on Marshal Nix's staff about the Doolin bunch having a couple of youthful camp followers, daughters of respectable farmers who had somehow got mixed up with the gang—perhaps by meeting some of them at a dance and being dazzled by the glamor and adventure of outlawry. Not knowing their names for certain, the marshals had dubbed one of them "Cattle Annie" and, because of her fondness for formal attire, called the other one "Little Breeches." Whatever their names, rumor had it the pair spied and carried messages for the outlaws; it would appear that they might also serve as lookouts.

As they looked him over, the smaller girl said to her companion, "What do you think?"

"I think he's got no business here," Annie replied. "What do *you* think, mister?" she demanded, her voice as sharp as the look in her eyes.

He shrugged and then offered the only suggestion he could think of at short notice. "I'm beginning to think I might be lost."

"Worse than that," the smaller girl retorted. "You're in big trouble! How about you keeping him here," she said to her friend, "and I'll go ask 'em what they want done with him."

Annie found that agreeable. "But first," she ordered Land with a gesture of her rifle, "you get down from that horse. Real careful!" Having no wish to rouse the anger of two excitable young females, he quickly obeyed, and Little Breeches stepped in and took the reins of the sorrel and led it over to join the other animals. Annie was still watching the prisoner like a hawk. She said, "Let's see both hands on top of your hat." And when he had obeyed that order, she barked, "Now you sit!"

He looked around for a rock or a log but saw nothing. The girl snapped at him, impatient and with a dangerous edge to her voice, "Mister, I told you to sit!" With the rifle pointing at him, he shrugged and let himself down awkwardly to the muddy ground, hands still locked on the top of his head. Satisfied, Annie told her companion, "That should take care of him. You get to riding." She added, "Don't take any more time than you have to. I think it's fixing to rain harder!"

Little Breeches caught up the reins of a mouse-gray horse. She still had the captured rifle, and now she picked up Land's revolver from the mud where she had discarded it, shoving it behind her cartridge belt. She found the stirrup and swung lithely astride. Looking down at the other girl, she said cheerfully, "I'll be back before you know it." She kicked the gray with her bootheel and sent it off at a good clip along the creek bank, in the same direction Land had been riding when he was stopped.

Unless he was mistaken, those words seemed to indicate she had no great distance to go for help. By riding blind, apparently he had come very close to stumbling upon the hideout he was looking for.

The girl named Annie had taken a position just out of his line of sight. Any slight movement she might make would be covered by the slithering whisper of the rain; nevertheless, he knew she was still standing there, on the alert, her rifle trained on him. Once when he tried to shift position a little, he heard her prompt warning: "You watch what you're doing! Don't try nothing funny. Keep those hands right where they are."

"This isn't the most comfortable place I ever sat," he pointed out gruffly. And because he thought he should at least keep up some pretense of ignorance, he asked, "Are you ready yet to tell me why you're acting like this?"

She retorted, "You ready to say what *you're* doin' in this back end of nowhere?" When he didn't answer, she said, "I didn't think so—and I got nothin' to say to you, either. So you might just as well save your breath!"

That put a stop to conversation. They waited, and the minutes stretched out and became a length of time that he had no way of measuring. He heard their horses stomping and moving around a little under the needling of the rain, heard them pull at leaves and blow their breath into the damp air. Presently the voice of the rain changed its pitch and loudness as it began to come down a little harder. Land began to grow acutely uncomfortable, body protesting against being forced to remain in one position.

Then, abruptly, a pair of riders were approaching through the steaming mist; Little Breeches sang out to announce their coming, and Annie made reply. The horses' hooves raised gouts of mud and slop as they hauled to a stand. The man Little Breeches had brought back with her looked down at the prisoner and said, "This is him?"

"It's him, Bill," she answered.

Land gave him a quick glance but knew at once that it couldn't be Bill Doolin. Even in the saddle, it was clear he lacked inches of the necessary six-feet-two that was almost the only thing the descriptions agreed on. This, then, would have to be a man named William Raidler, called "Little Bill" to distinguish him from the taller outlaw.

Cattle Annie spoke up. "He still won't tell me nothing."

"Maybe we can fix that," Raidler said. "Bring his horse." And as Little Breeches rode to fetch it, the outlaw swung down. "On your feet," he told the prisoner.

Land rose to meet his hostile stare. Raidler was a jug-eared, sallow-faced, thick-necked individual, probably in his middle twenties, who had to lift his head to rake the taller Jim Land with his narrow stare. "I don't know you," he said finally. "Maybe some of the others will. . . . Turn around."

Doing so, Land found himself again facing Cattle Annie and her rifle. But next moment, a cloth that smelled strongly of shred tobacco was whipped across his eyes and tied in place, effectively shutting away everything. Raidler's warning voice reminded him, "You're gonna be watched every minute. So don't touch that or try to take it off, not if you know what's good for you! Now climb on!"

The sorrel had been brought over. Moving blindly, Land groped for the stirrup and the saddle horn and lifted himself astride. He heard Raidler giving orders: "Annie, you lead his horse. We'll bring up the rear and see he don't make any funny moves." A moment later, the party moved out.

With his mount towed by its imprisoned reins, there was little Jim Land could do but brace himself against unexpected shifts of the saddle, both his hands piled on the pommel to make it clear he had no intentions of removing the blindfold. With at least one gun probably covering his every movement, he didn't feel ready just yet to offer a challenge.

As they moved on through the slithering rain, he was alert and busily trying to use his other senses to tell him what his eyes could not. There was little talk, hardly any sound except the whisper of the rain and the creak of saddle gear and the steady plodding of hooves on sodden ground. If it should start to come down much harder than it already was, he knew whatever sign they were leaving would be all too quickly obliterated. As best he could, he attempted to judge their direction and the passing of time, but found it harder than he expected in the confused and sightless world that had closed around him.

Some time later he realized their course had changed. The sorrel seemed to be climbing. Wet brush whipped against his legs and dragged across the skirts of his saddle; hooves struck echoes from stones underfoot. Abruptly his led horse was pulled sharply to the right, as though at a switchback turn; its hooves slipped awkwardly, and Land felt its muscles bunch. He braced himself as his animal clambered across a steep hump. Moments afterward, all motion ceased.

The rank smell of wet horseflesh hung heavy, and all around was the sound of the animals stomping and blowing. Land could hear leather creak as the other riders dismounted, but he stayed where he was until he felt the prod of a gun barrel against his leg, and Bill Raidler roughly ordered him out of the saddle. When his feet touched ground, a hand clamped upon his arm and pulled him about, and Raidler said in his ear, "Start walking."

The ground was uneven and rough, and he was given no time to test his footing, so that he stumbled repeatedly and once nearly fell headlong, with his captor's curses in his ears.

Then, abruptly, everything changed. A few last, climbing

steps and the drizzling rain was gone. A dark shadow fell
across him, while underfoot was smooth stone where boots
raised muffled echoes. Again he was pulled roughly about
and halted; a glow of light penetrated the cloth that covered
his eyes, and he felt heat against his face.

Raidler announced to an unseen audience, "Well—here he
is." Jim Land sensed the presence of others around him,
heard the sounds of breathing and the scrape of a boot sole as
someone changed position.

He knew he was being closely scrutinized, and the knowledge irritated him. Quite deliberately, he put up a hand and
pulled the knotted cloth from over his eyes.

At once, the muzzle of a gun was jabbed hard against his
side, and Little Bill Raidler's face, suffused with anger, confronted him. "By God," the outlaw cried tautly, "you were
warned!"

Land met the furious look without flinching. He cast a
quick glance around him, discovering that he stood within a
shallow, low-roofed cave, a natural formation in the native
limestone. Warmth and light flowed from the blaze in a ring
of blackened stones; light wavered on the walls and deeper
recesses of the cave, showing bedrolls and what looked to be
supplies stacked and covered by a tarp. It also showed, as
paler blotches against the shadows, the faces of the men who
stood and silently watched him. He spotted the two girls
among the others.

Jim Land looked again at Raidler. He said bluntly, "You
can either use that gun or take it out of my ribs. I just never
liked being stared at by people I couldn't see!"

At this the face of the smaller man, so close to his own,
twisted in almost uncontrollable rage. "You know, you're
really asking for it!" he gritted.

"Feisty sort, ain't he?" someone commented dryly.

Land turned his head to single out the speaker. There was
little enough to tell one of these men from another. They
were an indifferent lot, roughly dressed and hard bitten; they
appeared dirty and unshaven and not too well fed. He had
never seen any of them before, but he knew that despite
appearances they all had to be reckoned among the most
dangerous men in the territory.

Like the rest, the one who had spoken had a scruffy-looking mustache that covered much of his lower face. He asked the prisoner, "Now that you've had an eyeful, are you satisfied? Do you think you know what you've got yourself into?"

"I could make a guess," Land replied. "At least, I wouldn't suppose you're all holed up here because a picnic got rained out!"

The man seemed coldly amused. "Far as *you're* concerned, this is no picnic. . . ."

At that, Little Bill Raidler exploded. "Dammit, Bitter Creek! Quit wasting time! Hell, he knows us, all right—but we don't know the first thing about *him*!"

So this was George Newcomb—alias Bitter Creek, alias the Slaughter Kid! At one time a rider with the notorious Daltons, he was now a member of the Doolin gang. Jim Land looked at him with concealed interest as the outlaw responded to Raidler's exclamation with a shrug. "All right," Newcomb said. "So let's find out who he is. For a start, you might try searching him."

"Somebody put a gun on him, then."

Obligingly, Bitter Creek Newcomb brought out a long-barreled Colt and moved around where he could keep the prisoner covered without letting Raidler get in his way. Raidler thereupon holstered his own gun so as to use both hands. He ordered Land to raise his arms and then threw open the slicker and went in under it to search, first for any other weapons. Finding none, Raidler tried his clothing, and Land, who knew what was coming, kept his face impassive as he felt the outlaw digging into the inside pocket of his coat.

Raidler's eyes flickered with surprise at what he found there. He withdrew his hand, holding a paper and a bit of metal. As he stared at them, Land went tense, preparing for an outburst.

But there was an interruption. Two newcomers had just entered the scene—Jim Land heard the sounds of their boots, striding in through the cave opening. They halted. A voice demanded, sharp with suspicion at the sight of a stranger in the hideout, "What's going on here?"

Answering, Little Bill Raidler held up the badge he was

holding; the gleam of the fire danced and reflected from it as he said, "Would you believe the girls have caught us a deputy U.S. marshal?"

The voice behind Land said thunderously, "Lemme see that!"

Raidler tossed it to him, past the prisoner's shoulder. "According to this," he added, indicating the paper, "his name is Land. . . ."

"The hell it is!"

And then another voice—one that was all too familiar to Jim Land, one he had thought he might never hear again—said heavily, "Who else, Bill? This has got to be the one we heard about from that fellow at the Converse claim!"

Even a gun aimed at him couldn't stop Jim Land from wheeling about then. The two men who stood in the cave entrance were peeling out of their wet slickers, which they tossed over for the girls to dispose of. The tall one—as tall as Land, with the red-tinged mustache and stern blue eyes—he knew at once had to be the leader of these outlaws. And yet Jim Land scarcely noticed him.

His whole attention, at the moment, was centered on the one who entered just behind Bill Doolin. For he stood face to face at last with Turk Freese—the killer responsible for the one job Land had been forced to leave unfinished and the true cause that had brought him to this outlaw hideout in the wilds of Oklahoma Territory.

# Chapter Eleven

**B**ill Doolin studied the prisoner closely, with steely-eyed intensity. But instead of speaking to him directly, he first questioned Land's captors. He wanted to know where the two girls had first spotted him and how he had acted. And—most important—were they sure he was alone?

It was Little Breeches who answered. "We knew you'd be wanting to know that. Don't worry, Bill—we was real careful. We watched a good while before we pulled him in. Wasn't nobody with him."

"And whose smart idea was it to drag him right into the cave?"

"Mine, I guess," Little Bill Raidler admitted uneasily. "Nobody had any better suggestions. Of course, I blindfolded him first."

"Did you think that really made any difference?" Doolin swung his attention at last to the prisoner, his pale eyes seeming to probe deeply. "So!" he grunted. "You came hunting for us, did you? All by yourself! Well, you don't lack for nerve. What I want to know," he went on sharply, "is how you came so close. Somebody tip you off to this place?"

Land said coolly, "You don't really expect me to answer that."

That brought him a curse from Bitter Creek. Its tone gave Land warning, and he ducked his head, but too late. His skull seemed to split, and stars filled his vision as the barrel of

129

Newcomb's revolver clipped him. It wasn't hard enough to knock him out, but it was enough to stun; with Bill Doolin's angry protest in his ears, he felt the strength of his legs melt away. The next moment he was on hands and knees with his hat lying in front of him, waiting for his head to clear.

When the pain eased to a throbbing ache, he forced his head up. He found Bill Doolin squatting on his heels, rope-scarred hands dangling between his knees. The outlaw was watching him and scowling.

"You ain't helping yourself any," he pointed out gruffly. "Can't you see you're only making the boys restless? Well, all right—so you just went hunting on your own until you found us. I guess that makes sense. Now get up from there."

Land saw the way he grimaced with pain as he straightened up—it showed how that hurt leg must be bothering him. Doolin offered the prisoner a hand, but Land shook his head and made it to his feet without help, though he was still groggy and had to brace himself against the lancing pain that shot through his skull. Slowly it subsided. He looked at the hostile faces about him in the flickering light of the fire.

"It's up to me," Bill Doolin said heavily, "to decide what the hell we do with you. You have any suggestions?"

"I'm hardly the one you should ask," Land reminded him.

Bitter Creek Newcomb spoke up. "Bill, they're still holding Arkansas Tom in that federal jail at Guthrie. Maybe we got something here we can use to get him out."

"That's a thought." Doolin looked at Land in speculation. "Seems I heard you're the one who took him, that day at Ingalls, after he had all those other deputy marshals stumped. The man who could pull a stunt like that—single-handed—might be worth a trade. What do you think?"

"A trade? Me for Arkansas Tom?" Land shook his head. "You can forget that idea! Evett Nix is under too much pressure from Washington. He's only been able to lay hands on one member of the Doolin gang so far. It would cost the marshal his job to let him go—for anybody or any reason."

Bill Doolin studied on that a long moment. "If you say so," he decided finally, "then I got to believe it—you wouldn't deliberately close the door if there was any chance in it for you at all. But you can see it narrows my options."

"Sorry!" Jim Land commented, with mild sarcasm.

Turk Freese had been keeping silent, the scars on his face and the milky ruin of that one bad eye gleaming faintly in the light of the fire. "If this fellow's boss can't be made to deal for him, then he certainly ain't worth anything to *us*. I say get rid of him. And I don't mind being the one to do the job."

That got him a look from Bill Doolin. "You've already made it clear how little the idea of killing people bothers you. But I've never put a dead man on my record, and I'm not ready to start now." With every eye upon him, the outlaw leader swung away and took a turn about the cave. Jim Land noticed again how he favored his left leg at every step.

Suddenly, too, Land became aware that the rain had nearly stopped. The clouds must be breaking up; spears of sunlight showed past the mouth of the cave, where they turned the few drops that still fell into streaks of jeweled light.

Bill Doolin had reached his conclusion, and something in his look indicated he knew it was not going to be a popular one. He turned to face the silent members of his gang. "All right," he said sharply. "Not being the marshal, I don't have a jail or any place where I can stash someone until I got need of him." He turned to Little Bill Raidler. "You brought this lawman here. I want you and Bitter Creek to set him on his horse, put the blindfold back on, and take him out somewhere and lose him."

"You ain't saying you mean to let him go?" Turk Freese fairly shouted it.

"I still run this outfit, and that's what I'm saying!" Doolin stared at his men, inviting a challenge. When no one offered one, he again looked at Raidler and Newcomb. "You've got your orders," he said crisply and then added, "Wait!" He still had the captured deputy marshal's badge; he flipped it over, and Jim Land caught it out of the air.

For just a moment their eyes met, and as they did, something seemed to pass between them. Despite the gulf of difference that separated them, the only name Land could give to it was a kind of wary mutual respect. Accepting the badge, he nodded and put his feeling into a single word: "Thanks."

Turk Freese said sourly, "You giving him back his guns,

too?" But to this Doolin shook his head in emphatic denial. The prisoner's arms were roughly seized and the blindfold fitted into place. Moments later he was marched from the cave between the pair named to be his guards.

As the sound of their boots faded, Freese again broke the silence of the cave. "I hope you realize," he told his chief, "blindfold or not, he's gonna be back—and next time, he won't come alone. He'll have an army with him."

"Probably," Doolin agreed. "Only we won't be here."

"What the hell does *that* mean?"

"It means that this hideout has served its purpose—but now that the law has found it once, it's going to happen again. The sooner we leave the better. So get busy!" he ordered the gang crisply. "We're moving out."

The abrupt orders left them staring, openmouthed; still, they were too disciplined to argue about it. The gang fell to work—the men slow and grumbling a little, the two girls throwing themselves cheerfully into the task as though the whole thing were a game and an adventure, which to them it all probably was. Turk Freese watched, scowling, as bedrolls were assembled and equipment gathered. He had other, more important matters to concern him. Finding no one paying any attention to him, he suddenly turned and walked out beneath the overhang, into the sunlight.

By now the rain had stopped completely. Turk Freese followed the narrow and ill-defined path that led from the cave mouth to a sheltered hollow where the gang's horses fed on a fair stand of grass. Saddles and gear were stored under a pole lean-to; he fetched his own and quickly got it strapped on the back of a tough-jawed paint gelding. His rifle in the scabbard, he swung astride.

Raidler and Newcomb and their prisoner had a good lead, but at the moment he had no difficulty making out the direction they had taken. Later the sign would be much harder to read—when Bill Doolin ordered *Take him out and lose him,* what he meant was, *Don't leave any trail to help him find his way back!*

There was a determined set to his jaw as Freese kicked his mount after them. Whatever else they did, he didn't intend for them to lose Turk Freese!

\*   \*   \*

Until now Jim Land had had no real sense of the iron discipline Bill Doolin had over the members of his gang. It soon became clear enough from the behavior of these two who had been given charge of him. They showed how much they resented their assignment; Little Bill Raidler and Bitter Creek had no love for any lawman, and on their own they would have gladly finished him off rather than go to this unnecessary bother—only, the habit of following their boss's orders was too strong.

But they did it in their own way. When their rough handling on the path that led to the horses made the blindfolded Jim Land stumble and fall, they cursed him as they hauled him to his feet again. Land took this treatment without protest, seeing no good in provoking them. He was flung against his horse with a curt order to mount, and he did it as quickly as he was able.

Then someone took the reins, and once again he found himself being led helplessly over an invisible course. Deprived of sight, he worked hard with his other senses, trying to gain some notion of what was being done to him.

If their aim was to confuse him, they certainly managed. He could make neither head nor tail of the route they took. They climbed, only to go down steeper grades where he had to stand in the stirrups and grab blindly for the saddle horn in order to stay on the sorrel's back. Tree branches struck his unprotected face. At one point their horses dropped abruptly into a creek, so that spray drenched him, and afterward continued splashing upstream against its shallow current. When they quit the water eventually, the shoes of their mounts rang on bare rock where he knew they would be leaving no mark at all—nothing that would be of any help if he tried to backtrack later.

That, of course, was just what they had in mind.

A wind had risen. When at last he was brought to a halt, Land was aware of flickering shadows against the cloth covering his eyes; all about him tree branches and brush made a stirring, covering most other sounds. He eased his position in the saddle as he waited for some hint as to what came next.

Instead, there was nothing. Minutes passed. The horse under him became restless and stomped and moved around a little, but he heard no sound from his guards. Land thought he knew, then, the game they were playing with him. He reached up and tore off the blindfold, risking the bullet he had been promised if he did, and was not surprised to find himself alone.

This was a brushy knob of land in the flickering shadows of some windswept blackjack timber that made noise enough for the outlaws to ride quickly away and let him discover in his own time that they were gone.

They had picked a good place to do it. The ground here was flinty, poor for picking up their sign. He reasoned that he was still somewhere in the area south of the Cimarron, but had no idea how far he had been riding or in what direction, since leaving the hideout cave. It looked as though Raidler and Newcomb had indeed managed to lose him.

Before anything else, he wanted to get out of his slicker, an encumbrance now that the rain had stopped. He pulled it off without dismounting, standing in the stirrups; he was twisting about to fasten it in place behind the saddle when a rifle lashed out upon the stillness.

He froze. Echoes were confusing, but he thought the shot had come from somewhere to the left. His first thought was that his guards had changed their minds and doubled back to finish him off and then make up something to tell Bill Doolin afterward. He had barely had time to reach this conclusion when a second shot sounded.

This time a bullet struck an outcrop only yards below the spot where he sat. It raised a brief cloud of rock dust and screamed off in ricochet, a warning that his attacker had the range and was zeroing in. Jim Land didn't wait for more. He flung aside the slicker, yelled at the sorrel, and kicked it into a plunging start as he neck-reined it up and over the crest of the rise to his right, putting the rifle behind him.

This side of the hill was steeper, slick with dead grass underfoot and dropping away to a glimpse of a brushy watercourse below. He came down through the spindly stand of growth, drawing in for a moment at the edge of a brush thicket while he listened for sign of pursuit. For long moments he heard nothing except the movement of wind in the branches and the rush of the rain-swollen stream below him. But then, back just beyond the crest of the hill, an iron shoe rang on stone. Unarmed as he was, he had no defense but flight. Land hesitated no longer but plunged ahead down the hill.

Tree trunks whipped past as he helped the sorrel pick its way through them without losing speed. Just before him was the flash of sliding water and then, beyond, an open stretch of land barren of timber.

A scant pair of yards from the creek, disaster struck.

A third rifleshot came over, and though this one was fired from the back of a running horse, it found its target. Land never knew where it took the sorrel, but the horse stumbled, caught itself for two more pounding steps, and then, just as it reached the steep drop-off of the creek bank, its legs folded under it. Man and mount went over together in a wild spill.

Land had time to kick free of the stirrups, but not to leap clear. The creek received them both with a tremendous geyser. It was roiling and muddy, swollen by rain, and the bulk of the animal bore them down. Water closed over Land's head, and then he felt the bottom beneath his shoulders. He pushed against its resistance, to send him again to the surface. That was when alarm gripped him.

He could not move. He lay on his back with his right leg trapped, immobile, beneath the sorrel's weight.

Briefly and fiercely he fought to get free, using up his oxygen before he clamped control on himself as he saw it was useless. Head bursting and lungs burning with the need for air, Land faced his predicament—the blunt fact that there was nothing he could do to get out of this. But at that moment the dying horse made a final, convulsive effort and aided by the buoyancy of the water, half lifted itself; Land felt the weight roll off his trapped leg. Hastily he pulled it free, and a moment later he was pushing off from the bottom and breaking the roiling surface. There he sucked air deep into his lungs.

He fully expected to be met by a shout and another bullet, but his ordeal underwater could not have lasted nearly as long as it seemed. Jim Land looked hurriedly about him. The sorrel lay motionless now, its ebbing lifeblood staining the turbulent flow of the creek. There was no sign of pursuers, but danger had to be almost on top of him.

Right at his elbow, the near bank had been undercut by the water's action. Without a second's hesitation he flung himself into this hollow. It could not conceal him entirely, but a thin screen of brush clinging to the bank overhead should help; he caught at an exposed root to hold him against the tug of the current and waited with only his face above the surface. The roar of the water covered any other sound, and he could see nothing at all past the tangle of brush so close above his head.

Time seemed to crawl as the chill of the water ate deeper into him. Finally, under tension and impatient to know what was going on, Land risked a slight shift of position—and found he was peering up at the figure of a horseman on the bank almost directly above him. Startled, he made himself go motionless. Luckily the rider was staring off along the course of the creek, away from him; now he turned to look in the opposite direction. Land saw his features plainly—and it was Turk Freese!

That told him everything in a flash—who it was that had sneaked away from the cave and followed the prisoner and his escort and why he had waited until the guards had left before making his try with the rifle. Fortunately for Jim Land the first two bullets had missed; now Freese was left trying to figure out what had become of his intended victim.

Land could all but read his mind: Not seeing his body in the creek along with the dead sorrel, Freese would have to assume that he'd escaped, but not across the creek onto the open stretch beyond where he would have been instantly spotted.

The outlaw seemed to reach a conclusion. He jerked the reins, pulled his horse around, and gave it a swat with the barrel of his rifle; Turk Freese started off along the bank, heading downstream and apparently convinced his quarry was trying to escape by way of the creek itself.

Land waited only until his enemy was out of sight in the trees around the first bend of the creek, and at once clambered from his hiding place. With a last regretful look at the dead sorrel and at the saddle and gear he was unable to salvage, he splashed on across the creek—it was turbulent but scarcely waist deep—and found where he could climb the opposite bank without leaving too obvious a sign. Freese would be back soon enough, having found no trace downstream of the man he was hunting. It gave him very little time.

His nearest hope of finding cover was in a clump of leafless pecan trees, almost a quarter mile distant. He headed for them—hatless, soaked to the skin, and knifed by a chill wind that raked the dead grass and sent cloud shadows scuttling across the occasional patch of sun. He was little more than halfway to his goal when the drumming of hooves gave him warning. Just ahead the flats seemed broken by a shallow swale. With a burst of speed, Land made for that and flung himself prone.

The depression offered little protection, but it would serve if Freese didn't look too closely. Land risked lifting his head for a look back toward the creek just as Turk Freese flashed into view, flailing his horse with the rifle barrel. He went on without pause and disappeared again into the trees upstream, still hunting.

It roweled Jim Land to hide from an enemy like Turk Freese, but afoot and weaponless he had no chance of giving the man a fight. But there would be another time—he promised himself that.

He left the swale and went on toward the trees.


He walked for an hour. Autumn wind knifed through his soaked clothing, but exercise helped, and as the remnants of the storm clouds gradually scattered, the sun's rays soon dried him out. He took his bearings from the afternoon sun and bore northward, knowing the Cimarron lay somewhere in that direction.

Presently he came upon a wagon track and followed that for a distance; it led to a hollow among the rolling hills, where he saw the layout of a farm. Someone had worked hard on it. There were pasture and crops under fence, a set of substantial buildings, even the beginnings of a small orchard—

he saw apples and peaches, as well as a cow, chickens, and a pigpen.

A man was up on the roof of the house, nailing flattened tins over leaks that the recent rain had probably discovered. A woman came out to speak to him about something. Her skin looked darker than his; Land knew that whites, by marrying with Indians, could often obtain legal title to tribal land. That looked like the case here, and having checked the place out from a distance, he approached. The man on the roof gave no sign of noticing him. He descended his ladder as Land was coming up the last few yards—but when he turned around, there was a big revolver in his hand, almost casually covering the newcomer.

Black eyes in a lean, sunburnt face peered at Jim Land suspiciously, taking in his bedraggled appearance. The man with the gun said, "All right. Who are you? What do you want?"

Contrasting the neat layout of this place with Nels Antrim's slovenly horse ranch near Tulsa, Land made a decision. For answer he brought out his badge. The man's eyes narrowed; he looked at Land again and said gruffly, "I think you better come inside. Grub's ready. We can eat while we talk. . . ."

Sight of the food that the Indian woman silently placed on the table reminded Jim Land of how many hours it had been since he had had a decent meal, but even as he ate, the day drawing out reminded him he really didn't have time for this. He told no more than he had to, explaining merely that he had had a horse shot out from under him by outlaws and was badly in need of another, which he promised would be returned safely.

As it turned out, the farmer needed no details. He grunted angrily, "I got no use for them cussed outlaws. They've cleaned me out a number of times—took anything they felt like and then acted like they done me a favor by leaving me alive. At the moment I got no spare riding stock, but what the hell—I guess I can give you the loan of an animal and my personal saddle. I'm trusting you to see I get them back."

"You will," Jim Land assured him. When he left, riding back the way he had come, he not only had a horse and gear, but the farmer's own six-shooter and a handful of extra shells to fit it. The man's confidence and trust only added to his sense of the importance of what he had in mind to do.

The crossing of the nameless creek where he had lost Turk Freese appeared as he had left it. He rode over, pausing to look again regretfully at the carcass of the sorrel, almost wholly submerged beneath the rushing water. The sorrel had been a good animal. Now there only remained to see about the possibility of salvaging his saddle and gear; but in any event, that would have to wait. Instead he climbed the bank and started his borrowed horse—a chestnut gelding—toward the hill down which he had tumbled in precipitous flight from Turk Freese's rifle, some hours before.

He came upon his discarded slicker and retrieved it. What was more important, he found the clear prints of Freese's horse.

Without meaning to, or even thinking about it, Turk Freese had done Land a considerable favor. He had been so intent on stalking the prisoner and his guards that he hadn't even thought about the plain trail he himself was leaving. So he had undone all the effort put out by Bill Raidler and Bitter Creek in trying to follow their chief's orders. Even for someone less skilled than Land at reading sign, backtracking Freese should be a simple matter, as long as there was still light enough.

But it was late, the sun dropping toward the western horizon. The long, golden glow of late afternoon would soon fade, and this spurred him on anxiously. In fact, the swollen sun had slid from view and gray dusk was pouring up out of the hollows when, suddenly, he rounded a rocky spur and saw the dark mouth of the cave, facing him across a shallow canyon.

He drew rein quickly to stare at it.

This had to be the place. He could even glimpse a tree-lined hollow close by, which he judged to be where the gang put their horses. But he had to check it all out and be absolutely sure; once having made certain, he wasn't fool-hardy enough to think that he could take on the gang alone. His plan all along had been to return with enough men from the marshal's office to lay a cordon around the place and capture them through a concerted effort. But now, as he sat

and searched the layout, he felt a gnawing conviction that it
was too late for that.

As the light dimmed, a chill night wind was rising and
whipping at trees and brush around him. Yet there was no
hint of a fire. The opening remained dark, and Land had an
uneasy feeling that the hideout was deserted.

There was only one way to find out. He tied his borrowed
horse and went ahead on foot, gun in hand and moving
cautiously, hugging the shadows. Constantly wary of a look-
out posted against just this sort of reconnaissance, he found
his way to a point where he could look directly into the rock
corral. The silence there had already told him it was empty.
Actually seeing the place for the first time, he made out a
pole lean-to that was apparently for the storage of saddles and
gear. There was light enough for him to see that whatever
had been under it was gone.

Jim Land swore.

Crossing the corral, he found the stony path he had twice
been led over blindfolded and climbed it to the cave itself.
When he stepped into the entrance, nothing met him except
the sound of his own boots on stone.

Everything was gone—bedrolls, packs, and the pile of supplies he had noticed earlier, as well as the tarp that had
covered them. The ashes of the fire were a dark circle against
the limestone floor of the cave.

But then he saw something that sent him forward in disbelief, to drop to one knee. Laid out carefully, where he couldn't
miss them, were a rifle and a six-gun, with belt and holster.
Looking at them closely in the faint glimmer of dusk, he
knew that these were his own weapons! Squatting on his
heels, he picked up the revolver and stared at it in astonished
puzzlement.

What were they doing here? Why hadn't someone taken
them, along with all the other stuff, when the gang broke
camp?

There could be but one answer: Bill Doolin! Doolin had
known all along that Land would be back. Leaving his guns
for him, so prominently displayed, had been meant as a
gesture—a tribute to a worthy adversary and a challenge, a

dare for him to try the next confrontation in this war of wits
between them.

He must have known that Jim Land would understand the
challenge and would accept it.

# Chapter Twelve

Jim Land was astonished to see what had been accomplished on the Converse claim in a little over two weeks. The house, which at that time had not even been started, was now very near completion. He had always heard that a sod house went up fast when constructed by someone who knew what he was doing; on the other hand, he had a decent respect for just how much a square of sod, cut out of prairie earth, would weigh. Dake Parsons was tough, but he was getting on in years, and it didn't seem likely that Charlie Converse had been a great deal of help. The old ex-puncher would have been doing most of the job himself.

Yet the walls stood firm and tall enough to allow for settling. The ridgepole was in place, the rails laid in a slant against the comb of the ridge, with only the roof still waiting to go on. Yonder, on the adjoining homestead, the Tuttles had brought their own house almost as far along, undoubtedly copying every trick they learned from watching Dake Parsons.

Having returned the chestnut gelding to the farmer, Land had bought a roan to replace the sorrel Turk Freese had shot out from under him. Now, as he approached the Converse claim, Land thought at first there was no one at the homestead. The wagon and its team were missing, as was Parsons' own cow pony. He could see no one moving about the old army tent, which was the Converses' temporary living quarters, but drawing closer, he caught a tang of wood smoke. Rounding the tent, he saw that someone—Dake Parsons again—had built a quite respectable oven from stones collected at the creek below the claim, replacing the primitive fire ring. Enticing smells rose from the pots ranged on an iron sheet that formed its cooking surface.

And now, apparently hearing a rider, Beth Converse came from under the tied-back flap of the tent entrance. She wore an expectant look that turned to one of pleased surprise at seeing Jim Land. "Oh—it's you!" she cried. "I'm so glad to see you again!" But then she looked past him, and he caught the faint tug of concern in her brow, as she obviously failed to see the one whom she had been expecting.

He said quickly, "Is everything all right?"

"Of course," she said, though with what he thought could be false assurance. "When I heard you riding up, I thought you would be Dake. Charlie went into town yesterday to get a few things, and when he wasn't back by morning Dake saddled up to go see what might have kept him. But I'm sure there's nothing to worry about."

"I should think you might be uneasy, though, left alone out here."

"Oh, no." She indicated the adjoining claim with a nod of her head. "Our neighbors are handy, and they watch out for me. If worse came to worse, I have my gun—all it would take is one shot, and they'd be right here to help."

"That sounds like Vic Tuttle," he agreed with a smile. "I'm sure you're right."

As though suddenly remembering her manners, she exclaimed, "But won't you step down? It's almost noon, and I have some warmed-over stew on the fire. Maybe you'll help me eat it?"

"I certainly will. Though it's not the reason I stopped by."

"I never thought it was."

Glad of the chance to postpone for a little the true and serious purpose of his visit, Land put his horse on a good patch of grass, washed his hands at the spring, and returned to the tent. He found Beth had a plate of stew and biscuits and a mug of coffee waiting for him on the crude pine table. Seated across from her, he tried the stew and pronounced it

fine. Only then did he notice that she wasn't eating, but was
looking at him with a troubled expression.

"Jim," she said suddenly, "there's something I've been
hoping for a chance to tell you. It has to do with Bill Doolin.
And the other one—the one-eyed man you spoke about."

"Turk Freese . . ."

"You'll never believe it—but they were *here*. Almost a
week ago, they stopped to water their horses at our spring. I
have no idea where they had been or where they were
going."

Land could have told her they had been on their way from
the Woodward job to their cave hideout below the Cimarron,
but he kept silent and let her finish. "Doolin and Dake
Parsons knew each other, of course, and after hearing your
description, there was no chance I'd miss Turk Freese! But
poor Charlie was completely in the dark, and—I hate for you
to know this—but I'm afraid he told them about *you*. He
never meant to do it, of course; it just slipped out, before he
realized who they were. He felt terrible then."

"It really doesn't matter," Land said.

But she persisted. "I was watching Freese, and I saw the
look on his face. It frightened me! Jim, I think he hates
you—and since he knows you're here in Oklahoma, he may
even now be looking for you, trying to plan a trap!"

Beth sounded horrified at the very thought. Jim Land
pointed out, "But you see, there's no danger of that, now that
you've been able to warn me. So you mustn't let it worry you
anymore."

"You're not just saying this?"

"Of course not. It's the truth."

She seemed to be reassured. Land, for his part, had an
answer to the question that had brought him here today.
There had been the puzzling remark by Turk Freese, during
their confrontation in the cave—something about "that fellow
at the Converse claim." Jim Land had wanted to know what
that meant—if there had really been some inadvertent contact with the outlaws, he had to give these people some word
of warning. Apparently now that wouldn't be needed, and he
was relieved to let the matter drop.

A pleasant silence fell as they enjoyed their meal, listening to the trees and the nearby spring and an occasional ruffling of the tent as a gusting breeze caught it. Following the recent rain, the coming of October had brought a stretch of Indian summer; golden light, warm days and crisp nights had settled over the Cherokee Strip. Now as he looked out at the claim he had helped to stake, Jim Land commented, "If I were a stranger, seeing it for the first time, I'd say you have a right nice place here."

"Oh, I think so, too!" she quickly agreed. "I wasn't sure I would like it at first, being so different from anything I've ever known. But I've come to love the quiet and the land itself. I'm just afraid, now that he's here, that Charlie may be thinking he's taken on too much."

"That's understandable, him not being a country man the way I was. Frankly, I envy him the chance he has here. I can only hope you have an open winter and an early spring, so you can get on with the real work of proving up this claim."

Beth was looking at him with a frowning expression. Suddenly she told him, "There's something about you that strikes me as very strange, Jim Land."

"Not *too* strange, I hope."

She smiled. "No, of course not." And she went on, serious again: "It's just that—now that I know you better—I can't help but wonder what would attract a person like you into law work."

"It's not a bad question," he said slowly. "Wasn't anything I planned. But as a youngster in Illinois," he went on as she continued to watch his face as though seriously interested in an answer, "I'm afraid I was pretty restless—that's one thing, I guess, Bill Doolin and I have in common. My older brother inherited the farm when our folks died. He had his own set ways of doing things, and mine didn't always agree with them. Came a day when I decided there was no advantage in hanging around longer, fighting with him, so I left. Signed on with the army—and got sent to a dead-end post in New Mexico."

Land made a face over that memory. "Only took me a week to know *that* wasn't the excitement I'd been looking for! But I stuck it out and at the end of my hitch walked away from there—as fiddlefooted as ever, with nothing but one

month's pay in my pocket and a certain amount of skill I'd
picked up with a rifle and a pistol.

"First county seat town I wandered into, the sheriff was
looking for a part-time deputy. I applied and got the job
when he saw I could shoot. That was ten years ago. One
thing has led to another."

Beth asked, "Have you enjoyed it?"

"Enjoyed? That's hardly the word! Most of the time I just
figured I had a job that needed doing. The job I'm on now,
for instance."

He fingered the badge pinned to his coat, frowning. But
the steady and thoughtful regard of the woman across the
table from him somehow bothered him; it sent him to his
feet, to stand looking out the tent doorway. He said slowly,
"No, it's not been enough. There's so much more to life. So
many things a man wants and needs that I've never got hold
of."

He heard her quiet breathing, felt her presence beside
him. "What kind of things, Jim?"

Turning, he looked down into her earnest face—so close
that he suddenly felt his hands tighten into fists to keep from
seizing her and drawing her into his arms. Answering her, he
said hoarsely, "Some, at least, that I figure just aren't mine to
have."

From what he read in her look, he knew he had told more
than he'd meant for her to know. Suddenly he had to get
away from there.

Jim Land managed to excuse himself, but he could feel her
astonished stare following him as he went to his horse and
flung himself into the saddle. He rode away without allowing
himself to look back.


It had taken Dake Parsons some time to locate Charlie
Converse, even though the new town had been settling down
considerably since the first time he laid eyes on it. Much of
the floating population had been siphoned off and gone elsewhere, hunting for easier pickings. Someone had got together
and set up a town government to keep order; streets had
been surveyed and straightened, and much of the first confu-

sion of tents and shanties had given way to actual buildings, constructed from lumber freighted in by mule power.

It was in one of these new buildings, a big box of a saloon, that Parsons at last found the man he was looking for—he was seated at a table with bottle and glasses in front of him and a blowzy-looking redhead at his side. Charlie Converse looked awful, but the woman looked a good deal worse.

Parsons went over to the table, and ignoring Charlie's uncertain nod of greeting, he jerked his head at the woman and said gruffly, "Go on. Beat it!"

Bridling, she gave Converse a tug at the arm and demanded loudly, "You gonna let him talk to me like that?" Getting no response and seeing the dangerous expression on the old cowpuncher, she shrugged elaborately, rose, and wandered off. She left an aroma of cheap perfume that mingled with that of the whiskey.

Dropping into an empty chair, Parsons asked sourly as he watched her go, "That the best you could do?"

Charlie said heavily, "She looked better last night. Maybe because it was dark."

"Or because you were drunk!" Parsons considered the other man critically. Charlie's clothes were rumpled and spotted with dirt. His handsome face was haggard and unshaven, his eyes blotched with red. "How do you feel?"

The younger man gave a groan. "Rotten!" At which Parsons said, under his breath, "Glad to hear it!"

Charlie picked up his glass, saw it was empty, and mumbled, "I need another of these."

"That's the *last* thing you need! Come on—let's get out of here."

Charlie protested, but the older man got him on his feet and outside, where he steered him to an eat shack across the street. He put him on a stool and ordered, "Coffee, to begin with—black." He watched sternly as the other man forced it down with a shudder, whereupon he poured a second cup. By that time, he had an order of steak and fried eggs on the way.

Having long since had his own breakfast, he persuaded Charlie Converse to get some of the food down. By then Charlie seemed to have recovered from the worst of his hangover, but it had given way to a mood of depression. Elbows folded on the plank counter, he stared at his empty plate and blurted suddenly, "Dake, what in the name of God am I doing in this raw end of nowhere? Why do you suppose I ever thought there was something here I wanted—or that I had a chance of making a go of it on a homestead?"

"I've wondered about that a mite," Dake Parsons admitted. "But the way I look at it, no man's actually a failure till he convinces himself of it. Whereas it never hurt a man, either, to enter the game with some idea of the high cards in his hand—assuming of course he's holding any."

If that was an oblique reference to Charlie Converse's personal shortcomings, Charlie didn't seem to hear it. His face was a mask of despair just then, as he softly struck a fist upon the wood of the counter and moaned, "Can't I ever have *any* luck? Just once!"

Dake Parsons had a low tolerance for self-pity. He commented dryly, "*I'd* say your luck was running pretty good. I just found the wagon and team and the supplies you bought, still standing where I guess you must've left them tied all night—looked ripe, to me, for anybody at all to have taken off with the whole shebang. Anyway, I brought the horses some food and water, and they seemed grateful to get it."

Charlie Converse frowned as he heard that and even colored a little, as though with some feeling of shame for his neglect of the team. Parsons kept right after him. "You got any money left?"

He saw how the younger man made a sudden and anxious move toward his wallet. Reassured at finding it, he immediately became indignant. "Just how drunk did you think I *was* last night? Of course I've got money!"

"Good! Then you can be paying for your breakfast while I go fetch up the wagon. Miz Converse is all alone out there on the claim, waiting for us," he pointed out. "I'd imagine she's getting some worried, by now."

There was little talk as they rode back from town. Not sure that the other man was in shape to manage a team, Dake Parsons had tied his saddled pony on behind and handled the reins himself. Charlie Converse rode next to him on the hard seat, head hanging and forearms resting on knees, jolting loosely to the movement of the vehicle over uneven and trackless prairie. From his morose silence, the older man judged that he still wasn't feeling any too good. Parsons wasn't inclined to conversation, either. The mood he was in, he didn't trust himself to say much, for fear of saying more than he meant to and really starting a quarrel.

When they came in on the Tuttle homestead, Charlie stirred himself to remind the older man he had a purchase that Mrs. Tuttle had asked him to make for her; Parsons reined over that way so they could deliver it. Tuttle and his son were busy on their sod house, setting the crotches on which the ridgepole would eventually rest. Mrs. Tuttle was washing clothes in a tub, in front of the wagon-top extension that still served the family as a tent.

Dake Parsons pulled in and handed down the packages from the pile of stuff in the wagon bed. Mandy Tuttle was a plain, rawboned woman who wore her drab hair pulled to a knot at the nape of her neck. Parsons had her pegged for a troublemaker, and right now she was all eagerness to divulge something. She looked across Dake Parsons to the man beside him and began without any preliminaries.

"Lord knows I'm not one to meddle in someone's family affairs, Mr. Converse, but I wouldn't be doing my duty as a neighbor if I didn't tell you about the goings-on at your place today."

Charlie Converse was staring at her. "What are you talking about?" he snapped peevishly. "What goings-on?"

"Now, you understand," she insisted, "I purely hate to say a thing, but it just doesn't look right! I couldn't be positive from here who the man was, but it sure looked to me like that Land fellow I used to see around there. I just happened to notice him ride up, and because I never did trust that man, I figured I should keep an eye on him. Though I thought for sure he'd leave, soon as he realized you were gone and your wife there all by herself. But no, sir! They talked awhile, and then he got down off his saddle and went right in the tent with her. I have no idea how long the two of them were in there, together. . . ."

She had said all she needed to.

Dake Parsons thought, *Damned old biddy!* He never doubted

for a moment that whatever had happened between two people as honorable as Jim Land and Beth Converse must have been perfectly honest and aboveboard. But this woman's husband had been so obviously taken by his neighbor's handsome wife, that she might do or say anything to ease the smart of jealous pride.

Parsons opened his mouth, prepared to make light of her prying suspicions. But next moment he felt the reins being torn from his hands, and Charlie Converse was standing and shouting at the horses, flailing them with the rein ends. The startled animals leaped into their collars; the old wagon went rolling away from there with all its weathered timbers rattling and jouncing. Vic Tuttle's wife was left gaping, in midsentence.

"What the hell do you think you're—" Dake Parsons began, but further speech was jolted out of him. He had to cling to his place as the team fell into a dead run. Bags and boxes were flung about as the wheels struck unevenness in the hard ground.

A few brief moments brought them onto the Converse claim, and as they barreled in toward the tent Charlie stood and sawed at the reins. Parsons helped, with a boot on the brake handle; the horses finally came to a plunging halt. The older man hastily grabbed the leathers as Charlie flung them aside; he was getting the team settled when Charlie jumped down and hurried into the tent.

Beth had been occupied with some mending, but the commotion had brought her to her feet, laying it aside. As her husband ducked the tent flap and stood staring at her, she asked in a startled voice, "Is something wrong?"

Charlie was having trouble with his breathing. "I've got good reason to think so," he answered her question harshly and added, "How long was he here?" When Beth only looked at him, the heat of anger mounted through his stubbled cheeks. "It'll do you no good denying it. The Tuttle woman saw and told me."

She frowned in comprehension. "I think you mean Jim Land. Yes, he was here. He left about an hour ago."

"And why did he come?"

"No reason that I know of. He just stopped by."

"When he saw I wasn't around, I suppose!"

At that, Beth Converse stiffened. Her eyes widened and her face went pale. When she spoke again, her voice trembled slightly, but her tone was steady. "I don't know what Mrs. Tuttle saw or thinks she saw, but I think you're implying something that simply isn't true. It isn't true of Jim Land, and it isn't true of me!"

"No?" Charlie let a sneer pull at his lips. "I suppose he hasn't been playing up to you since the first day you met him! And it's plain to me you never did one goddamn thing to discourage him!"

She gasped. Her head lifted and her eyes shone with a suspicion of tears. "Charlie, that isn't fair!" she cried in a voice that choked. "You know it isn't! You—you have no right to suggest such a thing."

"No? Have you forgotten I'm your husband?"

"Have *you* forgotten it?" she came back at him. "If instead of listening to gossip, you'd been here to see for yourself—and not off somewhere with—"

The flat of his hand struck her cheek, the sound ringing sharply in the stillness. "By God," he shouted. "I'll not have that thrown up to me! Where I go and what I do is my business!"

The force of the blow had driven her half around, and she had to catch at the table's edge to steady herself. She stood as though stunned, her head hanging. Charlie Converse looked at his wife for a long moment, breathing hard, waiting for an answer. Getting none, he heeled about and strode out of the tent, batting the flap out of his way. There he paused.

Dake Parsons had not yet stirred from his place on the wagon seat, with the reins dangling loosely from his gnarled fists; it would have been plain to anyone he had been listening to the sounds of the quarrel. The men's glances met and held. Then, abruptly, Charlie Converse moved. He strode to the wagon and past it, to the tailgate where Parsons' saddled horse stood anchored by its reins. Without hesitation Charlie jerked them free, got the stirrup, and rather clumsily pulled himself into the saddle.

Too late, Dake Parsons realized what was happening. He rose to his feet with a shout as Charlie Converse turned the animal and gave it a kick, sending it off across the prairie in

the direction of town. "Hey!" Dake Parsons' angry yell went
after him. "Where do you think you're taking my pony?" But
by then he was gone.

Dake Parsons swore, long and luridly. Then he blew out
his cheeks in an angry and futile grimace. He wrapped the
reins he was holding to the brake handle and climbed stiffly
to the ground. For a moment he stood and looked over at the
tent, hesitating; finally he made a decision and headed for
there. At the opening he halted, looking in at Beth, who
stood leaning against the table with her face in her hands.
From the movement of her shoulders he could see that she
was crying.

When he spoke to her, awkwardly, she lifted her head, and
the print of Charlie's hand showed plainly on her cheek.
Dake Parsons scowled in indignation. "Hell! Did he do that?"
He clucked his tongue and shook his head. "I never meant to
listen," he said in gruff apology. "But I couldn't help hearing.
A fine way to treat you, especially after he—" Breaking off,
he grunted, "Sorry. That slipped out. It ain't my place to say
anything."

Tiredly she said, "It's all right. I know where he was last
night and what he was doing—it's nothing new. . . . Though
it just about broke my heart," she added, "the first time I
learned that Charlie was a man who could never be faithful."

"But then—to turn around like that and accuse *you!*"

She didn't even seem to hear. She touched her cheek, and
her eyes and her voice seemed dead as she said, in a strange
tone, "Charlie *hit* me! Whatever else, he's never done that
before!"

"Aw, dammit, girl!" Parsons cried, miserably. In sympathy
he put a gnarled hand on her shoulder, and at once she
turned and came into his arms and buried her face against his
chest. Awkwardly he held her, painfully aware of the dirty
shirt he wore, imbued with the smells of sweat and shag
tobacco. "Wish I had something useful to tell you," he said to
the top of her brown head. "But an old fool like me—what do
*I* know?"

She drew away to tell him seriously, "Don't say that!
You've been a good friend. I appreciate everything you've
done. Everything!" She added, "Where is he now?"

"Your husband? He took my pony and rode the hell away from here."

"Charlie stole your horse?" She was shocked.

Dake Parsons gave a shrug. "Don't worry about it. I have a notion where he'll be. If he don't bring my critter back in a day or so, I'll just go and collect him."

Beth frowned thoughtfully. "Then—you really think he's coming back?"

"Well, his claim is here, ain't it? And his woman. . . ."

She didn't answer immediately. She walked over to the opening and looked out upon the homestead and the nearly finished house. She said slowly, "I don't think he cares anything about this claim at all, anymore." And Parsons had to nod agreement, remembering some of the things he had heard from Charlie Converse earlier. It looked as though she was right. "And as for me," she went on, in the same tone, "if he does come, I don't think now I want him to find me here!"

"What?"

"I've tried hard, Dake," she insisted, and there was discouragement in the line of her shoulders as she stood with her back turned to him. "I swear I have! For three years, in every way I knew how. I wanted to make this marriage work. I loved Charlie so much—I wouldn't even let myself think about those other women. But now—since he struck me— everything's different between us. There's nothing left."

As though with a sudden resolution, she turned back into the tent, got a suitcase from its corner, placed it on the table, and opened it. She began gathering items of clothing and personal belongings. Watching, Dake Parsons blurted, "Well, I always thought you shoulda done it sooner. I never could figure he had a lot to him. . . . Where're you heading for?"

"St. Louis, I suppose. I've nobody left there, but it's a place I know. I'll catch the train at Tulsa."

As she closed the suitcase and snapped it shut, he said, "Is that all you're taking?"

"These are the only things I want. He's welcome to the rest." But then Beth looked around her with a wistful expression as she said slowly, "D'you know, somehow I really hate to leave this place. I had such dreams for it. But—" She sighed. "It has to be a clean break."

"You're only being smart," Dake Parsons declared. He took the suitcase from her. "I'll just put this in the wagon. I'll drive you to Tulsa," he added and waved aside her thanks. "That's all right," he insisted. "More than glad to do it. We can leave whenever you're ready."

# Chapter Thirteen

It had been a blustery day, and a tumbled rack of clouds lying along the western horizon promised an early, murky sunset. A ground wind blew in from the west, and it tailed Jim Land as he rode into a settlement just below the strip, some distance west of Tulsa. He was looking for a blacksmith, and so the rhythmic clang of a hammer striking metal, carried by the pummeling wind, was a welcome greeting.

Land followed it into the scatter of streets and houses and let it lead him to a flat-roofed structure where, amid billows of stinking smoke and a fountaining of sparks, the smith was battering a red-hot chunk of metal on his anvil. Jim Land watched him at his work, not dismounting, and waited until he had laid aside his maul and reached for the chain that worked the bellows of his forge. He spoke then into the relative quiet. "Don't want to interrupt you, but I've got a loose shoe here. Suppose you could fix it?"

"I've been known to," the smith told him. He was a big fellow, with the muscles for his trade and the shoulders to support them. He looked at the roan horse. "Will you be doing more riding today?"

"I'm not sure yet," Land said. "I might, but I'm beginning to think not. But first I want to get something to eat."

"All right. Tie him up there, and I'll get to him when I can."

Land thanked him and dismounted, adding, "It's the left

rear shoe." He left the roan at the hitching rack, having first
loosened the cinch and given the saddle a shake to ease the
set of it. Walking through the place, looking for somewhere
to eat, he argued with himself that it was too early in the day
to quit, but he was strongly tempted.

It had been one more in a string of frustrating days since
his finding of the cave hideout had caused the outlaws to
abandon it. Having once taken the fight to Bill Doolin and his
gang, Land hated to fall back into the old pattern of waiting
for another move and then trying to counter it. Yet every day
without news of a train or bank holdup brought the next
exploit one day closer.

Today he had spent three long hours staking out the Bee
Dunn place, a couple of miles south and east of Ingalls. Dunn
was a homestead rancher, with almost certain ties to the
members of the gang. Lately there had been rumors of activity, of comings and goings at his place, which, if true, could
mean the presence of some of Doolin's outlaws. In a brushy
thicket, with the roan tied near at hand, Jim Land had kept a
watch on the house and on a cave that was sunk into a high
slope overlooking the creek.

He caught glimpses of Dunn himself and of the man's sons
and thirteen-year-old daughter, Rosa, but no one else; at no
time did he see any of the family approach the cave, which
was reputedly used as sleeping quarters by outlaws. It had
been a boring and futile wait, but also a tense one, because of
the danger of discovery. He had finally mounted up and
withdrawn, convinced that it had been another day lost, and
a tiring one, too.

Right now he was mostly hungry. He found a restaurant,
but wasn't tempted to linger very long over the tough meat
and watery potatoes he was served there. Afterward, emerg-
ing with his meal heavy inside him, he paused to study the
low hang of the sun—swollen, almost ready to plunge behind
the pileup of clouds to the west. That was when someone
appeared at his elbow to ask in a derelict whine, "Friend,
would you happen to have the price of a drink?"

Land gave the whiskered panhandler an impatient glance
and then looked more closely. He said, "Oh. It's you."

The man bobbed his head, grinning as though he, too, had

just identified someone he knew. "Right you are, Marshal," he said. "Just ole Jack Boggs, big as life!" He appeared to be wearing the same decrepit clothing as the other time Land had seen him—at bay and confronted by a suspicious group of lawmen in Ransom's Saloon on the day of the Ingalls raid.

Jim Land asked shortly, "What happened? Did they finally get enough of you in Ingalls?"

"Marshal," the derelict told him in complete seriousness, "that town is dyin' on the vine! The Doolin boys used to bring in the cash and spread it around, real free and easy. But since you people chased them out, there ain't as much as a loose dime floating around. The place might as well close up shop!"

"How's that barber doing?"

"Smith?" He grimaced. "I can tell you, he ain't too popular after what he done to help dry up the town's prosperity! Sure nothing there for the likes of me anymore," Jack Boggs added. "I had a chance to hitch a ride, and I left!"

Land asked, half amused, "D'you like this town better?"

"No way it could be any worse, right now!" He caught at the man's other sleeve, as though to keep him there. "You know, I ain't forgotten," Boggs went on in an ingratiating tone, "you done me a favor that day in the saloon. That other marshal was all for tossin' me into jail and throwing the key away. Me, I been inside of jails. . . . I always got the shakes, awful bad!" He shuddered at the memory. "I just can't stand being locked up. So I appreciate you speaking up for me."

Jim Land gave a shrug. "I thought Duff Penner could be putting his time to better use. I didn't suppose you knew anything."

"All the same," Jack Boggs insisted, "I take it as a favor." And then he lowered his voice to a conspiratorial level. "Just maybe there's one I could do for you!"

"Don't strain yourself," Land said dryly. He turned and would have walked on, but the derelict scuttled around to block his path.

"I mean it, Marshal!" Boggs insisted. "I got information that's red hot—something I know you'd want to hear. Come to think of it," and his little eyes took on a sudden expression of craftiness, "this is much too good just to give away. Oughta be worth—" He grasped for a figure to indicate its value. "How about fifty dollars?"

But Jim Land's temper was growing thin. He shook free of the dirty hand pawing at his sleeve. "How about the price of the drink you wanted? That's as high as I go."

If Boggs was disappointed, his philosophical shrug didn't show it. "All right." But just then a couple of men came out of the eat shack and paused to talk. "Can we move on a spell?" the derelict suggested. "No reason the whole town has to hear this."

Land held his patience as they walked a few yards farther along the street, halting at last where no one was in earshot. "Say what you have to say."

"It's the Doolin gang," Jack Boggs said quickly. "I know where they aim to pull their next job!"

Land made no effort to hide his disbelief. "And how would you know that?"

"I heard talk."

"I see. More rumors!"

But the man insisted, "No! No! I overheard 'em making plans. It was a couple days ago, in the saloon right there across the street. I was minding my own business, sort of dozing, with my chair tilted back against the wall. Well, them partitions are just about like paper. All at once I realized I was listening to someone talking right in my ear—in one of the card rooms. Where I sat I could hear everything!"

He paused, and Land said curtly, "Go on."

Boggs drew a breath. "Only voice I could put a sure name to was the one doing most of the talking—an ugly son of a bitch named Turk Freese. He was laying it out for the rest and answering questions. And what he told 'em was that sights had been set on a bank that was ripe and prime for busting. When I kept listening, I soon found out he meant the bank at Tulsa."

"Tulsa? You're positive of that?"

"He said it more than once. According to Freese, with all the cattle that's been cleared off the strip and moved into the steam cars, account of the opening last month, the vault in that bank is plumb choked with beef money—just ripe for somebody to pick it off!"

Land was studying the sallow, whiskered face, giving no hint as to whether he believed anything he was being told. He said, "Did you happen to hear a voice that sounded like Doolin's?"

"I didn't, for a fact. I had an idea Turk Freese was filling in some of the other boys on a project that was already decided and in the works."

"By any chance was there a time mentioned or a date?"

Jack Boggs nodded vigorously. "I heard Thursday—sometime Thursday. Hey! That's tomorrow, ain't it?"

"Right!" Land said coldly. "And just what have you done with this information you've been sitting on for two days? Did you warn the authorities?"

"What authorities?" the man said with a grimace. "There ain't even a J.P. in this burg."

"You could have wired Tulsa."

"What with? Man, telegrams cost money! Anyway, who'd listen to me?"

"You expected *me* to," Jim Land pointed out. "And even pay for the privilege! Why shouldn't I think you made the whole thing up for my benefit?"

As though stung, the derelict fell back a step. In a tone of injured dignity he cried, "You think I'm *lying*! Well, then, I won't take up any more of your time!" And he actually turned away, his head haughtily erect. Jim Land sighed.

"Hold on," he said. "Here—I promised you." He took a silver dollar from his pocket. Golden light from the setting sun streaked as the coin spun and was caught. Jack Boggs, without another word, turned and walked away with his payment clutched in grimy fingers.

He left Jim Land with a dilemma.

His first impulse was to dismiss the whole thing as the invention of a fertile mind desperate for a drink. But then the doubts began: That talk about the vault of the Tulsa bank being filled with beef money raised familiar echoes of his own conversation with Oscar Halsell on a memorable day in Halsell's Livery. It held the ring of truth—and could someone like Jack Boggs actually have invented a detail like that?

No, this had to be taken seriously. Jim Land swore under his breath as he suddenly realized what he was in for.

If there was really to be an attempt on the Tulsa bank sometime tomorrow, he couldn't afford not to be there. Calculating the distance, he knew the only way he could be there in time was by starting now. It meant giving up any thought of catching up on his sleep. He had been looking forward to a night of well-deserved rest, but now that was out of the question. He would need to locate a fresh horse and hit the trail at once.

Then a new, alarming thought struck him: What if the thing was a trap? The gang knew him by sight. He could have been spotted immediately upon entering this town. Jack Boggs could have been primed and sent to tell him a yarn meant to lure him onto the trail to Tulsa, where an ambush could already be set up somewhere, waiting for him.

It was a chance he had to take. Unconsciously he adjusted the hang of his holstered gun, and then, wearily, he went looking for a fresh horse, as the sun dipped behind the rack of clouds resting on the wide horizon.

With the murky vanishing of the sun, a stronger, chilling gust of wind sprang up and followed Charlie Converse the final distance onto his homestead claim, pushing at him and whipping up the mane and tail of the plodding saddle horse. Depressed, head aching, he peered ahead, fully expecting to see a cheery blaze waiting and puzzled not to find one.

Yonder stood the wagon, and he could see the team staked out and grazing. Up on the roof of the sod house, Dake Parsons seemed to be putting the final lengths of sod in place against the comb of the ridgepole. Charlie Converse barely gave him a glance. He rode directly to the tent and dismounted, walked inside and then stood, staring dumbly about, still looking for Beth and unable to register the fact that he didn't see her.

He turned again and went outside, just as Parsons descended the homemade ladder and came toward him. If there was a look of wolfish anticipation on the old puncher's face, Converse failed to notice. Without preliminaries he demanded, "Where's my wife?"

Parsons cocked an eyebrow at him. He peered around

before saying blandly, "Well, now, I just don't see her—do you?"

Angrily Converse turned on him. "What kind of an answer is that? Do you know where she is or don't you?"

"You mean, right this minute?" Parsons shook his head, lips pursed. "Can't say I do. But I know she's long gone from *this* place. She's up and left you, Charlie!"

Charlie Converse stared back, feeling the warmth drain from his face. He stammered, "No—I don't believe it! She couldn't!"

"Maybe she couldn't, but she sure as hell has. Bound for Saint Looey, she said."

"But—*why?*"

"If you don't know that," Dake Parsons retorted coldly, "I don't suppose anyone could explain it to you. But I was more'n happy to oblige when she asked me to drive her into Tulsa, to the hotel, where she was gonna wait to catch the train. Afterward, I come on out here to wait for you to bring back my pony—and I see you have.

"Yeah," Parsons went on as Charlie's mouth worked on words that refused to come, "I figured sooner or later, you'd be showing up. And with nothing better to do while I waited, I went ahead putting a roof on your house. Dunno, I always been one that hated leaving a job partly finished. Anyway, there it is." He flung a hand toward the dark shape of the completed building. "You timed it real fine. There's your house, all ready to move in, and you scarcely had to turn a hand to it yourself. Not bad, Charlie—not bad!"

Converse had heard only part of what the old puncher told him. There was a roaring in his head as he reached and grabbed Dake Parsons by an arm, jerking him around. "Damn you!" he cried hoarsely. "Are you saying you *helped* her leave me? You'd dare to step in between a man and his lawful—"

"*Let go of me!*" Parsons spoke quietly, but at something in his tone, Charlie Converse made his fingers open. The older man stepped back, and his eyes were blazing.

"You sorry son of a bitch!" he gritted. "Don't it occur to you that little gal has stood by you through every failure and every half-baked scheme of yours for longer'n you had any right to expect? And the times you thought you were getting away with things behind her back—why, hell! She knew all about those women, but trying to save her marriage and do the best she could with the mistake she'd made was worth more to her than her pride. I don't imagine it ever got through to you, just what a special gal you had there. When you raised your hand to her, though—that was the end! That was the day you lost it all!"

He was visibly trembling with anger as his voice choked off and the two men stood confronted, glaring at each other. Charlie Converse found that his own voice was shaking as he began, "Nobody has ever talked this way to me. . . ."

"Then by God it's time somebody did!" Parsons cut him off. "And right now, before I say too much, I'm takin' my pony and I'm gone! I'm off for Nevada," he added bluntly. "Cook your own supper—if you know how; I'm eatin' in town. I don't aim to spend another minute in your company. You ain't worthy for me to know!"

And he heeled around without another word and strode to where his sack and bedroll lay strapped and ready for the trail—almost as though he'd known this was the day Converse would be showing up. He went to where the other man had left the dun with reins dragging and saddle still in place. Dake Parsons checked his cinch and leaped astride with an agility that belied his years. A word to the pony lifted it into a lope westward across the prairie, where the last sullen light of dusk was fading.

Charlie Converse stood like a man turned to stone, alone with his wagon and his tent and his empty house, a chill night settling about him.

# Chapter Fourteen

During the night an intermittent icy rain had pummeled sections of Oklahoma Territory, making life miserable for a traveler working against the clock through the long hours of darkness, but at least that rain appeared to have settled the thick dust of Tulsa's Main Street. Now the low clouds had broken in an alternating flow of shadow and brightness as a morning sun drew wavering mist from the puddles and flooded wheel ruts.

So far as Jim Land could see, the scene before him was a normal and peaceful one. The town of Tulsa was going about its ordinary business. At the bank, customers entered and left, pausing on the plank sidewalk to exchange greetings and then go on about their affairs. There was no hint of anything wrong.

He appeared to have made it in time—assuming that the threat to Tulsa's bank was something more than the invention of a derelict trying to cadge a handout. Jim Land no longer knew what he thought or if he was capable of making sense at all. He knew only that he was light-headed from fatigue after a night without sleep except for such fitful dozing as he could manage in the saddle. But the normality of this morning scene made him doubt the urgency that had brought him here.

So he didn't ride across the muddy street to the bank, nor did he consider inquiring about local law. He didn't feel like bringing ridicule to the office of the federal marshal by spreading an alarm concerning an emergency that might not arise. For the moment he preferred to watch and wait. He reined in at the hitching rack that fronted the hotel opposite the bank building and let himself stiffly down from saddle.

The animal he had ridden through the night, a tough little black mare, had stood up well to the hours of steady traveling. It deserved a stall, a rubdown, and a good bait of oats, but there remained a chance he might be needing it again in a hurry; the best he was able to do just now was to tie it where it could reach a nearby water trough. As the horse gratefully sank its muzzle, he gave its neck a friendly pat and promised, "You'll be taken care of, girl, soon as I can see to it."

The slicker Jim Land had worn during much of the ride was in its place behind the saddle. He took off his rain-soaked hat, worked it into better shape, and gave his coat a tug to settle the hang of it. A short time earlier, during one of his infrequent stops for rest, he had washed most of the trail stains off himself in a brook and had broken out his razor and soap for a hurried shave; so he supposed he looked reasonably presentable as he went tiredly up the veranda steps and inside the hotel.

Going through the lobby, he entered the dining room, with its carpet underfoot and ranks of white-clothed tables. Apparently, despite the lateness of the hour, breakfast was still being served, though most of the tables were empty, their litter of dirty dishes being cleared away. In one corner, a couple of men lingered over what looked to be a discussion of important business. Jim Land went directly to the windows fronting the street and found a table that gave him a good view of the bank building opposite. He laid his hat on the seat of another chair and prepared himself for a vigil combined with the welcome prospect of a good, hot meal.

He was carefully studying the bank's layout when quick footsteps approached his table; he didn't look up at the woman until her politely spoken "May I take your order?" made his head jerk around in disbelief.

"Beth!" he exclaimed. "What on earth are you doing *here*?"

Neatly dressed in shirtwaist and skirt and frilled white

apron, Beth Converse seemed as surprised as he. But she told him, with a hint of a smile tugging wryly at a corner of her mouth, "It looks as though I'm waiting tables."

Although it was less than a week since he had seen her, to Jim Land she looked changed—thinner, somehow, and with a faint, dark stain beneath her eyes, as though worry or sleeplessness had taken their toll. "But—what in the world?" The words stumbled from him in incoherent questions unable to make themselves take shape. "Where's your husband?" he finally managed and looked past her, half expecting to find him in the nearly empty dining room.

The faint smile faded, and haggard marks of grief took over in her lovely face. "That's something I don't really know," she admitted and then added quickly, in response to something she read in his eyes, "No, he hasn't left me. I'm afraid—I'm the one that's left him!"

Jim Land was on his feet then, kicking back his chair. "You don't mean it! When did this happen?"

"Let me see. . . ." Beth seemed to have to think about it, as though trying to force time into perspective. "Was it four days ago? I think so. It was the same afternoon you came by the claim. When Charlie got back from town, I'm afraid we had a row about—something." Land noticed the faint pause and the evasion. With a quick shake of her head she said, "I'd rather not go into it. But it's over. It's all over!" Suddenly her lower lip was trembling and she caught it between white, even teeth to steady it. She added quickly, "This isn't getting your breakfast!"

Land dismissed that. "Never mind that. I want to know about *you*. Where are you staying? What do you plan to do now?"

"I'm not too sure yet, but for a start I suppose I should go back where I came from. Since I had no money, I've been working here. I've got a little room I can afford in a boarding-house, and I've saved almost enough for the train fare home. Afterward?" She made a small gesture.

Jim Land looked at her a long moment and then turned for another glance into the street. All was quiet out there, giving no hint that this would be anything but a normal autumn day. Meanwhile, food was suddenly the furthest thing from his mind. "We have to talk," he exclaimed. "Please! I want to help you if there's any way I can."

This time the grateful smile she gave him erased some of the anguish from her eyes. "Dear Jim!" she said. "You're always there, aren't you—ready to help. But I'm afraid this is a time when I can see nothing for you to do."

"All the same . . ."

At his insistence she hesitated and then said, "Just a moment, then." He watched her move gracefully among the tables to the lobby. When she returned, he was standing and staring moodily out the window at the play of cloud shadow and the traffic in the street. Beth had removed her frilly apron. She told him, "The manager says I can have ten minutes—the morning shift is almost finished, anyway. We can use the parlor; there's no one in there."

As they went through the lobby, a man that Jim Land took to be the hotel's manager was at the desk in conversation with the day clerk. He gave the stranger a curious stare but nodded and smiled at Beth; it didn't surprise Land that she would have already won friends for herself, even in the few days she had been working here.

She preceded him into the parlor, a comfortable room complete with carpet and window drapes, overstuffed furniture, and a writing table for the hotel's guests, even a rubber plant large enough to fill one corner. Except for themselves the room was vacant at this hour. Land closed the double doors and went immediately to the big windows facing the veranda. He was relieved to see they gave him an even better view of the bank than he had had from the dining room.

Satisfied on that score for the moment, he turned away to find Beth frowning at his behavior. "What's going on, Jim?" she said anxiously. "Are you expecting trouble?"

"Just being careful," he assured her. "Right now it's you that I'm concerned about." He went to her; in a stillness that was broken only by distant sounds from the street and from elsewhere in the hotel building, he looked at her and said, "D'you know, I've found that it can help sometimes just to talk things over with a friend."

She nodded wordlessly. Now that they were alone, he

could see her letting down some of the courageous front she had put on. She looked desolated. Land drew a breath; there was a suggestion that he had to make, much as he hated being the one to offer it. "Do you suppose perhaps you should reconsider and go back to him?"

Pain crossed her features. She said in a muffled voice, "Don't tell me to do that, Jim!"

"I can't tell you to do anything," he said quietly. "I'm only trying to find out what you're really thinking."

"If you mean, have I wondered whether I've made a mistake—I've wondered about it a lot! And I know I didn't! Charlie can't help being the way he is," she went on while Jim Land listened gravely. "But neither can I help being me! I tried to be what I thought he wanted in a wife. I really tried hard, Jim! But—" She let a helpless shake of the head finish the sentence and dropped her eyes.

"What's just as important," Land reminded her, "could he ever be the husband you wanted?"

"I thought so once. At first everything was fine for us. But it wasn't long before the need for money began to get in the way, and it changed him. I think, before long, it began to make him resent me. And I suppose when a man feels like that . . ."

*He begins looking around*—that was the thought she left unfinished. Jim Land's jaw tightened; he could feel himself start to boil at the thought of any man doing that to her. But a possibility that was even worse made him ask, "Has he ever—*struck* you?"

Her silence told him the answer. He found himself gripping her shoulders in a way that made her raise her troubled look to his. And the words poured out of him, in a voice roughened with feeling: "I'm sorry, Beth. That's something I can't be reasonable about! I never intended for you to know this, but the truth is that I think I've been falling in love with you ever since we met! I once told you I was a restless man," he went on. "I've had all that burnt out of me through the years. There's nothing of it left. I came from the land; I'd like nothing better than a chance to go back to it, once the job I'm on is finished.

"But not alone! Not after seeing you on that homestead

claim. I know now that what I really want is a place just like that—with someone just like you! Well, there it is," he finished. "The plain truth! I hope you aren't angry."

She looked at him, stunned. But he could find no trace of anger. Her clear, brown eyes had never been that close to his. Her lips parted and silently formed his name. And there was no way he could have kept, then, from bending his head and kissing her. When she returned the kiss, he took her gently into his arms and felt hers move up and tighten.

All at once he stiffened, with an exclamation. Beth said, "What is it?" and instantly freed herself, turning to follow his stare toward the windows and the street, where a familiar team and wagon had just halted at the hitching rail beside Land's borrowed mare. She gasped as she saw Charlie Converse awkwardly climbing down and starting for the steps of the hotel veranda. "He's looking for *me*!"

"He doesn't have to find you."

"Oh, I can't be that much of a coward! No, Jim—I have to face him." When he still tried to hold her back, she shook her head and managed a smile; and though her face looked ashen he was forced to let her go. He watched her lift her head and set her shoulders, preparing for an ordeal. Then she went to the lobby door and opened it.

Land followed her that far, but there held back, knowing he could do nothing now but watch. Charlie Converse was at the desk, talking excitedly to the clerk; the gist of his questioning was clear when the latter glanced past him toward the parlor entrance, starting to say something just as Beth stepped through. Charlie turned around with an exclamation at the sight of his wife. At once he moved toward her across the lobby, obviously not noticing Jim Land, who had halted just beyond the doorway.

For a moment husband and wife looked at each other, until Beth found her voice to say, "Are you all right?" Charlie didn't look all right. He was haggard and unshaven, with a wild expression on his face. The words began to tumble out of him.

"I've been on the road all night. I never really hoped to find you— When I got back to our claim, Dake Parsons told me about bringing you to Tulsa and dropping you here at the hotel. He said you'd be on your way to Missouri by this time. But I had to come anyway." His red-rimmed eyes anxiously searched her face. "Beth, does this mean that you weren't serious after all? That maybe you've thought some more about it and changed your mind about leaving me?"

In a voice that told of the effort this was costing her, she said, "No. I'm sorry, Charlie. I'd like us to be friends, if we can. But I can't come back."

"But I *need* you!" He reached and seized both her hands, grasping them desperately. "Please!" he cried brokenly, oblivious of the desk clerk watching them, openmouthed. "Don't do this to me! I'm not saying I don't deserve it—before he rode away, last evening, that old fellow Parsons gave me a tongue-lashing, and I had to admit that every word he said was true!" Land saw that Beth was trying to free her hands, but gave it up with shoulders sagging when the man tightened his grip and refused to let go. His voice took on almost a note of hysteria.

"I can't get by alone! I'll do anything—apologize for anything I've ever done to you. And I take back all the things I said about you and Jim Land. That was just craziness and jealousy talking. . . ." All at once Beth was crying, and Land turned cold at the thought that she might surrender to this abject pleading.

In that moment, with his words of retraction still ringing in the lobby's stillness, Charlie Converse looked past her and caught sight of the man he had accused. Their looks met and held.

"Converse," Land said coldly, "whatever you may be thinking about this, you're wrong! This wasn't planned—we met just now, by accident. You haven't got a damned thing to be jealous about!" He waited for an answer, but the other man said nothing, and his expression told even less. Jim Land looked at Beth; her head was averted, and there was no clue to be had as to what she was thinking or feeling or what effect her husband's words had been having. But clearly, Jim Land could do nothing here; husband and wife were going to have to settle this.

He turned and walked past them, across the lobby and

outside, taking a turmoil of feelings with him and knowing
that his own fate, too, rested on whatever they decided.

Land halted at the edge of the veranda steps, looking upon
the muddy street with eyes that scarcely registered the trio of
horsemen who had just ridden up to a hitching rail that
fronted the squat bank building across from him. One remained in the saddle, but the other pair were dismounting,
moving easily and without haste. His mind too full of other
matters, Jim Land only really noticed them when the largest
of the three turned to duck beneath the pole and he caught a
glimpse of the man's face. It was Turk Freese.

Instantly alert, in the next glance he knew the other pair.
But these two were no part of the Doolin gang. The stocky
figure starting into the bank at Freese's elbow was the horse
rancher Nels Antrim, and therefore it wasn't too surprising
that the gaunt, slope-shouldered man who stayed with the
horses should be Antrim's friend—the drifter Sid Yount.

What two petty crooks of that caliber were doing, taking
part in this job, Land couldn't imagine and had no time to
wonder about. He was already breaking loose from where he
stood and drawing his gun. He rounded the tailgate of Charlie Converse's wagon and was in the open street, heading for
the bank, even as Freese and Antrim disappeared inside. Sid
Yount, still on horseback, caught sight at once of the lawman.
His head jerked back, and Land saw his whiskered face go
slack with astonishment. But a gun came up in his fist, and he
triggered at the man running toward him through the slop
and mud of Main Street.

He had fired too hastily. The bullet went wild, and before
he could manage another shot, Jim Land got off a better one.
The sound of the guns mingled, bouncing against the sounding boards of false-fronted buildings. Sid Yount's arms flew
wide. The impact of the bullet drove him sideways off his
saddle, to strike the hitching rail beside him with a splitting
impact and then roll loosely over it to the boardwalk, where
he lay unmoving.

Yount had been holding the other pair of horses by their
reins. Now free and terrified by the guns, all three animals
broke in panic and bolted, scattering wildly, with their hooves
raising geysers of muddy water.

The morning routine of Tulsa's Main Street had been smashed in a matter of seconds. All along the block, voices were shouting and doors slamming, townspeople rushing to escape the sudden danger that had burst in their midst. But Jim Land kept going without breaking stride. He was within a few yards of the bank when, without warning, the big front window went out in an explosion of glittering shards. He glimpsed the bulky figure of Turk Freese, holding the six-shooter with which he had smashed the glass. Now the weapon tipped with flame, and there was a burst of powder smoke. Land almost thought he heard the bullet streak past him; he fired back and saw his enemy retreat a step into the bank's shadowy interior.

Then the outlaw's gun fired again. Land felt the smashing blow that took him somewhere near the center of his body. There was no pain, but he knew he was falling; the sound he heard, as he went down and the gun dropped from his fingers, was a woman's shrill cry. It sounded like Beth Converse.

In the lobby, Beth heard the initial exchange of gunfire and felt herself turn cold with the certainty that Jim Land must be involved. She stared at Charlie and heard herself choke out the words, "It's Jim!" Knowing only that she must learn what was happening, she turned then and hurried toward the door with Charlie's startled cry of protest following her.

As she burst out upon the hotel veranda, a riderless horse went galloping past with reins and stirrups flying, confusing her and obstructing her view of what was going on in the street. She halted at the edge of the steps, trying to bring things into focus; and now Charlie came up behind her, and she felt his hand on her arm and heard him saying hoarsely, 'Beth! Don't do this! You could get yourself killed!"

She ignored him, for she had discovered Jim Land.

He was alone out there in the street, and he was hurt. She saw him stagger and catch his footing. A cry of horror distended her throat as she watched him pitch backward into the mud. At that moment everything else was forgotten. Beth pulled loose from Charlie's protesting hand, and then she was running on legs that shook so they seemed barely able to support her. Somehow she reached Jim Land and went down on her knees. His eyes were closed. She touched his face, and as his coat fell open and she got a glimpse of blood, a sobbing gasp broke from her.

Only then did she become aware of someone approaching. Still kneeling, she lifted her head and saw the shape of the man striding toward them, outlined against the facade of the bank building with its shattered window. Beth lifted her head farther, and as the bulky figure came to a stand, towering over her, she looked into the face she knew all too well— knife-scarred, with that one milky, damaged eye and the other that gleamed as he saw his enemy lying helpless before him.

Turk Freese lifted a smoking revolver. His mouth twisted. "He's still breathin'! Get out of my way while I finish him!"

Even as he spoke Jim Land was stirring, as the first shock of the bullet appeared to leave him. Seeing him move spurred Beth to defiance. *"No!"* She spread her arms as though she would shield the hurt man with her own body.

Fury seized the outlaw. Bending, he trapped Beth's arm in one big hand and hauled her to her feet, thrusting her aside so that he could get a clear shot at his victim. But at once she was back, flinging herself at him and striking out with her fists and all her desperate strength. Turk Freese swore and tried to push her away. She caught her ankle in a wheel rut and almost lost her footing, but kept her grip on his arm and dragged him off balance. Cursing with impatience, the big man turned on her then, and the revolver swung up, barrel poised to strike.

Until this moment Charlie Converse had been standing beside his wagon, motionless as a man in shock, heedless of the team horses, which had been badly spooked by the action only a little distance from where they stood. But what he saw happening to Beth must have broken through somehow and reminded him there was a revolver loaded and ready under the wagon seat. He climbed up a spoke of the front wheel, groped, and got the weapon. And with his shaking arm steadied against the iron rim of a wheel, Charlie Converse managed to aim and work the trigger.

But he was no marksman. His desperate effort missed its target, yet came close enough to startle Turk Freese. The ugly head jerked around; the one good eye spotted Converse preparing to try again. Without hesitation, Freese tore Beth's grip loose from his arm, sending her sprawling. And his revolver dropped into line, as with a look of contempt he threw a shot at the man by the wagon.

The bullet didn't miss. Charlie Converse made a convulsive movement as it struck him. He stood for a moment as though pinned against the big wheel of the wagon, and then he seemed to crumple and went sliding down it.

But between them, the valiant efforts of Beth and Charlie had granted Jim Land the respite he needed to fight through the numbing shock of the bullet that had felled him. He half raised himself and saw his own revolver lying directly in front of him. Gathering his strength, he reached toward it. Turk Freese must have caught the movement from a corner of his one sound eye, for at once he wheeled about and turned his smoking weapon on his enemy, even as Land's fingers touched the metal of the gun and closed on it.

The reports came almost together. But this time it was Turk Freese's bullet that knocked up a gout of mud, harmlessly, only inches from where Land crouched before him. A look of vast surprise washed across the outlaw's face. A massive hand groped toward his chest. And then the life went out of his remaining eye, and Turk Freese dropped headlong, the way a tree falls.

The trail that had brought Jim Land from Texas to Oklahoma Territory had reached its end at last.

# Chapter Fifteen

With the echoes of gunfire ringing in his head and the mingled smells of powder smoke and muddy earth, Jim Land found the strength to pull himself to his feet. He staggered and caught himself. Then a strong arm was around his waist to steady him, and he looked down into Beth Converse's brown eyes. Her clothes, like his own, were soaked and muddy; there was a streak of mud across one cheek, and her hair had come down from its pins during the struggle with Turk Freese. But she had never looked better to him than now, as he realized she was apparently unhurt and none the worse for what had happened.

He managed a tight grin. "I'd say we look like quite a pair just now!"

She saw nothing amusing in the situation. "Are you badly hurt?" she demanded anxiously.

"I'll be all right." He was looking past her, where her husband lay crumpled and motionless beside the wagon. "I think Charlie needs you worse," he told her as gently as he could. She turned quickly to look, and he heard her gasp in anguish. He could tell that she was torn between her concerns. "Go on," he urged as she hesitated. "Don't worry about me."

The moment she left him, Jim Land realized how much he had needed the support of her steadying arm. All his mental processes were dulled. He had a sensation of standing on a

174

slowly spinning turntable, with Turk Freese sprawled at his feet and turning with him. He had to brace his legs to keep from falling. All around him, he could hear the street coming back to life in a growing hum of activity, as townspeople grew bolder after the shooting ceased.

Somewhere in his mind a voice was warning him that it still wasn't over. While trying to make sense of this, he shoved a hand under his coat and felt the warm wetness of blood. The wound was beginning to catch fire with the passing of the initial shock; he couldn't tell yet how seriously he had been hurt, but the furrow that had been plowed across his ribs seemed to be bleeding. He switched his gun to his left hand while he dug out a handkerchief and fumbled it beneath the blood-soaked shirt to try to stanch the flow.

But when he moved to take the revolver again with his right hand, the fingers felt wooden and as thick as sausages. Unable to control them, he felt the weapon slip free. He stood blankly looking down at it in the mud in front of his boots. And at that moment he understood the warning his brain had tried to give him.

There was still one bank robber unaccounted for.

Nels Antrim came bursting from the door of the bank, trampling broken window glass. The horse rancher had lost his hat somewhere. In one hand he carried a canvas bag that looked to have been partly and hastily filled with money; in the other he held a big, pearl-handled six-gun. He raised it, staring wild-eyed around him, shocked to see his comrades lying dead and the horses, meant for a getaway, long since vanished.

Then his eyes fell upon the lawman who had blown his well-laid plan to ruins. He saw Jim Land standing empty-handed in front of him, and a grimace lifted the upper lip from the rancher's crooked teeth. He twice had missed a chance at this man; this time at least—the thought showed in his bearded face—there was no way he could miss.

The look melted into one almost of blank surprise. Amid the echoes of a gunshot, the man's stocky figure began to weave a little. Nels Antrim suddenly went to one knee. He again raised the heavy six-gun, but it began to wobble in his hand, and then he bowed his head and tumbled slowly forward. The canvas sack fell from his hand; coins and bills spilled out of it. And Jim Land, still dazed and not sure what had happened, looked around as a buggy with a man and woman on the seat and a lathered horse between the shafts drew to a halt just beside him.

The horse, a roan, had obviously been traveling, and it took a firm hand on the reins to quiet it. In his other hand, the driver had the gun with which he had killed Nels Antrim. It rested on his knee, in such a way that Jim Land realized its muzzle was pointed, almost negligently, in his direction. Registering that, he lifted his eyes and met the piercing blue stare of Bill Doolin.

The outlaw's look passed over him, not missing the blood that was beginning to soak through the material of his coat or the fact there was no weapon in his hand or in his holster. He glanced again at the stiffening shape of Nels Antrim and said bluntly, "Looks like I barely got here in time to do any good. But I see you're at least still on your feet."

Land found his voice. "Another second and I wouldn't have been. He had me cold!"

Now Doolin was looking at the body of Turk Freese, sprawled not far from them in the middle of the wide thoroughfare. "Freese?" And at the other's nod, "You killed him?"

"That's right."

He said it defiantly, but Doolin showed no particular displeasure. His only comment to that was, "Somebody was bound to." But then he leaned closer, and his manner became intently serious.

"I want you to understand, this was none of my idea. It was Turk Freese's doing, all the way—and he was mighty careful to keep me from learning about it. Most of the beef money in that bank vault belongs to my old boss, Mr. Halsell, and Freese knew I'd never stand for the gang touching a penny of it. I figure I owe that much, at least, to the man who befriended and trusted me when I was a young fellow and needed a start in life. So Freese had to go outside the gang for somebody to help him with the job."

"The pair he got wouldn't have been hard to persuade," Land told him. "I happen to know they both had a grudge against Halsell—I was on hand the day he ran them both out of town. Likely they were glad enough of a chance to get back at him."

"Well, somehow the word got out what Freese was up to, but it reached me almost too late. We were on our way to Kansas, looking for a safer place for my wife to stay. I took a chance and changed our route by way of Tulsa, hoping I could do something to stop him. It appears you've saved me the trouble."

Jim Land had been aware of the woman who shared the seat with Doolin. He gave the outlaw's wife a closer look—and this time, astonishingly enough, recognized her. It was the pretty dark-haired woman from Ingalls, and so at last he could understand her antagonism on that day of the raid toward any man who wore a badge—even the one who had saved her friend's hotel from the torch. Even now, as he nodded to her, she only returned his look without expression.

He was beginning to feel light-headed and to wonder how long he could stay on his feet. Yet when he turned back to the outlaw, he spoke crisply as he said, "A damned good thing for me you showed up, Doolin. But I'll tell you now—if you're coming back to Oklahoma to pick up where you left off, then this isn't going to make any difference. So you might as well go ahead and pull that trigger."

The pale eyes appeared to ice over. Bill Doolin glanced down at the gun in his fingers, still pointed at the unarmed man who stood before him. But then something changed in the outlaw's face. Deliberately he slid the revolver into its holster and took up the reins. He said, "I may be back—I may not. Edie's gonna have a baby. There's nothing like that to make a man take a good, hard look at himself. I figure I've got some choices to make."

A moment longer, their looks met. Jim Land heard himself saying quietly, "I hope you make the right ones." And on that he stepped back, and without another word Bill Doolin flicked the reins against his horse's back, and the roan stepped forward. The rig, containing the man and woman and a pile of boxes and other baggage in the rear, rolled on up the street, heading north. Jim Land, watching it go, could imagine the reaction of anyone observing this scene who might guess who the driver really was.

For now, in the aftermath of the gun battle, the street was beginning to swarm with humanity. He saw the ones who came pouring out of the bank to surround the bodies of Antrim and Yount. A teller in eyeshade and sleeve protectors had snatched up the money sack and was anxiously gathering the coins and bills that had spilled out of it. An excited babble of voices rose on every hand.

For Jim Land, the light-headedness remained, but the world no longer threatened to spin away from under him. The fiery pain of the bullet that had raked across his ribs was settling somewhat to a throbbing ache. For a moment he contemplated his fallen revolver, lying in the mud, and then risked leaning to pick it up.

As he straightened with it, he saw a man come hurrying toward him from the group before the bank. A deputy sheriff's badge was pinned to the man's coat, and Land stood and waited for him.

The deputy was a spare and lanky figure, middle-aged, with a grizzled mustache that looked as though he had a habit of chewing on it. He was wagging his head as he exclaimed, "Man, man! Looks like I just missed one hell of a shoot-out! But damned if I can get a clear picture from anyone. Some say one thing, some another. And just who the hell are *you*, anyway?"

For answer Land took the badge from his pocket. At sight of it, the man gave him a look that held a hint of respect. "Federal man, huh? Did you kill 'em all? Or only part of 'em?"

"I used up my share of bullets."

"Looks like you took one, too!"

Land gingerly touched the place. "I guess I'll live."

The deputy was already examining the body of Turk Freese. "Ugly son of a bitch," he muttered, and placed the dead man's hat on his face to cover it. He straightened again and, arms akimbo, glanced around the muddy street that resembled a battlefield. He shook his head and blew out his cheeks. "The only one of these that I remember seeing before was that fellow Antrim. We've had an eye on him and on that so-called horse ranch of his, north of town. But I never knew he went in for holding up banks!"

Dryly, Land said, "He won't be trying it again."

"Funny thing." The man fixed him with a sharp glance. "I got a witness who says he saw you kill the other two, but not Antrim. He insists it was someone else done it—the one I caught just a glimpse of, driving off in a rig. Could that be so?"

"I reckon it could," Land admitted.

"But who was he?"

Jim Land hesitated only a moment before he answered. "Far as I'm concerned, it was a fellow who saved my life. . . ."

The lawman appeared to accept that. "Well, I'd say you both deserve medals! Having our bank cleaned out would've been a real blow for Tulsa—to say nothing of Mr. Halsell or the other big depositors. Look," he went on, a man harried by his responsibilities, "I'm hoping for more details from you later. All right?" He got Jim Land's nod. Starting to turn away, he paused to eye the blood on the other man's clothing. "You better be getting that looked at! Doc Allen should be on his way. I sent for him—I figure the young fellow lyin' by the wagon there won't be lasting much longer. . . ."

Land realized with a start that he had forgotten about Charlie Converse. He saw now that a crowd had gathered about the wagon, and he started for it at once, moving cautiously, hoarding his strength.

A hand caught at his arm, and he looked into the face of the old doctor. John Allen had come without a hat, his hair forming a halo of white above his bony features. "Land? I didn't realize it was *you* I was looking for. They just told me there'd been shooting and I was needed."

"Wrong man," Land told him. "I'm still on my feet. Yonder's the one who really needs you."

One look and the doctor was hurrying to shove and pull bystanders aside, ordering them in angry tones to make way and give the injured man decent room. As the crowd moved back, Land was able to see Charlie Converse lying with his upper body propped against the wagon wheel, and Beth down on her knees. Jim Land worked his way to a place just behind her. As a precaution he took hold of the wagon box to steady himself.

He had seen too many men die to be mistaken now about

Charlie Converse. Charlie's eyes were closed, his head thrown back, his skin a sickly color shining with sweat; every shallow breath stirred a faint pink froth at the corners of his mouth. Doc Allen, hunkered down beside him, had placed his bag on the ground and opened it; but when he saw the wreckage Turk Freese's bullet had done, he glanced up at Land through shaggy eyebrows and slowly shook his head.

Beth saw the gesture; a low moan of understanding broke from her, and Land dropped a hand upon her shoulder, in a clumsy attempt to comfort her. The doctor, with a clean cloth, gently wiped some of the clammy sweat from the dying man's face. Charlie Converse's eyes wavered open, and he saw his wife and Jim Land. But there was no hint of the old jealousy as he found the voice to say faintly, "Still think I wasn't too far wrong about the feeling between you two. It's all right," he told his wife before she could speak. "I don't mind. He'll be a whole lot better for you than I ever was."

Beth tried to say something, but only a sob came out. She reached and touched her husband's cheek and then let the hand fall.

Charlie turned to the doctor. He gestured feebly toward the opening of his coat, as he mumbled, "Pocket . . . for her . . ." Understanding, Allen reached and from the inner pocket brought out the leather wallet, considerably thinner than when Jim Land had retrieved it from the men who had stolen it. Allen handed the wallet to Beth, who pressed it to her bosom as her husband said, his voice momentarily stronger, "Still a little money left—not as much as there should have been. And the registration . . . for our claim. Hang on to it. Only wish I had . . . something more to give you."

"You gave your life for me!" she choked out. Charlie seemed to consider the thought, and he nodded a little.

"Guess I did at that, didn't I?" he said, almost in a tone of satisfaction. "One thing at least I can be proud of. . . ."

He took a quick, indrawn breath then let it out again and was gone, his head falling forward. Beth pressed both hands to her mouth. She was crying as Jim Land tightened his grip on her shoulder.

\*       \*       \*

A few hours later the hullabaloo and excitement of Tulsa's bank robbery had settled; a clean afternoon wind scoured the dusty street where men had died. Jim Land climbed the stair of a rooming house on Boston Avenue, his hand on the stair rail to give him balance. He moved so as not to stir the banked fires of pain. He knocked at the door he had been directed to, and after a moment Beth Converse opened it.

She had had some time to compose herself after the morning's ordeal. She seemed her usual neat and attractive self, though Land, knowing her, could see the pallor in her features, the lines of grief about her eyes. She stared, seeing him at her door. "Why, Jim!" she exclaimed.

He said, with a hint of dry humor, "You've got a suspicious landlady! But she said I could come up for a few minutes, if we left the door open. And I had to see you," he added. Without answering, she drew back for him to enter. Her room was small but adequately furnished, probably suited to her purposes; Land registered little more than this. His whole concern was with her as he asked anxiously, "How are you feeling?"

It was a moment before she answered. "I guess the word is numb." She pushed a hand into the thickness of her brown hair and then smoothed it again. "Now that the first shock is over," she went on in the same uncertain tone, "I understand what has happened, but somewhere inside I just haven't taken it in yet!" Her eyes searched his face. "But—*you*, Jim! Should you really be on your feet?"

"Doc Allen doesn't like it," he admitted. "But I'm moving easy. The way he's got me strapped up, I can't do much of anything else."

"Won't you have a seat?"

Beth indicated a chair, but it looked too comfortable, and he shook his head. "If I sit down, I may not want to get up again. Don't worry about me. I'll mend in good time. Even Allen admits it."

An awkward silence fell over them. It was as though Charlie's tragic passing had opened an impassible gulf between this moment and that earlier one when they had kissed in the parlor of the hotel; they faced each other now with almost the formality of strangers. Jim Land found himself studying her expression, trying to read some hint of what lay behind it, but not succeeding.

He drew a breath. "I was needing to know if you've made any decisions."

"Yes, I have. I'm going to stay. I want Charlie to lie in the Tulsa cemetery. This was where he hoped to find some of those things he'd always looked for." She went on to explain the conclusions she had reached in hours of silent debate. "And though he never found them, I hope very much to keep what he left for me." She meant the registration certificate, which Jim Land saw lying on the table beside her husband's battered wallet. "I don't know how well I'll manage alone," she finished. "But I mean to try."

Land nodded approval; he tried not to show the great surge of relief her words sent through him. What he said was, "You know, you have until spring before anything more has to be done to hold the claim. And by that time I should be whole again and able to help."

"Oh, no!" she cried. "You've done far too much for me!"

"Not nearly as much as I'd like." He went on before she could interrupt, "You're not the only one who's been making decisions today. I've chalked up a few myself. First—I'll be turning in my badge soon. I'm not much use to Marshal Nix in this shape, and by the time I'm mended I may not have a job, anyway. Bill Doolin has left Oklahoma; somehow I don't think he's going to be back. And Turk Freese is taken care of—the end of something that's been weighing on me for more than two years.

"Without a leader, the rest of the Doolin gang won't be much of a problem for the marshal and his staff. He's got enough good men; they don't need me. In fact, I'd just as soon not be around to try to take any of the credit away from them."

Beth was looking at him with an odd expression. "You really mean you would give up this work you've been doing so many years? I'm afraid I wouldn't be telling the truth if I said I'm not glad!" She hesitated. "But—afterward? What happens then?"

Jim Land faced her. He would have liked to put his arms around her, but he kept them at his sides as he answered,

"There are still decisions to face. Why not give them a while? Later on we'll be able to think more clearly about other things—now just isn't the time for settling them. I'm willing to wait."

She nodded. "All right, Jim." But he took the slight smile she gave him, and the tentative touch of her fingers on his hand, as a token and a promise.

# Epilogue

The outlaws who had ruled the roost in Oklahoma Territory did not long survive its opening to settlement or the concerted efforts of Marshal Nix and his capable staff. Within two years of the 1893 Cherokee Strip land rush, most of the Doolin gang were dead or in prison.

In May 1895, Bitter Creek Newcomb was killed at the Dunn ranch, probably a victim of treachery by the family that for years had been friends and cronies of the outlaws—they had turned informers to save themselves from prosecution. In September, Little Bill Raidler was ambushed by lawmen and seriously wounded; tried and sentenced to ten years' imprisonment at Columbus, Ohio, he was paroled in 1903 because of his crippling injuries, and he returned to Oklahoma, where he became a storekeeper for the few remaining years of his life.

Arkansas Tom Jones (his true name was Roy Daugherty) stood trial in May 1894 for the killing of the three deputies during the Ingalls raid, and he was sentenced to fifty years in Lansing prison. He was pardoned in 1910. Back in Oklahoma, supposedly reformed, he actually joined with Nix and other lawmen in the making of a movie, *The Passing of the Oklahoma Outlaws*, in which he played himself. But by 1916 he was robbing banks again and was in and out of prison. In 1924, he was killed by police at Joplin, Missouri, after pulling his last job.

Cattle Annie (Annie McDoulet) and Little Breeches (Jennie Stevens) were arrested in August 1895, convicted of horse stealing, and both being minors, sent to reformatories in Massachusetts. After a few months Annie was released and turned to settlement work in New York, where two years later she died of tuberculosis at Bellevue hospital. Jennie, released in October 1896, returned to Oklahoma and disappeared from history; years later, one report had her living respectably and raising a family in Tulsa.

As for Bill Doolin, after leaving Oklahoma Territory, he hid out for a while in New Mexico, where he became friendly with Eugene Manlove Rhodes, the famous Western novelist. During this time attorneys were plea-bargaining, trying to arrange Doolin's surrender in return for a reduced prison sentence. These efforts failing, he eventually rejoined his wife and son in Kansas.

By then, however, his crippling leg wound had become painfully rheumatic, and he journeyed to Eureka Springs, Arkansas, in an effort to seek relief in the mineral baths. A tip led to his capture there on January 15, 1895, and his return to Oklahoma—though he was spared the humiliation of traveling in irons, on giving his promise not to make a break for it, a promise he kept.

But the Doolin story was not quite finished. The following July, while awaiting trial, he pulled a daring escape from the federal jail at Guthrie, taking nine other prisoners with him. A month-long, all-out manhunt followed, with posses combing the Cimarron country and all his other former haunts in an effort to track him down. Finally—once again through the treacherous Dunn family—the marshal's office learned that Bill Doolin was at the town of Lawson (now Quay, Oklahoma), where Edie's parents were living and where he had gone to pick up his family and take them somewhere far from Oklahoma for a fresh start at an honest life. On an August evening in 1896, a posse that included federal marshals, two of the Dunns, and a couple of local youths, one of whom was the fiancé of sixteen-year-old Rosa Dunn, ambushed him with his wagon fully loaded and ready to depart. Bill Doolin fell riddled with bullets and buckshot.

An era in Oklahoma history had ended.

READ THIS THRILLING PREVIEW
OF A BOLD NEW SERIES
OF THE AMERICAN WEST
FROM THE AUTHOR AND THE PRODUCERS
OF WHITE INDIAN AND PONY EXPRESS

# RIO GRANDE

BOOK ONE IN
# THE TAMING OF
# THE WEST

BY DONALD CLAYTON PORTER

*The time is the early 1860s; the place is the desert country of Arizona and New Mexico, where U.S. Army forces face not only the incursions of rebel war parties bent on conquering the West for the Confederacy, but also hostile Indians determined to drive out all white men.*

Lieutenant Kevin O'Reilly, U.S. Army, had been sent into Navajo country as part of Major Emery Church's advance unit. This assignment delighted the big Irishman since it meant he would most likely see again the beautiful Navajo girl who had captured his heart. But so far there had only been the endless patrols into the countryside, chasing down bands of Navajo, parleying with them to get them to move to the reservation. There had been no sign of the girl . . . until perhaps today.

Kevin yanked his horse to an abrupt stop. The distant crackle of army carbines was shattering his concentration on the tracks of the Navajo band he and his six-man patrol had been following. The sound of the rifle fire alarmed O'Reilly, for among the footprints beneath his mount's feet were the small, dainty impressions left by the passage of a young woman—and the tracks led in the direction of the rifle fire!

He turned to Private Mike Connor, the broad-shouldered Irishman riding alongside. It was Mike who, at the last meeting with the Navajo chiefs sometime ago, had prevented O'Reilly from striking out at the ugly Navajo brave that had accosted the lovely Indian girl. Kevin now noted that Mike's face wore a frown as he cocked an ear to the slight northerly breeze.

"How far away is the shooting, Mike?" O'Reilly heard the tension in his own voice.

Connor glanced at his friend. "Mile and a half, maybe two miles. Sound carries far on a day like this. Now, Kevin, we don't know what it means. Could be a hunting party. And even if 'twas a skirmish, we don't know your Navajo maiden is in it. Try to relax and have some faith. Believe in the luck o' the Irish. After all, there be many Navajo women." His voice trailed off as O'Reilly touched spurs to his horse and moved at a swift lope toward the sound of the gunfire. Mike kneed his own horse into motion, waving the other troopers forward. "By the saints, let it not be his Navajo," Mike muttered to himself. "If Kevin is to find her, let it not be this way."

They covered the distance in a very few minutes. Kevin already was off his mount and moving among the huddled bodies in the shallow ravine when Mike and the other troopers caught up. The scene before them shocked the veteran soldiers. Eleven Navajo bodies, including four women and two young children, were sprawled about the ravine. Two of the adult men wore the robes of tribal chieftains.

Kevin looked up, face pale. "She's not here, Mike. But, my God, why? We were supposed to parley with the Indians, not wipe them out. Yet here are eleven Navajo slaughtered like so many sheep—and not one of them is armed." O'Reilly sank to his knees, gently lifted the dead body of a young girl, perhaps eight years old, and cradled the bloody head against his jacket.

Mike Connor stepped from his horse, moved from first one body to another, then straightened. "I know the two chiefs," he said, aware of the tightness in his own voice. "Cuello and Castellito. They sought peace. They were going to come to the reservation willingly. And this is what they ran into. . . ."

Kevin O'Reilly carefully placed the dead girl on the sand, then covered her with a blanket that had been wrapped around the frail shoulders. He felt the tightening in his chest as the sickness inside him gave way to a growing fury.

"I'll know who did this, Mike. And when I do . . ."

Connor saw the powerful hands of his friend clench and unclench. He knew that when the explosion came, someone would pay. "All the work we've done," O'Reilly said through lips drawn thin, "all the effort to convince the Indians to come in peacefully. Gone in a volley of rifle fire in an ambush. The rest will never come in now, Mike."

" 'Tis the truth you speak, my friend," Connor said. He turned to a pair of white-faced young troopers. "Bury them as best you can," he said. "I'm going to ride a small circle to see what I can find."

Connor returned in less than a quarter of an hour. He slid from his mount in front of the lieutenant, who was wielding a trenching tool alongside the troopers.

"Kevin," Connor said, "I'm no threat to Kit Carson at reading sign. But this was an army patrol that did in the Navajo. And it don't take no expert scout to put a name on a horse that moves with a left hind foot turned out so sharp."

Connor sighed to ease his own growing fury. "I didn't see it happen, Kevin, any more than you did— but that hind foot belongs to a Tennessee walker that's rode by just one man. It appears that our Major Emery Church was the man who set this ambush up."

Kevin straightened. "Then, by God," he said, the edge on his voice as keen as that of his trenching tool, "the major will pay!"

Mike sighed. "Hold up a minute, you hot-tempered Irishman," he said. "Do you think Church's report will be the truth of what happened? Will General Carleton take your word and mine—a junior officer and a single trooper—against that of a major? No, my friend. Trouble you don't need, you or your young Navajo maiden."

Connor fetched his own trenching tool from his pack and turned to digging hard and deep as he talked, welcoming the exertion. It would help to burn away his own disgust. He tossed a spadeful in a growing pile at the mouth of the small grave. "No, Kevin, let us not speak of this to the major, as we have no proof. The damage has been done."

Kevin straightened after placing a tiny bundle in the bottom of a grave.

"There's fact in your words, Mike. But, by God, someone will know of this besides us. Colonel Carson is on his way to take over the Navajo campaign, I hear. And Kit Carson will need no proof!"

Assuming full command over Major Church's smaller advance units, Colonel Kit Carson moved to Fort Wingate, located just on the fringes of Navajo country in Arizona. General Carleton, meanwhile, remained in Santa Fe, eagerly waiting for Carson's reports about the patrols that were being sent out to subdue the Navajo and bring them to the reservation.

"Our plan," Carson told his subordinate officers, "may seem harsh on the surface. But in the long run it will save lives on both sides and bring a relatively quick end to the Navajo problem. Our purpose here is not to kill Indians, but to subdue them. Thus, by destroying their homes, burning their crops and orchards, gathering their sheep from them, and providing them food, medical aid, and clothing, we can get them to surrender."

*Carson meets with the chiefs of the Navajo and sets forth terms of peace. Some of the chiefs want to accept, but others, including one named Gallegos, angrily reject the terms.*

*Following this meeting, the colonel and his immediate subordinate, Lieutenant Colonel Ted Henderson, adjourn to Carson's office.*

A knock sounded on the door. "Come in," Carson called.

The door swung open. Ted Henderson noticed that the tall lieutenant who entered almost had to duck to clear the upper frame of the doorway. The broad-shouldered young officer saluted, his fingers trembling slightly against the campaign cap.

"Lieutenant Kevin O'Reilly, sir, respectfully requesting an audience with the commanding officer."

Carson casually returned the salute. "Come on in, Lieutenant. Sit down. What's on your mind?"

O'Reilly swallowed, his nervousness now obvious to Ted.

"Sir, I could be—brought to court-martial for

this, but—well, my conscience just couldn't take it any longer." O'Reilly cleared his throat. "Major Church," he said, "is guilty of serious crimes against the Navajo."

Ted saw Carson's eyes narrow, and he waited for the lieutenant to proceed.

"There was the matter of an ambush, sir—two chiefs—"

"Wait a minute, Lieutenant O'Reilly." Carson reached for a paper on his desk and handed it to Ted. "Colonel Henderson, will you please read for us Major Church's official report on the incident for the lieutenant's benefit."

Ted read the report aloud, watching as the husky lieutenant's eyes widened in disbelief.

"But—but sir, that's not how it happened," O'Reilly stammered.

"Then why don't you tell us what did happen," Ted said.

O'Reilly shuffled his feet. "There was an ambush, all right, sir. But it wasn't the Navajo chiefs who were responsible. Cuello and Castellito were not even armed! It had to be Major Church's patrol that staged the ambush, not the Indians!"

Carson sighed, sank heavily into a chair. "Will you swear to that under oath?"

O'Reilly scratched an ear nervously. "Yes, sir. And so will Private Connor. But it would just be the word of me and Mike against that of an officer commissioned in the United States Army. But if you ask, sir, of course, I will testify. And I will have the satisfaction of knowing I've told the truth, even if no one else does. But, Colonel Carson—"

"Yes, Lieutenant?"

"There may be even more mischief afoot, sir. Just before sunset, sir, Major Church and about thirty of his men rode out on patrol. I—I'm afraid they have something more in mind than just checking out the country."

Ted saw alarm flash into Carson's eyes. "Which way were they headed, Lieutenant?"

"North, sir."

Carson turned to Ted. "Any chance of catching up with them, Colonel Henderson?"

Ted shook his head. "There's no moon tonight; we would be searching on blind luck. And they have fresh mounts and a head start."

"Then," Carson said with a sigh heavy with dread, "I suppose we will just have to wait until sunup." He turned to the young officer and held out a hand. "Lieutenant O'Reilly, you did the right thing in coming to us with your story. It took courage for a junior officer to complain about the field conduct of his superior officer. I thank you. And when Major Church returns, your name will not be mentioned in our—uh—discussion."

In the soft gray light of early dawn, the bedlam of yells, whoops, and fast-moving hoofbeats jarred Ted Henderson from a fitful doze. He hastily pulled on his boots and, strapping his pistol belt about his waist, stepped from the small room which served as his quarters near Carson's command post. Ted felt the muscles in his jaw tighten, the hair on his forearms stiffen, as he watched a mass of riders whipping their mounts across the parade ground. He glanced at Carson's quarters. A light burned in the window, and Ted was sure the colonel had been awake the entire night.

With long, angry strides, Ted crossed the few feet to Carson's combination office and living quarters, fighting the growing tension in his stomach. He stepped onto the small porch as Kit Carson, his blond hair askew, opened the door.

The two officers stood rigid and silent as Major Emery Church, heading the detail riding in, brutally yanked his lathered horse to a halt before them. Ted's heart skipped as he saw the blanket-wrapped bundle clutched in Church's right hand.

Church tossed the reins of his exhausted mount to a nearby trooper, then delivered a sardonic salute in the direction of the two officers. Neither Carson nor Ted returned the gesture.

"Come into my office, Major Church." Ted heard the flinty edge on Carson's voice. Waiting until Carson had stepped into the room, followed by the major, dusty and grinning, Ted entered and carefully closed the door. The heavy wood muffled the babble of excited voices from the parade ground outside.

"Explain yourself, Major. I ordered no night patrols." Carson's controlled voice did not match the expression in the narrow eyes illuminated by a single oil lamp on the commanding officer's desk.

Ted noted the ill-concealed glitter of contempt in the major's eyes. Knowing a clash was more than possible between the two, Ted casually stepped off to one side, placing himself a pace away from a point between the two men.

"Somebody had to do something besides talk," Church snorted. "So I did it."

With a flourish, the major flung open the blanket, spilling the bundled, grisly contents on the floor at Carson's feet. Ted heard his own sharp intake of breath. A gory pile of Indian scalps lay at his feet.

Church casually flipped a small scalp over with the toe of his boot. "That," he said, "is the only way to tame Indians."

Ted moved by instinct, catching Kit Carson's arm in a powerful grip as the colonel drew back to swing at the major. "Kit! Don't do it! Striking a junior officer will cost you the command, and we need you now more than ever! This animal isn't worth it!"

"Well, well," Church's sarcasm rang in Ted's ears, "the famous Kit Carson has a bodyguard now."

The slender thread of control that held Ted's own temper snapped. He whirled to face the major and advanced a step. Church instinctively retreated. Ted glared into the smaller man's eyes, pinning him to the spot like a bug nailed to the floor.

"Major Church," Ted said, surprised at the even, conversational tone in his voice that belied the fury now churning in his belly, "but for the fact that we are both in uniform, I would give you the damnedest beating you have ever seen in your miserable life." He noticed Church's hand ease toward the holstered pistol at his hip.

"Go ahead, Church! Try it if you've got the guts! You'll find out you aren't going against weak old men and kids. Go ahead, please. Pull a weapon on a superior officer, and I'll kill you on the spot!"

Ted advanced a step, then another, until the retreating major's back came into contact with the wall. Ted found a small measure of satisfaction in the sudden flash of fear in the major's eyes as Church suddenly realized the infuriated officer before him meant every word. Ted pushed his face close to Church's.

"Major, your stupidity is equaled only by your gutless taste for Indian blood. This butchery has turned what could have been a negotiated peace into a long and bloody campaign that will cost many lives!" Ted reached out and plucked Church's pistol from its holster. "You wanted blood, Major," he said, cocking the weapon, "well, by God, you have it. And it might very well be your own."

Church's eyes, now bright with fear, followed the path of the pistol muzzle as Ted raised it slowly from waist level, pointing it at Church's forehead. Then, deliberately, Ted lowered the weapon.

"Major Church, you are confined to quarters until your superior officers decide on your punishment," Kit Carson commanded. "As for myself, I would prefer to hang you in the center of the parade ground to show the Navajo how white man's justice really works!"

Kit stalked to the door. He flung it open with such force it almost left the hinges. "Get Sergeant Major Armbrister over here, on the double!" he yelled to a nearby trooper.

He stepped back into the room, noticing that some color was beginning to return to Major Emery Church's face. "If you so much as poke your nose from your quarters, Church, I will personally bite it off. Do I make myself clear?"

Church turned to Ted. "You haven't heard the last of this, Henderson," he said, hate dancing in his eyes. "I'll get you for this."

"Any time, any place, Major—but out of uniform.

I'll not disgrace the United States Army by smashing a snake in blue!"

Frank Armbrister, stepping through the door, took in the situation at a glance.

"Frank, I want you to escort Major Church back to his quarters. Arrange for a guard at his door at all times. If he wants to go out for anything other than the latrine, I am to be informed at once," Carson said.

"Yes, Colonel. I'll take care of it."

"And Frank," Ted added, "should Major Church make any attempt to escape or ignore your instructions, I would not be at all surprised to receive your report that he had met with a severe accident."

"Yes, sir. A man can get hurt real bad around here if he isn't careful," Armbrister said, one eye closing in a slow wink. "Now, Major, will you come along with me?" Armbrister took the major's arm.

At the door, Church turned and glared at Ted for a moment, eyes flashing hatred. "I'll kill you for this, Henderson—mark my words."

"Sergeant, did you just hear this officer threaten the life of a superior?"

"Yes, sir. Spoke right up and said it, he did."

"Don't forget that, Sergeant. You might have to repeat it under oath one day."

Armbrister nodded, then escorted Church through the door into the light of a new day. Ted turned to Kit Carson, noting the hot fire still burning in the colonel's eyes. "So what do we do with this loathsome Indian scalper, Kit?" he asked.

"I know what I'd like to do—hand him over to the Navajo as a gesture of goodwill," Carson said, "but we might as well face facts. No court-martial panel is going to take action against him. In their view, what Church did would be an action against an enemy in time of war." Carson sat heavily in the rawhide chair behind his desk. "But if you will write out the report stating exactly what happened and its probable impact on the campaign against the Navajo, General Carleton should find it interesting reading."

A tentative knock on the door brought Carson's

voice to a halt. Ted called, "Come in," and Kevin O'Reilly, face lined in worry, stepped into the room.

"Begging your pardon, Colonel Carson—I heard what happened. I—I must examine the scalps that were brought in. I understand there were women and children killed by Church and his men."

"Certainly, Lieutenant," Carson said, "and from the tone of your voice and the expression on your face, I hope you do not find what you search for. After that, would you please see that the remains are given a decent burial?"

Gingerly, O'Reilly picked his way through the scalps, hoping he would not be sick in front of his two commanding officers. At length he looked up.

Ted could see the relief in the young officer's eyes despite the pale face.

"It—it isn't here, sir," O'Reilly said. Carefully and with a reverent touch, the big Irishman began placing the scalps back onto the blood-stained blanket in which they had arrived.

"For your sake, Lieutenant, I'm glad to hear that," Carson said. He turned to Ted.

"Colonel Henderson, we have a most unpleasant but necessary duty before us. I need you to assemble some messengers, people the Navajo may listen to. I must send my personal apologies to the various Navajo chiefs for this atrocity and all other committed by Church—and my personal promise it will never happen again." Carson sighed. "I don't think they will listen," he said, "but I must try. I will go in person to the chief of the band massacred in this most recent incident. You take charge here. Your patrols can work in the vicinity of the fort."

Ted nodded "Myself, Yellow Crow, Frank Armbrister, and Albert Jonas will carry your message. I will find others as well."

"Sir?"

Ted looked up as Kevin O'Reilly stood, the blood-stained bundle held respectfully in his arms. "Yes, Lieutenant?"

"I would like to volunteer to deliver one of the messages."

"Do you speak Navajo?"

"Pretty well, sir. I've been spending a lot of time learning."

Carson nodded. "Very well, Lieutenant. Take no more than a couple of troopers with you—and you realize, of course, that the Navajo may kill you on sight?"

"I'll take the chance, Colonel Carson. And thank you." O'Reilly turned to go.

"Lieutenant," Carson said, his voice soft, "if you tell me which Navajo you search for, perhaps our other men might be of help."

The lieutenant paused at the door. "I don't even know her name, sir," he said, "but I have reason to believe she is with Gallegos's band, possibly a relative. She's—the most beautiful woman I've ever seen."

"Then go with God, Lieutenant. And I hope you find her."

Wind Flower gently brushed a stray strand of black hair back into place behind an ear. She breathed deeply the crisp, cedar-scented air of the secluded branch of the Canyon de Chelly, and she felt the spirits which guarded the sacred place flow about her, bright comfort.

Pride swelled in her breast as she listened to her father near the conclusion of his speech. Few bands of the Navajo, she thought, were so fortunate as to have as strong and just a leader as her father, Gallegos. His rich voice carried easily to where she sat, a respectful distance from the circle of braves around her father.

"You have heard the words of the white soldier," Gallegos concluded, "and they are the same words the Navajo have heard before, words that mean no more than the passage of wind through the trees. Now the Navajo must prepare for war! The spirits shall guide his arrows, and from the scared grounds of this canyon he shall ride against the soldiers, strike hard and fast, and drive the blue-coated ones from the land of the Navajo!"

Wind Flower heard the mutters of assent from the

braves, then suddenly felt a discomfort deep within and knew she was being watched. Fifty feet away, the squat, ugly figure of Choshay stood, his eyes glaring at her. Wind Flower felt a chill settle about her shoulders.

Choshay had become obsessed, she thought, since her father had banned him from the ranks of his warriors and warned him never again to approach Wind Flower. So far Choshay had kept his distance, yet Wind Flower continued to carry the thin, razor-sharp skinning knife in its sheath strapped against her thigh. The old ones, the gossipy grandmothers who knew more of tribal intrigues than the leaders themselves, had spoken of Choshay's growing band of warriors—mostly outcasts like himself—and their killing of white women and children on frequent raids from the holy canyon. His cache of big guns, even horses, continued to grow, and the whispering ones said he had accumulated much dried meat and corn in a spot known only to himself.

Wind Flower knew that she was wise to worry, for one day Choshay might become strong enough to challenge Gallegos for control of the Canyon de Chelly and its inhabitants; only his fear of Gallegos had kept him at a distance so far. But when Gallegos led his warriors from the canyon to defeat the soldiers, then Choshay might seize the opportunity to gain control. She suppressed an inward shudder. Choshay, she vowed, would never touch her body; Wind Flower would plunge the skinning knife into her own breast first. Death would be more welcome than his filthy touch.

Wind Flower rose, brushing the loose sand from her soft deerskin dress. Gallegos had finished his oration, gaining the enthusiastic support of his braves, and now they would be planning the details of their war against the white man. That left much for a woman to do. Meat and parched corn must be prepared for the warriors, crops had to be gathered, sheep had to be tended, blankets had to be made to shield the Navajo bodies from the cold that would come.

Making her way back to her own hut, she paused at her grandfather's lodge to see if he were in need of anything. But the sight that greeted her stilled her tongue.

The old man sat hunched over the sacred sand paintings, wrinkles of many years deepening in the weathered, tired face. Wind Flower had seen that expression before, and she knew the sand paintings spoke to the revered old one of troubled times to come.

Lieutenant Kevin O'Reilly forced his leaden legs to carry him the final few steps to the top of the high mesa overlooking one end of the Canyon de Chelly. He raised a hand, signaling the footsore and bone-tired infantry company behind him to halt. He scanned the countryside with care and saw the smoke from numerous fires, the blackened, charred land where fields of corn once stood.

Satisfied at last that no Navajo warriors lay in ambush, he waved his soldiers forward. Tall stalks of heavily eared corn stretched over several acres before them. This was the Indian corn that grew late in the season and remained on the stalks right up until the first snow.

Kevin O'Reilly did not need to tell his troops what to do; by now they were ruthlessly efficient in the destruction of Indian crops. At his hand signal, they deployed in the familiar skirmish lines at the edges of the cornfield. Within minutes, flames licked at the sun-dried stalks, and with the gusting winds, the field soon would become a short-lived and raging inferno. All that would be left would be another scar on the face of the land.

A glimpse of movement within the cornfield caught his eye. He stared through the steadily growing circle of flames, hoping an innocent deer or antelope had not been trapped in the ring of fire.

His heart leaped in dismay as the movement suddenly snapped into focus through the heat waves shimmering above the field—a slightly built figure, long hair swirling, raced from one point to another, seeking a way to escape the nearing flames. It was a woman trapped there, O'Reilly realized.

The lieutenant reacted without thinking, tossing his rifle aside and plunging through a small opening in the ring of flames into swirling, choking smoke. He stood for a moment, confused and disoriented by the smoke and shimmering heat, eyes watering in protest. Then he spotted her again, only a few feet away.

O'Reilly squared his bull-like shoulders and plowed through the cornstalks. The slender figure, taken by surprise, tried to twist free of the powerful grip on her arm. O'Reilly shouted in the Navajo tongue above the growing crackle of flames. "Man help!" He momentarily realized his grip, stripped out of his greatcoat, tossed the heavy garment over the small body, and scooped up the girl. He glanced about, feeling the first wash of fear, looking for a break in the circle of flames. He found none, and there was no time to search. Running at top speed, he dashed toward the nearest flames, felt the slap of fire against his body, and then broke through into the fresh clean air, stumbling into the arms of a sergeant.

Ignoring the hands that slapped at his smoldering clothing, O'Reilly whipped the greatcoat from the slender figure.

Recognition hit him with a jolt—the high cheekbones, chiseled face, brown eyes wide with fear—the girl from Salt River! Unable for a moment to speak, O'Reilly simply stared. The object of his long search was now within his arms! The woman's eyes softened as she touched his face and his forearms, and O'Reilly became aware he had suffered some minor burns in his dash through the flames. The touch broke his trance.

"Daughter—daughter is safe now," he said in his good Navajo. "No harm will come to her from the fire or the soldiers."

She bowed her head slightly, and O'Reilly was pleased that the flames had not scorched the thick black hair which fell almost to her waist. He reached out as though to stroke it, then checked the impulse as the girl once more raised her eyes.

Wind Flower felt her heart pound within her breast as she looked into the strong but gentle face before her.

"Twice now," she said, her voice musical in the flowery Navajo tongue, "white brave has saved Wind Flower. Once from the ugly one, Choshay, and now from the fire. The daughter of Gallegos thanks the brave soldier not once, but twice, for the gift of life."

Through the daze of a swirling brain almost overwhelmed by the beauty of the woman and the just-ended struggle to save her life, Kevin O'Reilly heard a low whistle at his side.

"The daughter of Gallegos," the sergeant repeated. "Lieutenant, you don't realize what a prize you have here."

"Sergeant," O'Reilly replied in a choked voice, "no man alive realizes just how much of a prize . . . " He could not seem to pull his eyes away from her face, her beauty, the tenderness he saw in her large, long-lashed brown eyes.

"If Gallegos will negotiate for anything," the sergeant said, "it's this girl. He'll pay almost any price to get her back."

"No!" O'Reilly's sharp tone surprised even himself. "It will be her choice; I'll not hold her captive!"

"But, Lieutenant!"

O'Reilly cut the protest short with a quick wave of the hand. "Wind Flower is free to choose," he said in Navajo. "It is white brave's hope, his dream, that Wind Flower will come with him, that she will join her people who have already come to the white settlement. But if she wishes to return to her people, no white hand will be raised against her."

Wind Flower looked steadily at this big soldier in blue. She knew what she had to do.